Nine Folds Make a Paper Swan

Ruth Gilligan is an Irish novelist and journalist. Her debut novel *Forget* reached number one on the Irish bestsellers list when she was eighteen, making her the youngest person in Ireland ever to do so, while her subsequent books *Somewhere In Between* and *Can You See Me?* were both published while she was still at university. She writes and reviews for the *Irish Times*, the *Irish Independent*, the *TLS* and the *Guardian*, and she teaches creative writing at the University of Birmingham.

Nine Folds
Make a
Paper Swan

Ruth Gilligan

Atlantic Books
LONDON

First published in hardback and trade paperback in Great Britain
in 2016 by Atlantic Books, an imprint of Atlantic Books Ltd.

This paperback edition published in Great Britain in 2017
by Atlantic Books.

10 9 8 7 6 5 4 3 2 1

A CIP catalogue record for this book is available from the British Library.

Paperback ISBN: 978 1 78239 859 2
E-book ISBN: 978 1 78239 858 5

Printed in Great Britain by CPI Group (UK) Ltd, Croydon CR0 4YY

Atlantic Books
An Imprint of Atlantic Books Ltd
Ormond House
26–27 Boswell Street
London
WC1N 3JZ

For Debbie, where it all began
and
For Alex, until the end.

There are those of us who haven't yet told our stories, or refuse to tell them, and so we become them: we hide away inside the memory until we can no longer stand the shell or the shock – perhaps that's me, or perhaps I must tell it before it's forgotten or becomes, like everything else, something else.

—Colum McCann, *Zoli*

Prologue

I n the bloodless light of the foyer she feels herself nothing but a
stranger.

The all-smiles nurse leads her through. Visitors' Book. Auto-
graph please. A set of coded doors and then a waft of luncheon
smells, almost solid on the air. Cream of mushroom soup.

The first room is laid out with tables and chairs, the aftermath
of last night's Festive Bingo. Old games for old folks, two little
ducks. She surveys, clutching her parcel to her chest; spots a left-
over scorecard that has fallen to the floor. But she admits there is
a polish to the place she hadn't been expecting, a vase of lilies on
the sideboard and the surfaces wiped so clean you could almost see
your face in them, even if after three days without sleep she would
probably just prefer to look away.

In the next room, a parliament of armchairs curves around a television – a *Father Ted* rerun – the volume turned all the way down to
mute. Only, she can just make out a hum of classical music playing
somewhere near, which turns the priests into a sort of silent film,
a farce of dog collars and fags and mouths mouthing *go on, Father,
you will you will you will.*

The television's audience, though, won't resist the distraction;

a ripple of heads for the arrival; wrinkled necks strained tight, young again. And eyes that cannot seem to place her – is she somebody's granddaughter? A niece? Whose turn is it for a visitor anyway? Usually Sammy Harris is the safest bet, more relatives than marbles left in him these days. Or even Betty O'Meara – an age since she has had one – not after her brood decided to emigrate to Canada, something to do with these 'recessionary times', a second chance buried underneath the snow.

The imposter herself only has eyes for the floor. Still she hugs her parcel as she follows the nurse out towards the conservatory where another scatter of them sit, framed in the frail light.

Until, tucked up in the corner, they find him.

He wears a tatty shirt. A tie. A little hat, poised atop his head. It is a Jewish hat, apparently, though the symbolism is overshadowed by the other men's jealousy – covers his bald patch nicely, so it does. He sits unmoving, staring out at the back garden where a cluster of pigeons takes lumps out of the mangy ground.

Two little ducks, lucky for some.

But the onlookers now are too curious for the birds, because this here is a revelation – the first visitor the old man has ever received – in here for years, like, and not a single one! Of course, they all have their theories about him, half-baked stuff whispered round. Even the staff, sneaking into the Records Room for a go of his file to see what family, if any, he has left; what his story could possibly be. The folder, though, doesn't say a word. Totally empty. The most vigilant Home for the Elderly in all of Dublin, yet somehow he has slipped through the cracks.

The nurse leaves the unlikely pair to it, still-lifed in silence. The classical music changes track. The girl looks exhausted. After a while the old man stands and leads her off down the corridor, much to the others' annoyance – just when things were getting interesting – before they reach his room and step inside and finally, it is her turn to stare.

The entire bedroom has been covered. All four walls, from carpet to ceiling, bristle with layer upon layer of paper. Foolscap. Narrow-lined. Printer plain. Not a hint of wall left peeking. Each page is covered too in line after line of the old man's handwriting – he transcribes another sheet every day, then pins it up with all the rest, stabbed deep with the rusty tacks he keeps in a drawer beside his bed. It is the strangest of rituals, the other folks think; odder, even, than most. Wonder sometimes if he kept going forever would the walls just close right in? Crushed to death by his own words and how about that for a way to go, eh?

The staff, meanwhile, try to have a read when they can – any excuse to nip into his room. To change his bed linen. To drop off his laundry. Tricky at first to find your way with the scrawl, but the words themselves, ah, now we're talking. Melt your bloody heart:

> *What about a man and a woman who court via pigeon mail,*
> *until the woman falls in love with the pigeon instead?*
> *It all started on Clanbrassil Street in 1941, an unlikely place*
> *for love.*

'And do you suppose they are his memories?' they speculate then, back in the staffroom over builder's tea and biscuits that have been touched by too many fingers. 'Events like, from his past?'

'Or just ideas from his imagination? Maybe he was a writer in his previous life?'

'Jaysus, and I wonder what was I in mine?'

Under the weight of confusion the girl sits – a wooden chair at the foot of the bed – still holding her strange bundle to her chest. Whereas the old man seems to have grown lively, skipping about, running his fingers along the overlaps of paper like the feathers of a swan that might take flight.

She bites her nail; flicks a white half-moon to the floor.

When the burden becomes too much she holds it up, an offering.

He pauses; takes it from her.

Unwrapped, it is a book, a hefty thing with a black leather cover and gold letters indented so deep they catch the bit of sunlight finding its way in through the window to watch.

The tome looks so heavy in the old man's lap – a paperweight as if he might blow away.

Slowly, the girl begins to talk, presumably to explain about the gift. That it is a great read? A family heirloom? No one is sure. Only that the more she speaks the further he seems to sink, lower and lower back into himself like he has just been told the most Godawful news. While she sprouts the other way, quicker now, reasserting the natural order, higher and higher until she is standing, smiling, a real beauty as it turns out, despite the cut of her; despite how she suddenly has to go, just like that, slamming the door behind her with an end-of-the-world bang.

The draught makes the pages on the walls flutter, a whisper that only the old man can hear. Though for the entire visit, he hasn't uttered a word.

Two days later, the walls have shed their plumage. A large envelope sits stuffed on the chair, sealed with the single bit of spit he managed to get going in the mirror that morning. The pins are clustered on the bedside table like a set of teeth, bared.

He waits until after lunch to take the nurse aside. The address on the envelope is in the same, stuttering hand they know so well – the last words, it turns out, he will ever write – and above it, the name is the same as the one from the Visitors' Book the other day; the one that exited so quickly she didn't even have time to sign herself out again so now it reads as if, really, she never left.

The residents have finished their soup and squabble over the Penguin bars brought out for dessert. They go calm again as they trade the feeble jokes hidden under the wrappers' seams:

'Why do seagulls always fly over the sea?'

'Because if they flew over bays they would be bay-gulls, and they're made out of bread.'

A drizzle of half-laughs. A lash of glances in his direction. But the old man is too distracted to notice, only nods a 'thank you' to the nurse then shambles back to the naked room, empty save for that single book – the black leather wedge with the gold indents; the gaffer tape stuck crooked down the spine to hold the wonk of a thing in place.

He picks it up. He stares at the title, still struggling to believe. And then he reads, knowing he might not stop, not tomorrow or even the tomorrow after that when the pigeons have flown off somewhere better again, resisting the urge to come home. Because in the end, it is the only story to have survived.

part one | In the beginning...

1901

'What if, in the beginning, they arrived by sea and then, in the end, they left by sea too, each in their own way?

'*North.*

'*South.*

'*East.*

'*West.*

'Never once looking back?

'Because maybe that's all a compass can really show – the different ways a family falls apart. The pull of magnets, and the push of other dreams.'

Ruth heard the sound of bone before she felt it. The crack was clean, just below the shrivel of her knuckle; her body lurched forward from where it sat on the bed to land on that single, snappable point.

'Tateh!' she cried out for her father next to her in the darkness. 'Tatehithinkihavebrokenmy—' the panic colliding all her words into one.

But the ship's moan was so loud it drowned her out, its very own version of pain.

The prow buckled beneath the force of the crash, the impact

rippling along the hull. The waves leapt acrobatic. The propeller paused mid-propel. While above, the Atlantic stars spelled out a Morse code of dots.

S-O-S

Save our souls

Sinking our ship

Below deck, the bunk beds were nearly wrenched free from their fixings, the wood already gnarled with splinters that seemed sharp enough to prick the darkness and bleed it out, like a bullock drained the kosher way. As it happened, the ship itself had been for cattle once, herds of beasts sailing off towards the foreign slaughterhouses, the white-pink sinews of their shoulders knotted tightly together, hooves ankle-deep in the muck-splattered straw.

But now the stench of it was back again – the cold, meaty waft of fear.

Because the boat had crashed. An almighty thud. Ruth wondered if it was an iceberg they had hit. Or maybe a whale – she could still remember that story the rabbi used to tell; still see the gulp of his throat as he acted out the moment poor Jonah was swallowed. Whole. But of course, she knew that this here was a different story; a different tale with a full cast of characters – two passengers per bed and sixty beds in total sailing from Riga to America on a promise of could-bes, suddenly thrown forward with hands out to stop the fall and bones that snapped in two like pencils.

'Tateh—'

'All right, Bubbeleh. All right, I am here.'

For a moment, Ruth forgot about the throb.

It was the first time her father had spoken in hours. In fact, he had been practically silent for days now, leaving her lonely there on the top bunk, nothing to play with and nothing to listen to except for other people's prayers; other people's vomit as it backwashed on the floor below – ten whole days of seasickness worth. Unless, of course, homesickness spews just the same.

Her finger seared again. Eight years without breaking a bone, and now this.

And it had been strangest of all, her father's silence next to her, because at the beginning of the journey he had barely drawn breath, filling the below-deck shadows with the usual stream of his latest ideas:

'What about a famous mural painter who is tortured by being forced to watch his creations get covered with layer after layer of white paint?'

'Or a man and a woman who court via pigeon mail, until the woman falls in love with the pigeon instead?'

'Or—'

Until his wife had had enough – a lash of impatience from the bunk below. 'Moshe!' she cried. 'Won't you give us any peace?'

Even in the blackness Ruth could sense her father's blush. 'It's all right, Tateh,' she tried. 'It is just too dark for stories. We…we cannot picture a thing.'

She had always wondered what her father did with his unused ideas – stones in his pockets, weighing him down, heavier even than the mounds of baggage they had managed to lug through the snow, across the Latvian border, up to Riga, down the port, along the gangplank to this – an entire existence condensed into a schleppable load. There were the stockings and the pans; the shabbat candelabras; a compass wedged hard against a little leg making a *NorthSouthEastWest* bruise. And then of course there were Uncle

Dovid's letters sent back from America, nearly as sacred to the family now as the Torah scrolls themselves. In fact, probably even more so. Because the ancient words could only tell them their past.

In the beginning...

Whereas these letters told the story of their future.

'Tell it again, Tateh,' Esther had asked when they first set sail. 'I want to hear it again.' Ruth's beautiful sister Esther commanding their father's voice to repeat his brother's words.

So he had done as he was told; had adjusted his window-thick glasses and filled the bloated belly of the boat with tales of all the things that awaited them across the Atlantic. He told them about Manhattan with its buildings that scraped the sky; about the flag lined with stripes and a fistful of stars; about the giant lady with a crown and a torch who welcomed the weary ships in.

And it was only a few more days until their own ship would arrive – two weeks at sea, they had been told. Despite her nausea, Ruth had been counting. And she had even used her compass to try to plot a map in her head, a bit like the one Tateh had had pinned to his attic wall, back where they had come from. It was a yellowed thing, with crosshatch lines for the ocean and a red dot for 'New York'. *Can you see it, Bubbeleh, can you?* Only, the dot had been pointed to so many times that eventually it had disappeared, rubbed away by the poke of desperate fingertips, as if the place never existed at all.

And now her finger was broken.

She turned to ask her Tateh for a kiss; to feel the bush of his beard up against her. But suddenly he seemed busy with other things, the bash of the boat bringing him back to life. He clambered his way down from the bunk and reached up for Ruth to follow. Confused, she let herself be lifted, her hand stashed tight into her chest, before he took her other hand and led her on through the blackness, a wobble in her legs from the waves underneath. And soon there were other legs too, other hands and other wobbles as the rest of the passengers began to follow behind, the pied piper and the rats.

'What's happening?' they whispered, half-terror half-delight. 'Did somebody say...*arrived*?'

Ruth climbed the ladder to the deck as best she could, though she was clumsy in Esther's old shoes, the buckles chafing stockings chafing goosepimple flesh. Once across the gangplank she felt the scuff of dry land beneath her; a breeze that was surprisingly warm. But a fresh batch of whispers had already started to spread, a new confusion doing the rounds.

'Arrived? But—'

'Nu, America is early.'

Ruth checked the sky as if the answer to their questions might be there, but it was just as lightless out here as it was under the deck – the middle of the American night. She half-remembered how Tateh had mentioned something about 'time differences', not that anyone had really bothered to hear – they had just assumed it was another of his silly ideas – a story all about clocks. Ruth wanted to ask him about it now, to get him to explain, only he and Mame were babbling something else in a language she didn't know. Russian? Lithuanian? She could never tell – used to think they were just special phrases only grown-ups were allowed to say until Esther had explained it was called 'different tongues'. So now the world had time differences and tongue differences and how did they know they weren't just different worlds altogether? And why was no one sure if this was even the right one for America?

As soon as she saw her, though, Ruth's head went mute.

The people around her stopped. Dead. Sea leg sways gone still. Their breaths stopped too, the whole cloud of them held tight in anticipation. But also in concentration. Because what if this was it – the moment they had been sailing for? The one they would have to remember now for the rest of their lives, to translate into words again and again for generations to come?

Arrived.

America.

The beginning?

Ruth tried to force some words of her own to stop her head from spinning away. She started with the ones she had been practising. 'New York' and 'Subway tunnel'. 'Centre Park' where they would go to play and learn the names of different trees. And of course there was 'Liberty' too – wasn't that the woman's name? The one who stood now down the end of the port, a floppy crown on her head and an eager smile dimly lit by the yellow torch she held in her hand, guiding them in just like Uncle Dovid had said.

In a way, she looked smaller than Ruth had expected. In fact, totally different to the image in her head. But despite her father's genes she had always struggled with her imagination, so really, what would she know? She just hoped that that side of her would grow up when the rest of her did, to make them all proud at last.

Still nobody around her spoke, unready to believe. Ruth looked at her Tateh, waiting for him to confirm. Or maybe even to call out a greeting – he was the only one amongst them who could speak any American yet, a whole library of borrowed dictionaries piled on the attic floor, building blocks for little girls to make forts. And Ruth wondered now if an idea stayed the same no matter how many times you translated it? And what about a family, she wondered? Or even, a love?

But despite these questions, her father gave no answers. Nothing. The only time Ruth had, or ever would, see him lost for words. So she knew then that yes, they must have made it – that this here must be it.

Arrived.

America.

The beginning.

The right world at last, too perfect even to be said aloud.

While behind them Cork City lay slouched in sleep, snoring off last night's dregs, dreaming of anything other than the unexpected arrival of a Russian slaughterhouse ship.

There is always a beginning before the beginning, and this one had started with a plague of rats.

He had been an aspiring young playwright in a village called Akmian, which meant 'a river full of stones'. He sometimes went swimming to check if the rumours were true. He had a younger brother and a brand new wife and a skull that was full itself – an endless stutter of ideas like a tick or a twitch until one about a plague just stuck.

He felt the scurry of it, running through his dreams.

He wrote for five years, five years on one wooden, time-knotted desk, high away in an attic room where pillars of notes and ideas towered on every side – one sneeze and the pages would fly. While out in the shtetl, the locals all thought him crazy – calls his wife the Princess of the Bees and writes a play about rats?

'Nu, inside his head must be a zoo.'

'Noah's Ark, two by two!'

But once finished, something about the play caught on. First in the shtetl's tiny shed theatre, the local ramshackle treat; then in the town of Vilnius; then eventually it caught on in Moscow. And every night in the Empire's biggest city, beneath the ceilings dripping gold, the audience would gaze at the swarms of rodents; at the valiant hero who did not slaughter them, but rather rhymed the rats to death with his poetry and wit. Though the biggest joke of all was that no one could ever know the name of the man who had created this magic. *Anonymous* said the theatre programme. *Anobody*. A genius with a pockmarked face and a pair of bottle-thick specs forbidden to catch even a glimpse of his own work.

Since 1882 it had been illegal for Jews to move to Moscow. So said the May Laws. The no-you-May-not Laws. After the assassination of the Tsar the conspiracy theories had rippled out from St Petersburg, all eyes burning on the underdogs. Until eventually, the truth came out – that yes, there had been a Jewish man involved. Just one. And not even in the killing – not in the hurling of the bomb or the years of conspiracy, just in the hiding, to give the rest of them a place to disappear under the cracks of his floorboards because his people had had a history of being refused such a luxury, so now, who was he to do the same?

In the end, he was a hanged man.

From that moment onwards, it was his people who were forced to hide. Banished from the big cities; forbidden to own land or to take up certain jobs.

To see their masterpieces on stage.

Until one of them begged and an exception was made – a one-night exception for the Ratman.

It took him an entire day to get there – a bus from Akmian then a local train to Moscow, the carriages filled with prostitutes heading to work. Each clutched a bottle of vodka in one hand and a bright yellow permit in the other, both needed to appease the guards. Yet, at the sight of the patchwork of fishnets the playwright didn't so much as flinch. 'Sorry to disturb, ladies, but is this seat taken?' He buried himself amongst them with a smile as their cleavages ricketed along in time with the tracks. The scent of musk lightened heads. The snow chucked fistfuls of itself at the windows. And the more they gossiped the more he began to listen, enthralled, flattering them with a kind of attention they had never known in all their lonely lives, so that soon he felt the slick of their ruby lips upon his earlobes, whispering, begging for more. Either down the back of the train or in the icy Moscow alleyways where they made their dens. 'Come on,' they pleaded. 'We don't even charge you...' Just one chance to steam up the glasses of the Akmian genius who spoke to them nicer than any boychik ever had.

But 'no', he eventually managed. 'No thank you.' He had his Princess of the Bees waiting back home. And besides, the Commandments decreed – Mitzvah 570 to be precise – that there should be no intercourse with a woman outside of marriage.

The ladies cackled at that; the ladies who made a living out of those who flouted Mitzvah 570.

Eventually they waved him goodbye as he made his way towards the theatre's back door. He smuggled up to the cheapest seats in the house and looked down at the gilded faces looking up to his rats in awe.

By the time he returned to the shtetl it was the following afternoon, yet he knew his Princess wouldn't have slept a breath.

'So?' she asked. 'How was it?' Her black eyes had turned grey in the winter light.

'Exquisite.' He pulled her to him. Still his ears rang with the douse of the applause. 'Austėja, I have been…I think…' The same sound as torrential rain. 'I think it is time for us to leave.'

She gazed out the window beyond his shoulder. The snowflakes landed soft thuds on the ledge. 'Moshe,' she said, suddenly. 'You have something on your ear.'

He grabbed the stain between his fingers, ruby red. 'I must have cut it,' he replied. 'Shaving.' Even though he had been growing his beard since the day they were married, a hive for the honeybees.

It took them ten whole years to save; ten years and two daughters and one brother Dovid gone on ahead to work. A long wait. And then a crumpled letter arrived with some extra money for four tickets on an orange-rusted cattle ship – yet another beast to add to the zoo.

To America.

As well as packing his bags before he left, the playwright had learned his pillars of notes by heart, then built a giant bonfire in the middle of the Market Square. The whole shtetl gathered round to watch the flames feasting on years and years of work, their eyes streaming from the smoke almost as if they were upset; almost as if it were the man himself being burned.

'In the beginning,' he joked, perpetual patron of the upbeat, 'God cremated the heavens and the earth!'

But even hours after the embers died, still the stragglers stood, staring, thinking of other lands. While mothers snarled at sons to breathe in the fumes, just in case the genius was infectious.

The following day they began their schlep, all the way to Latvia and onto the ship where the captain smashed a bottle on the prow – an ancient tradition to launch them out to sea. A bit like a groom breaking a glass on his wedding day to remember, always, the destruction of Jerusalem. A sailor married to his vessel. Though everyone knew the story of the playwright's nuptials when the glass had refused to crack.

The chuppah had been a beautiful thing, the roses mangled into a perfect arch above the soon-to-be-happy couple. But below it the groom had started to sweat, stamping his foot upon the lump that just wouldn't flatten, while his almost-bride watched on, forcing a smile, trying to find some symbolism in the glitch – that their bond was unbreakable? Not a single flaw or weakness? Until, finally, another foot stepped in – Dovid's foot – putting them out of their misery as the crowd cheered and the Princess of the Bees kissed her husband, sucking away the panic and also the flicker of doubt as to which brother she had really married that afternoon; which one she wished she had.

But now, after ten days at sea, they had sailed away from that life. Those whispers. The Akmian playwright with his rats safely stashed in his pocket ready to be translated to a magical place called 'Broadway' where everyone would know his nobody name, the exhaustion worth it at last, the roses tossed on stage like a flock of birds scooped up to carry home for his wife, to keep her his and always his.

These were the things he had prayed for; the things he saw now as he slept in the dirt of a dockside shed. While all around him the ship's passengers lay dreaming their own versions of American dreams.

*

Ruth was the first to open her eyes.

The throb of her hand had woken her, pulsing its way through her sleep. She breathed in. Metal and sweat. An aftertaste of sea.

It had been late last night – long past her bedtime – when the woman down the end of the port had led them here. Lady Liberty. Not a statue at all, as it turned out , but a landlady, touting for business; offering a place where they could rest their poor, tired heads. They had followed her in silence, exhaustion winning out over a thousand questions, each of them just content for the moment to sleep on solid ground again. Though actually, Ruth had found it strange dropping off without Mame and Esther below her. She had liked being in the top bunk on the ship, feeling their words as they vibrated beneath – secrets they never let her hear but at least now she could feel.

She checked her finger. Already the base had begun to blacken.

Beside her, her father snored, eight hours of ideas clogging his nostrils. The white patch of baldness gleamed out from the crown of his head, the first bit of him to come into the world usually hidden away beneath the circle of his kippah.

Next to him in the dust her mother's curls mingled with her big sister's – a carpet of black, oily and slick. Like the story Tateh used to tell about the trio of women who spent their lives knitting – a widow, a spinster and a divorcee – alone except for each other and their needles and wool. Until one day they had an argument and tried to pull apart, only to discover that they had knitted themselves together – their clothes, their hair, even their eyelashes, bound into one.

Mame had warned him to stop. She said it would give the girls nightmares.

'But Austėja,' Tateh had protested, eyes vast with the confusion, 'it is supposed to be a metaphor. For family.'

Her family had begun to wake now, limbs stiff from awkward folds, and then the other bodies across the floor stirred too. Ruth watched as they opened their eyes one by one, each face registering a split second between waking and realising; remembering where they were.

America.

Arrived.

A sleep-crusty grin. And a look around for a bucket so that the men could wash their hands to begin their brand new day; their brand new everything.

'Have a look for one outside, girls, would you? There's bound to be one by the port.' It was Leb Epstein who made the request, drowsy up on elbows, his gut still resting firmly on the ground.

He was a tailor who had come from the very same shtetl as Ruth and her family, accompanied by his thin little wife. She always looked at your shadow instead of at you as if her eyes were too skinny to fit too much at once. The couple planned to travel to America first and save enough money through waistcoats and pleats to send back to the rest of their clan, just like Uncle Dovid had for them – letters of advice; certificates of introduction; pale pink flushes from sisters-in-law that couldn't always be hidden.

Ruth put her left hand behind her back. 'A bucket, Mr Epstein? Yessir.' She repeated the word in her head as she beelined for the door, *abucket abucket abucket.*

She had always been eager to make herself useful; to help the adults wherever she could – barely able to walk before she had sought out the orders, the chores, the tasks that made her feel more important than she really was. Sometimes the villagers laughed at her diligence; told her she had a very old soul for her eight little years. But this morning especially she just needed an excuse – anything to get outside.

Ruth eased the shed door open, a low groan off the hinges as if they had been sleeping too. She craned her neck, preparing herself for the New York view. The skyscrapers. The cabs. The peanut vendors on every corner – every single one – Uncle Dovid wrote that he worried he was about to turn into a peanut! And Ruth thought now it sounded a bit like one of her father's ideas, *A Plague of Peanuts! The Incredible Salty Man!* So she wondered if that counted as imagining; if maybe she should try and tell Tateh. *Guess what, guess what, America has fixed me!* Or if maybe she should just stay shtum and stop trying too hard to please?

Outside the shed, America hadn't tried at all.

The dock was deserted, quiet as an inhale.

There were no sailors.

No peanut vendors.

Nobody.

Ruth craned a little further.

Beyond the empty quay the sea was empty too. There was no sign of their ship – not even an orange-rusted bruise smudged against the port – while above, the sky stretched away uninterrupted, untouched, no buildings or scrapers at all. Like an uncracked glass on a wedding day, Ruth thought – an omen she hadn't ever understood.

Until now.

Behind the shed the warehouses sat in rows, abandoned. Smashed-out windows. A barrel leaking a tongue of rust where the rainwater had spilled. The only sign of life was the maul of seagulls overhead, their wings making hard work of the breezeless air, currents that just wouldn't run.

'Right, you runt.' Ruth's big sister suddenly appeared next to her, eyeing the dockside wasteland. 'Where would we find a pump?' Not that, really, they looked like sisters at all. Even at ten, Esther was much too like their mother – the wool-thick hair; the black eyes; the stare that cut like wire – whereas Ruth, as Esther always liked to remind her, had been born deformed, one of her eyes green and the other one brown.

Ruth never understood why the world didn't look different colours out of each one.

But this morning, the world just looked wrong. Felt wrong. Not even a shudder from the trains running under the ground – had Uncle Dovid just been making them up? And where was Liberty this morning, Ruth wanted to know – there had been no word from her either – so what if it had all just been a big fat trick?

'Esther...' She looked at her hand. The blackness had travelled even higher. 'Esther, are you sure...' She wondered if the nail would fall off soon; if the seagulls would swoop down to peck it up.

And normally she wouldn't have said a thing about her confusion. She didn't like to complain. Most of all, didn't like how cruel her sister could be with her weaknesses. All of them.

But this was different – this was everything.

Or at least, it was supposed to be.

'Esther, are you sure this is New York?'

Two days before they began their journey Tateh had taken the girls up to his attic, almost empty now that his papers had been carried off for the fire. He told them they could each choose one remaining item to take with them when they left – a souvenir from this life to the next.

Of course, Esther had gone first; had marched right up to the Shakespeare that sat on the top shelf of the bookcase, swathed in pale blue leather – another cow in another life. She had struggled to even carry the ton-weight down, let alone for thousands of miles, but it seemed the impracticality was precisely what had made their father smile; the perfect after-his-own-heart choice.

His second daughter had opted for the compass. It was hidden half-forgotten in the clutter of the desk, a mere four words in total. *North, South, East, West.* But even as she held it Ruth had felt better; had run her unbroken finger around the rim so that her nail made a sound along the ridges, a buzz that almost drowned all the other noises out.

This morning, Esther's voice was loudest of all. 'Stupid girl!' it cried, the disdain filling the whole span of her mouth. 'Don't you remember what Uncle Dovid said?' It was a voice for the stage, her father always boasted – the finest legacy he could have hoped for. The only one, really, he would ever need. 'Ellis Island,' it said now. 'He *told* us we had to come to Ellis Island first before we were allowed in.' Reading from a script everyone else seemed to know – everyone except for Ruth. 'All right?'

And to any audience the gesture that followed would have just looked like a kindness, a sibling affection, as Esther smiled and took her little sister's hand in hers. 'That's why Tateh and Mr Epstein are about to go to the Immigration Office.' She gave it a tug, a squeeze of reassurance. 'That's why you are shooing off with them too.' And then a twist. An extra snap. A whimper barely heard. 'You didn't think we'd travelled all that way for *this*, did you?'

Two hours later, having woken from her faint, Ruth sat on the tram with her father and his friend, stiffening her face into a smile, nice and wide like her sister had shown her. And maybe someday, years from now, they would come to look alike, maybe even be loved alike. An American family healed better again, the scars you could barely see.

Just as long as she ignored the pull in her pocket where the compass tried to drag her down. It must be broken too, she told herself, the magnets somehow mangled when the boat slammed the shore, because as they boarded the tram she had checked it, just to be sure.

She had stood at the edge of the dock and gazed out at the Atlantic, knowing the sea was meant to be *East*. The arrow had dithered, stuttering like a lip before tears. And then it had fallen down. *South*. The sea spreading off the bottom of Ireland and away.

So Ruth smiled a little harder now, telling herself that once Tateh and his rats were rich and famous he would buy her a new one that worked, the four points back where they belonged again.

In the end, the smiles turned out to be more like a plague. A transatlantic epidemic.

They were only in the Immigration Office five minutes before the laughter caught on, the flatcapped men behind the giant oak counter in stitches at the Ratman's wit.

'New York?' they screeched as they regarded the stranger with his scrap of a hat and his bush of a beard – a nest for the seagulls who squawked outside, taking the mick themselves. 'America?'

While his face turned as pale as the tiny patch of white on the crown of his head. Or as white as a spot on a map that desperate fingers have pointed at again and again and again. Until it is gone.

In time, so many stories would be spooled out of that moment it would become impossible to count.

Some said that when their boat found land there had been cries of 'Cork! Cork!', but that in their exhaustion they had heard 'New York! New York!' instead; didn't notice the difference for weeks.

Others claimed they had somehow known the English word for pork, and thought that that was what the sailors were heckling – 'Pork! Pork!' – a barrage of un-kosher threats to run them off the ship.

Other times it was just that the captain had told them this was the last stop, 'only up the road' from America; only a short, final shimmy in the wilderness – sure, they would be there in time for tea.

But for Ruth and her family, there was only one story; one version of the heartache.

After two weeks they sent Tateh off again, this time to the Housing Office on Lynch's Quay, to try to find them somewhere to stay. Mame insisted it was just a temporary measure, just a matter of pride – anything to get them out of that shed. 'We may be your family, Moshe, but we are not your rats.'

So the paperwork shoved them off towards an abandoned red-brick terrace, the houses huddled together like a crowd trying for warmth. Hibernian Buildings, they were called. Celtic Crescent. Monarea Terrace. Down the road from the port, as if the family could still be called up for the second leg of their journey at any moment.

They scalded the place with boiling water every day for a week, to annihilate the native germs. Mame refused to unpack a thing, insisting the bundles remain untouched. 'Temporary, remember – what did I tell you?' But soon Tateh put up a mezuzah outside the front door, another matter of pride. Then he coaxed the girls to unwrap a couple of items they had lugged halfway across the globe (or, as it turned out, only a quarter of the way). So now there was a tub of tealeaves in the kitchen, a snag of lace around the window, a copy of Shakespeare and the Talmud sitting on the shelf, the latter with the words of different Rabbis written side by side.

And every Friday as Ruth sat side by side with her family for dinner, she could almost forget about everything else; could almost ignore the rage and the resentment that lay ahead that evening as soon as the girls had been banished to bed.

Because they had become nightly by now, her parents' arguments – rituals forming even in the worst of times. It went food then prayers then pleas and regrets; the high pitch of her father's optimism and the lash of her mother's anger reaching up the stairs to the landing where Ruth sat, crouched in her nightdress, a covert Jewish playwright in the highest stalls of a gilded Moscow theatre.

She cracked her knuckles one by one. The fourth one wouldn't give.

'But Moshe, I have told you,' she heard her mother cry now, the line almost on cue. 'We do not belong in this place.'

She spied the back of Mame's head, the neck tensed into bones, before it thrust itself forward for the usual swerve – the same-old new line of attack. 'And what about Dovid?'

'Nu, what *about* Dovid?'

'Moshe, he is over there all by himself.'

'Austėja, why must I keep telling you it does not matter about my brother Dovid?'

It was the only time Ruth heard her father raise his voice. It sounded like a stranger's sound.

She checked behind to the bedroom door, though she knew Esther wouldn't stir. Even during the day her sister barely bothered to listen, unwavering in her allegiances: 'How am I supposed to become a famous actress,' she had sobbed, 'in some country I've never even heard of?'

'But Esther,' Ruth had tried to console her, eager to please as ever, 'I think they speak English here too.' Because she had heard them out in the street, all right, the melody in their talk; the bounce and skip to their tone; the word 'boy' after every lovely line.

'Look, my dear.' Downstairs now, Tateh was panting like he had been running, the heat of it steaming the inside of his specs. They said he was practically blind and yet still he was able to see things that no one else could. 'My darling Austėja, I will do it – I will write another play.' As he spoke he took a step closer to his wife. He seemed calmer in her orbit. 'Not the rats, but a new one. I am telling you, there is something…I can feel it already.' He had even enquired already after one of those newfangled typewriter contraptions – just the thing to set him off. 'Nu, can you imagine it,' he had exclaimed. 'Letters flying through the air! Only, they do say that sometimes the letters get stuck…'

Lttrs flyingthrough thea ir!

And Ruth smiled now as she thought of it, because it sounded a bit like her own words; how they sometimes congealed whenever she got nervous.

Wehaveeachotheristhatnotenough?

MamewhatistheIrishwordforhome?

Doesthesecondchildalwaysgetlovedsecondbest?

'Just...just let me do this,' Tateh concluded now. 'Let me do it for you?' Until it came, the highlight of the ritual. 'For my Princess of the Bees?' The silly pet name and the only story in the world the playwright refused to tell.

His daughters had pleaded with him over the years, begging for even the gist of the tale:

'Tateh, why do you always call her that?'

'What are the bees?'

'Mame?'

But even Esther had failed to prise the truth from their mother's lips, so instead they could only wonder at the flicker in her stone-black eyes whenever it was mentioned – somewhere between a warning and a delight. Sometimes, recently, the only sign of life that was left.

The Princess of the Bees.

Through the silence below the footsteps clipped away. Ruth turned and sprinted back to bed before she was caught and smacked to sleep, a hot face on a cold pillow. Only, as she lay there, she realised that tonight had been different. Because this time, Mame hadn't objected – hadn't said no, in any language – the ritual evolved and witnessed by two different-coloured eyes.

And Ruth remembered how Tateh once told her that bees sometimes communicated not by sound, but by sight; by watching each other dance. A 'waggle' they called it, making shapes with their flight that could be turned into maps for the others to follow. So then, no matter what, the rest of the hive would never get lost.

April

Date: 15th May 1958
Name: Shem Sweeney
Location: Lavatory
Status: Diabolical

I watched the words as they leaked from my pen, my whole body sinking with the relief of it – sweet release before my bloody eyes.

To be honest, I must have been a sight to behold myself, the gangle of me sat there on the filthy toilet lid, feet hovering off the ground to try and avoid the sop off the lethal-looking puddles below.

Some were so thick they had begun to form a skin. My gut did a churn over itself.

Being brutal, I was an awful scrawn of a lad; much taller than I should have been, given Jews tend to be on the shorter, stockier side, though my Ima did once say that her Abba (may his memory be blessed) had been a six-footer himself, bones so big they took the piss. Not that I ever got to meet the lad, mind you – he died before my time – and no photos either, apparently.

been an early enough growth spurt, mine, which I sup-
osed was kind of ironic given all my body's failures in the years
that followed, but that evening I was eighteen years of age as I sat
on the jacks, scrawling away like a mad yoke. In my left hand I held
a half-masticated biro, the tip going like the clappers, while in my
right I clutched the old timetable I had managed to nick from outside the nuns' dormitory when nobody was looking. It was the best
thing about being silent, to be honest – I got fierce good at going
unnoticed. Some might say, too bloody good.

Day 14

Items of note:

1) *I miss my Ima*

2) *The food is diabolical*

3) *I miss my Ima*

I read the points back to myself one at a time; saw where the pen
had leaned that bit too hard. But I couldn't help it, because it was an
entire fortnight now since I had arrived in this Godforsaken place,
and still I hadn't written a thing – all my thoughts, my frustrations,
clogged up with no release – I was going out of my skull! Until that
morning I had managed to smuggle the bic on the sly; had waited for
a chance to sneak off to the first floor lavs and then finally indulged
in my guilty pleasure. Sweet fucking release!

But no, that sounded all wrong. Like I was some kind of pervert.
Like I had nipped off with an under-the-counter for a you-know-
what – same as all the lads in school who used to boast about the
trajectory of their respective semen squirts. *And com'ere, do Jewies
have to hold theirs differently?* No, I could only imagine what the nuns

would have said if I was up to all of that. Though to be honest, they probably would've been just as furious if they had found me here now, given I was strictly forbidden to do any writing whatsoever while 'undergoing my treatment'.

They say masturbation makes you go blind. I was just mute. And what makes that go?

> *Roommate Diagnosis: Abysmal.*
> *Utter wanker/masturbator extraordinaire.*
> *In fact, must be blind as a bat.*

I smiled at the feeble joke, these days few and far between, though up on the wall, Jesus didn't seem to get it. Jesus on the cross. Because every room in that hellhole had a figurine just like it nailed, crooked, on high – even there in the jacks, hardly the most sacred of surroundings.

The lid beneath me was cracked, ice-cold through the fabric of my arse. In front of me the stall door was riddled with splinters, the flakes of paint long shredded or maybe even picked away by those who sat here shitting. Hiding. Praying. And I noticed one punter had obviously enjoyed his little session so much that he had carved a satisfied 'AH' into the grain. Must have been a non-speaker like myself, I decided, capturing the relief of the moment the only way he knew how:

Ahhhhhhhh.

I picked up my page now to do the same – a sigh of content-ment, scribbled down the timetable margin. But no, there had been enough writing for one day. Because God alone knew how long this scrap of paper was going to have to last me, so no need to use it up in one greedy go. Not when there was so much else still inside me, gagging to get out.

I stood up, slowly, careful to avoid the worst of the flood. I clicked my neck left and right; patted my head for my kippah, still not used to the fact that it was gone.

The nuns had confiscated it the minute I had been admitted, despite my Abba's fury. He didn't say a word when they took away my clothes. My insoles. My toothbrush. My beloved flashcards – the only means of communication I had left with the world. But as soon as they requested that circle of cotton from my skull he had gone nuts: 'Now just a minute,' he spat. 'I was *assured* there would be absolutely *no* religious discrim—'

'We understand, Mr Sweeney. But we just feel—'

'May I *remind* you that I could have *chucked* the boy into one of the *state* facilities, but I *specifically* chose to go private on the basis that the *standard*—'

'Joseph,' my Ima blurted, like she had just remembered something she'd forgotten.

My father's name echoed down the damp of the asylum hallway where we stood, three Jews and an Ursuline nun. It sounded like the opening line of a terrible joke.

'Joseph,' my mother repeated. 'Come on now.' Though her country lilt was barely audible over the din of the rain.

It had been Pathetic Fallacy, the weather that afternoon.

Murphy's Law.

Or more like Murphy's Phallus, pissing on us all.

'Sure, Joseph, it doesn't really matter. Don't—'

'Well, of course *you* would say that, Máire,' my father snapped, spitting the strange remark at the side of my mother's headscarf, the one that always hid her lovely blonde hair from view.

The flecks of his saliva glistened beneath the institutional lights so white they were almost green.

So slowly, I had unclipped my skullcap and handed it over to the Matron, Sister Monica, a flash of a smile across her beady eyes – a flicker of everything that was to come before—

Dingaling!

But now it was done; now the bell was ringing, the toll of it shrill across the toilet tiles.

Dingaling!

Time for bed. Time to sprint downstairs back to my ward and my room before the nuns found me missing. God only knew the bollocking they would line up for me if they noticed I was gone.

Dingaling!

I folded the paper as small as it would go. I reached for the lock, shuddering at the riddle of germs. But I had no choice, so I grabbed it with my left hand and then my right – always needing it to be equal, balanced out – before I scuttled away past the clogged-up sink, the tiny hole at the back filtering off what scummy drizzle it could. Sweet release.

I paused to watch for a moment, savouring as best I could. And then, without a sound, I was gone.

I hammered the stairs two at a time, bouncing my hands along the banisters as I went, *left then right then left then right then left*. I turned down the corridor, empty except for the corrugated jut of the radiators, the pipes inside them clicking like throats. The walls were lined with portraits of all the saints (*go marching in*), each one caged away in their frame as if they had been locked up here themselves, hundreds of years ago, and never released; never cured.

In St Jude's Ward the usual scrum was under way, nuns cattle-herding stragglers towards their pokey-arsed beds. One lad had done a protest piss in the middle of the floor and was refusing to clean it up. Apparently Jude was the patron saint of lost causes, the poor fecker, and yet it was actually kind of ironic given that down here we were supposed to be the most 'curable' patients of the lot. 'Rats in the attic' the Irish saying went for the deranged, so at Montague House they seemed to have taken the phrase literally and stashed all the proper hystericals on the upstairs floors – crazier the higher you went – whereas down here, there was supposedly still a whiff of hope. Maybe.

Soon the Common Room was empty, nothing left but the reek of itself; a pool of wet half-smeared.

According to the rumours, this had been the living room, back when the House still belonged to a certain Lord and Lady Montague. The story went that their son had gone a whole clatter of sandwiches short of a picnic, so when the old pair popped their clogs they left their crumbling pile of bricks and mortar and bad memories to the nuns to be regurgitated as an institution for the 'superior correction of seats of thought'.

I always thought it sounded funny, that. '*Seats* of thought'. I'd never really heard of minds for sitting before – do a headstand 'til the blood rushes up.

Speaking of chairs, the ones here were fecked across the floor, a couple of tatty newspapers strewn alongside. I heard a voice behind that made me jump, but it was only the radio in the corner, a boxy yoke that was always turned to shite-talk instead of the music channels. I would have killed for a bit of rock'n'roll; or even some Connie Francis, the hit of the moment – 'Who's Sorry Now?' – well, I'm afraid to say that I am, Connie, 'cause I can't bloody hear your song! Instead the nuns kept the dial fixed on the news or the depressing talky programmes; voices grumbling all the usual sca – economic woe, unemployment, emigration – people fleeing the country like rats from a sinking ship. Though to be honest, Ireland probably wasn't sinking a bit these days; was probably floating higher and higher what with all that weight off her shoulders.

I checked round the corner for the other lads, the regular crowd, like. Enda Flaherty and Eoin Moore. Tourettes Tony – my favourite of the lot. And you would have known if Tony was still up, all right, would have heard him as he knocked about the place, blurting 'ANUS' at the top of his lungs.

'NUN'S ANUS!'

The sisters glaring at him every time as if it were the devil on his tongue, licked with a lovely Monaghan lilt. While the few of us who were still tuned into this world would giggle our nuts off, the attention only making him worse.

'SHAVED ANUS BIBLE HUMPERS!'

Yes, Tony was my favourite. Not that I knew him or anything, just watched from the sidelines, making a few notes in my head. To be honest, a tiny bit of me always hoped that it was just a joke – that he was just putting it on to be funny. Now that, that really would've been something worth smiling for.

I savoured the notion as I reached my bedroom, turning the corner with my left foot first – always the left – to stop a dose of the panics kicking in. But as soon as I arrived I felt a different kind of panic, because it seemed the old man had waited up. For me.

'And so he deigns to join us. Where have you been – picking your hole?'

My roommate, Alfred Huff. The wanker himself.

I hovered on the threshold unable to move, a deer mangled in the headlights. Inside, our room was an absolute scut of a thing – it must have been one of the Montagues' storage cupboards; a pantry at best. I could have sworn the reek of pickle still lingered. Mind you, there was barely any air for it to cling to now between the pair of jaded camp beds shoved together, the arses sagging in tandem, and the narrow wardrobe wedged into the corner like a coffin upright. Otherwise, there was nothing but the room's single shelf crammed with an assortment of battered-looking books which Alf had warned me not to even think about touching. So instead I could only stare up at the terrace of spines, each one wrinkled like his ugly mug or like a teabag that had been squished to death for one last piss-weak brew.

I cranked my neck to make it calm. *Left then right then left then right then left.*

'Nu? What has you spazzing like that? You after getting the epilepsy on top of everything else?'

His words made me still again, rigid with the anger. The blush. Though there was a hint of irony this time to ease the blow. Because out of anyone, your man wasn't one to talk about spazzing – an awful bout of the tremors off him, his hands forever on the jitter like a pair of chattered teeth.

But for the moment it was time to set my own hands to work. I stepped inside and unbuttoned my shirt; shoved the paper scrap under my pillow for safekeeping, the princess and the proverbial pea.

L-M-N-O...

But no, there was no good in the letters any more – already I could feel the solace from the upstairs lavs vanishing, just like that.

I kicked off my shoes. They didn't let us have laces.

And I knew that it was pathetic; that I should have been immune to the old fogey by now. Sure, he had been a cretin to me from day one, the first person I was introduced to right after my parents had said their goodbyes.

Ima's face had been skiddy with tears as she glanced back over her shoulder. Though it was always over her right one – I didn't like that – wanted to beg her to balance it up with the left one as well. Or even just to let me count her tears; to put a number on the chaos.

But before the day was out, Alfred Huff had put down something else instead. 'Quite the ride, your Ima,' he sneered, wrinkled lips curled fat around the smut. 'Shame you won't be seeing her again, eh?'

I stripped down to my regulation underpants and dressed up into my regulation PJs, the fabric flimsy over the jut of my bones. I lay down with the scratch of the blanket. I was half a shin too tall for the bed. I closed my eyes, but above me the lights were still going gaudy, so instead I just stared at the glare of the bulb. And waited.

To be honest, the fact that he was such a prick was just a shame, really – one more to add to the list. Because in another life, Alf and I could have probably been...friends. Something. Sure, we were the only two Jews in the place! My Abba had been bloody delighted when he had heard who I would be rooming with, even if it was just some old cripple in a wheelchair with a pair of gammy hands. And I supposed I had been almost relieved myself, knowing I would only have to shack up with one other person – the rest of the St Jude's lads were all fecked together in the master dormitory, row after endless row – a whole chorus of crazy through the night that would surely scupper your dreams.

But most of all, I had thought to myself how, out of anyone, your man would understand my silence; would appreciate why I had stood there at the pulpit on the day of my Bar Mitzvah, five years ago now, and gone shtum – not a single word since.

'Sweeney. Huff. Goodnight!'

The pantry switch clicked off; the darkness collapsed in on us both. Already I could hear Alf's snores – he was always the first asleep – liked to get out of there as quickly as he could.

I rolled onto my side. *Left then right then left then right then left.* I curled my knees into my gut like a foetus. An unborn eejit.

But no, despite the fact that Alf might have understood – that we might have even been…mates, something – it seemed he had decided to go the other way instead and use my religion, our religion, against me.

When I first arrived he had been out in the yard playing checkers with Enda Flaherty. It was the only time I had seen Enda sitting down since – usually he was too busy shuffling around the House's corridors, his slippers torn ragged with the mileage. It was probably why Alf was friends with him, to be honest, that perpetual wandering – the closest thing to a Jew he could find in Montague House.

Until me.

They were arranged around a ramshackle wicker table, the weft and warp of it still slick from the rain. Alf stooped forward from his dented wheelchair, his legs half-gone and his grey hand quivering over a pile of red counters.

I flicked my eyes across the board. Two more moves and the game was his.

'Alf, there is someone I'd like you to meet.' It was Sister Frances who did the honours – from what I could tell, the youngest nun of the bunch. She was a pretty thing too – a touch of the Grace Kelly about her – enough at least that her presence attracted the attention of the other patients lolloping, gormless, nearby. 'His name,' she said gently, 'is Shem.'

Shem, eldest son of Noah; aged ninety-eight the year of the flood. Even if I had always been shite at swimming – too much limb to figure out how to float.

'Looking lovely today, Franny,' Alf replied, a gruff voice in a hotch-potch accent. 'Is that a new lipstick you're parading?' He sucked his teeth to *tut tut tut*. 'And you with your vow against vanity?'

The pretty nun looked to the ground. I could have sworn I saw her blush. 'Well, I'm introducing you specifically, Alf,' she continued, 'because Shem here will be sharing a room with you from now—'

'He'll be *what*?' Alf growled as he hefted a counter to the right, claiming three blacks for his trouble.

I checked again. A decent position. One more turn to go.

'I *said*, he'll be sharing a room with you from—'

'Arra now, you remember it is fierce cruel to be pulling me leg, Fran, given me circumstances. Sure, I've had that room to meself since—'

'Yes, I *understand* that, Alf, but Sister Monica has decided it would be for the best since ye are both...*brothers in faith* so to speak.'

At this, finally, he looked up; scanned my scrawny figure as if for proof.

I felt the other yard-timers follow suit.

Tourettes Tony proclaimed something about my anus.

Alf's eyes frisked me all the way down and up, shameless into every crack. Though to be honest, they weren't the eyes I had expected, so much younger than the haggard rest, and a dimple scooped out of the middle of his chin that gave a strangely fetching touch. It reminded me of your man Kirk Douglas, and wasn't he a Jew and all?

Our stares met, just for a second. I looked away to the sky. Even with the rain gone, still there wasn't a bird in sight.

'Hmm,' Alf finally pronounced as he returned to his game. I stood rigid, watching the shake of his hands. 'Bit lanky for a Jewman, wouldn't you say? Nu, did your Ima not force-feed you up like the rest of us?'

At the mention of her, though, I flinched. *What did you say about my Ima?* But of course, I couldn't ask him, or answer; could only pine for the flashcards that had just been taken off me, a longing like a phantom limb. I wondered if Alf ever got that for his legs.

'I *said*,' he repeated, his impatience beginning to mount, 'you look like a bit of a shmendrick to me, no?'

The other patients shuffled closer, nosy for the awkward scene – the old man and the shmendrick, the pipsqueak.

'Can't have had many kneidlach fecked your way of a Friday night.' The Yiddish tests thrown my way now too, words that only my father ever used. 'Nu?'

No?

Nu?

Eh?

And questions had always been the worst for me – an ask without an answer – the imbalance of it alone enough to get me riled. So the lads at school would all gather in a circle like kids looking for a story, but instead it was to batter me with questions, gobs like dogs asking hundreds and hundreds while I shuffled for a flashcard that would answer even some of them, even one of them, fingers fidgeting quicker and quicker until—

Paper cut. Droplets of red upon the page. The same colour as a nun's smutty lips.

'I'm afraid, Alf,' Sister Frances sighed, 'I'm afraid Shem is actually...The boy's a mute.'

A ripple of whispers buffered against me as the strangers took in the news. Only it didn't soften the blow. Because the laughter that came was a vicious thing, there on his throat somewhere phlegmy and sore. 'Mute shmute!' The dimple in his chin bouncing up and down like a babby on a lap. 'Go away with you, Franny, sure, who ever heard of a Jew who can't...' Until his eyes saw that no, Sister Frances wasn't joking. That no, Shem Sweeney wasn't speaking.

No nu never.

'Sure, that's unnatural.' His laughter began to fade. 'Like a duck who can't swim. A...a Paddy allergic to spuds. Jaysus, without a voice sure, he's not even really a *Jew* for fuck's—'

'Now, Alf, there's no need for that.'

But by then I had stopped listening. Because I had heard it all before, for five whole years – five empty years – and I was only an eejit for thinking this lad or this place would be any different.

I turned and dragged myself back inside, walking away like my parents had done that very afternoon while I had just stood there in the hallway dripping, waving. Like a deaf person clapping – that's what they do, you know – shove both hands in the air and move them from side to side, showing their appreciation silently instead.

Back in the room now, Alf let off a groan in his sleep, hefting around so that his stumps knotted up with the sheets. While beside him, I buried my face into the pillow, trying to swallow the lump that had formed in my throat so that even if I could talk, figured out how to again, the words would have only got stuck.

The yell of the bell had me up the following morning, lamenting another day. I made my bed and checked for my paper scrap. It was exactly where I had tucked it.

Once dressed, the timetable kicked off as per usual, the Montague House routine. There was Wake Up at one end and Curfew at the other; Work Hour out in the yard, half-arsed with our pointless tasks. All three meals were set in stone, different shades of canteen slop, including dinner at an ungodly five o'clock so that by the time you actually made it to bed that night your stomach was already going insane, an accidental hunger strike that wouldn't let you cave whether you wanted to or not.

In better news, Games Hour fell once a week, a sixty-minute hurrah that saw me step out from the sidelines to trounce them all at Scrabble – the only mode of expression I had left. Although, it seemed these days I wasn't the only one fixated on my words (or more precisely, my lack thereof), because as part of the never-ending routine, Wednesday afternoons meant a visit from the local GP.

Doctor Lally was a stubby chap who wore creased suits and a moustache that looked almost definitely stuck on. He gawped at each of us for half an hour a pop in the stuffy confines of the back office, the naked bulb over our heads definitely more interrogational than medicinal.

It was an unfortunate name, 'Lally'. Doctor for the 'do lally'.

'And how's about you this week, Mr Sweeney?'

I squatted before the splintered desk, an unnaturally high jut off my knees. I spotted another 'AH' carved into the wood, just like the one in the toilet stall. More relief? I wondered, settling myself. Or maybe, this time, a scream?

'A deep breath, remember,' Lally went on. 'And then the words do be bouncing off the lips like a...well, like a bouncy ball.'

Each week he led me through a variety of routines, the ones I had already tried with all the other stubby eejits before him.

Exercises.

Tongue stretches.

Diagrams of the inner throat, Lally tentative as he held them up as if he half-expected me to lash out; as if I had some kind of phobia of gobs. When actually, an obsession would have been closer to the mark – the first thing I noticed about people these days – the plumpness of lips. The dinge of teeth. The sliver of tongue you got with certain syllables.

Ls were my favourite.

L-l-l-l-l-l-lovely.

L-l-l-l-l-l-lally.

One Wednesday he even made me fixate on my own mouth in the mirror while he explained how I should try and reacquaint myself with it 'like...well, like a long lost pal', even though I wanted to tell him I'd never really had any friends apart from my Ima so he would need to be a bit more specific.

And then the following week he asked me would I mind if he touched it. 'Now if you could just...just open up, boy.'

Oh the irony, I thought, the spit sopping down my throat. *Yes, if only I could.*

But I played along with his whims all the same, humouring him while it lasted. Because I knew it was only a matter of time before Lally, like all of the others, gave up on the whole attempt; resorted instead to finding some alternative means through which I could communicate with the world, as if anything came even remotely close.

For some reason they always started with sign language, using fingers instead of tongues. I only knew what it was because we'd had a deaf lad at school who went at it with his brother all wrists and thumbs, a lifelong game of charades.

One word.

Sounds like 'yelp'.

Starts with H.

But despite the doctors' attempts I never went in for all of that, too worried my fingers might try and spell out the thing that had sent me silent in the first place. Then I would have no choice but to tighten my joints too. Early arthritis. Or as I always thought it should have been called, *Early can't-write-is.*

So in the end, I had decided to just scribble my conversations instead; had found some notelets in my father's drawer and began to carry them around wherever I went, all piled up like a deck for a trick: *Pick a card, any card!*

Or like notes for a speech: *Ladies and gentlemen, unaccustomed as I am to public speaking…*

If only they knew.

To be honest, it had worked well enough – a means to an end, like, for a while. I had even managed to devise a system whereby each phrase I wrote was intoned with a set of dots and dashes – a bit like Hebrew accent marks, or fadas in Irish – to try and capture at least some of the sound. Five years of:

YES PLÊASE

Half a decade of:

THÁNKS A MÌLLION

Literally millions of them. Of:

I LOVE YOU TÓÒ

The accents like eyebrows raised in surprise. Or maybe it was doubt? And then there was his lesser-used cousin:

I LOVE YOU TWÒ

The last word ripped away then stuck back on with a load of Sello-tape, though it was always a lot flimsier than the rest, like it could fall off at any minute.

And I had once tried to just write out the truth on a flashcard and swallow it. Whole. I'd decided it could be a way to purge myself, or more precisely, to ingest the bloody thing so then at least it would be in me, a part of me, in a way other than my speechlessness.

But I choked – halfway down my gullet and the thing was up again, a lump of pulp upon the floor. So no, it seemed I couldn't even manage that.

'Right, well, I'm afraid time is up,' Lally announced, a cheer in his voice that masked the relief surprisingly well. 'But I do be feeling the progress coming, no bother. So I'll be seeing you next Wednesday, all right?'

I nodded vaguely as I left the office, ducking my head extra low under the doorframe.

And later that afternoon I watched out the window as Lally lowered himself into his Morris Minor, a dent in the curve of the roof like a skull. And as he drove away I wondered where he was headed – where was his home? What was his mother like? And most of all, did he have a secret about her the way I did about mine?

So April continued, the cruellest month I think some gobshite once said, though I'm not sure why he had such a vendetta against these thirty days in particular. To be honest, if nothing else I was starting to get used to the routine of the place – I had always needed that sort of regularity, that rigidity – so I was grand at least to sleepwalk through the motions.

But for all the monotony, as the month drew to a close I began to feel it, low down in my gut.

I had never been away from my mother for a prolonged period of time – not even close. There had been a three-day weekend in fourth year, a schoolboy camping trip off to Dalkey Island where Liam Mackey thought it would be gas altogether to hide a rasher under my pillow, the princess and the pig.

But this was the longest period yet, and it had started to take its toll.

I had scoured the place for a telephone; a chance to hear even a sneak of her voice – just a confused 'Hello?' would be more than enough – two 'l's from her pinky-red tongue. Or I saw some of the other patients scribbling letters – barely literate pen pals with the outside world – but obviously I was still banned from anything like that. So the only thing I had were my secret sessions up in the first-floor jacks, the highlight of the weekly routine by a country bloody mile.

The germs still gave me the skits – stiff as a plank as I sat there and wrote.

Each night I would jot down everything I could remember about her, to be sure that I wouldn't forget. I wrote about the shape of her lips, the bottom one so much fatter than the top as if trying to buoy it up; about the way I called her 'Ima', the Hebrew word for 'Mum', even though she had always been hopeless at the language herself. And I also wrote down everything I had to remember to tell her as soon as I got out of this place; as soon as my father realised that this was a pointless bloody exercise and we would just have to make do as was, the silence here to stay. *Consider it another child, lads! The sibling I never had!*

So I wrote about the nuns and the rotten dinners; about Tourettes Tony and his anuses and fecks. And I wrote about my roommate Alf, the absolute cretin; about how relentless he was with his torture, the main whack of his days now spent shrivelled into his chair, complaining about my very existence:

'Sister Monica, it's a bleedin' disgrace I've been shacked up with this little freak!'

'They always say look out for the quiet ones – sure, what if he shtups me in me sleep?'

Only, between his cruelty and my mother's beauty, I realised that I had started to run out of space, the stolen page crammed full to burst. It wouldn't be long before I would have to steal another one. Or maybe devise some kind of shorthand for my gommy woes.

S-O-S

Shitty old Shem

Suffocator of stationery

And then I remembered when I was younger I could never tell the difference between the two spellings of the word. 'Stationery' and 'stationary'. So close, and yet…So my Ima had taught me that *sta-tion-E-ry* was for *pEEEEEEns* and stuff, whereas *sta-tion-A-ry* was when I stood still, in the one spot, and she ran *a-wAAAAAAy*, using the sounds of the matching letters to stick them together in my head. At the time, though, the second scenario had made me cry so loudly that she had had to come closer to me than ever; had pressed my head into the hollow of her chest until the panic of it all dried up.

I left the toilets behind and smeared my hands on my shorts, thirty times each side. But when I made it back to bed that night I couldn't manage sleep, the panic of the memory written all over my dreams.

And then, when it could get no worse, the cretin came looking for me.

It was the final day of the month, the furthest from April Fools', though to be honest, my loneliness was beginning to drive me so mad I almost felt an affinity with the gobshites around me. A kindred gombeen spirit.

We were out in the yard for Work Hour, twenty of us in total, each with a broom in hand and instructions to brush up the dust, no matter that our scrapings only made its splutter worse. A black, emphysemic hock.

Above us, the sky was completely blank, like someone had forgotten to colour it in.

We must have been some scene to behold, every manner of retard you could imagine out there – a comedy if it weren't so bloody tragic. And an irony to it too, given Montague House was meant to be as good as it got – the crème de la curdled crème of the country's lunatic facilities. Apparently there were about twenty thousand of us across the nation in total, locked up without a key – more per capita than the Soviet bloody Union.

Ireland, the Isle of Saints and Scholars. And Psychos.

Of course, long before I arrived I had heard all the horror stories about places like this; the schoolboy rumours, usually to do with taunts of 'your ma' getting 'locked up' for being a 'whore'. Apparently the patients all crawled around on shite-crusted floors, guzzling their meals from troughs. Farms not hospitals, the dead buried outside in one giant hole, flesh atop unknown flesh.

But by now my father had heard enough about mass graves to last him a lifetime, so to his measly credit, he had taken no risks; had put his money where his son's mouth wasn't and gone private, to Montague House – practically a holiday compared to those other hellholes.

Wish you were here!
And I wasn't.

'Shmendrick, can I have a word?'

I saw his wheels crunch in beside me before I saw the rest of him. My whole body ached, knackered with the work and the heat. And now this.

He locked his chair into place with his fidgety hands, all set for his attack. I saw a stain of red on the cuff of his shirt, hard to tell if it was blood or grub.

For a moment I didn't move and neither did he, his question still the only thing between us. Though I realised he must have known I was feeling even weaker than usual these days, pining for my Ima more than ever, because when he finally opened his gob again he annihilated me in one fell swoop: 'Listen, Shmendrick, I'm after finding…this.' In the shake of his palm the scrap of paper looked more pathetic than I remembered. A tiny yoke, and yet it was about to capsize the whole bloody thing.

I felt the weight of my body as it slumped into the broom, six and a half feet of skin and bones and *oh fuck*. Because how the hell had I managed to let the thing go missing? Usually I was so careful – tucked it down into the secretest of cracks where no one could ever find it. But I supposed I had just been distracted lately, my mind off the game and off with her instead, clinging to our memories for dear life.

But now there weren't going to be any more of them. Because he would turn me in; would hand me over to the nuns to bang me up on the top floor with all the other rats in the attic, a plague of spastication and not an antidote in sight.

I played the notion over in my head. I thought my breakfast might chuck up on his wheels.

But of course, Alf wasn't finished with just me yet, going in for a second round. 'You see, Shmendrick, I have…I have a proposition for you.'

I looked at him now, the clouds of dust settling between us as he began to lay out his terms. I saw the liver spots on his temple and the little bum chin; saw the trouser legs that flopped downwards from his knees and didn't lead to feet. I wondered what he had done with all his shoes. And by the time I managed to catch up with what he was saying I had to double take, because the stuff he was coming out with was the strangest shite I think I'd ever heard. First there was something about a 'change' in him ever since I had arrived; about the first time in years he had shared a room with someone else, and about this load of 'memories' that was after coming back.

'Only,' he said now, his voice dropping a little lower, 'I want to get them...on paper, like. But I can't...Me shakes won't...'

He paused. I glanced at him glancing at the scrap. The fidget of his hand gave it a life of its very own.

He said that he could find us a place to meet; that he could get me pen and paper, on the sly of course. 'And look, I know I've been a bit...' He stopped then, the apology less than half-born. I stubbed my toe into the dirt, kicking 'til it went sore. 'But if you do this for me, Shmendrick, I promise I'll...I'll...'

I waited for the next words to come – surely an undercut that would knock the wind out of my gut. But when it didn't arrive I looked up, and Alf looked back, the light catching something different in him, something I hadn't seen before, a sadness in his eyes I think I almost believed. 'Shmendrick, I'll...' He glanced away, hoking a crust from his eyelid, a bit of dust that must have got lost. Before he found me all over again: 'I promise...I'll help get you back to your Ima.'

Friday

Neither says a word as he drives her home.

The car doors are locked, the windows fogged white as if they have been fucking for the last ten minutes instead of just sitting there, accelerating, breathing all the things they aren't quite ready to say aloud.

In her lap, the unopened present sits snug as a sleeping child.

Beneath it, her little black dress is all creases – a shame really, after she bothered to go and get the thing pressed, to try to look the part. It was her first ever venture to Paradise Dry Cleaners, though she had passed the place a thousand times before; had felt the hot, chemical air gushing out onto the footpath, maybe, yes, a bit like the climate of some Paradise far far away.

This, though, is Hampstead Garden Suburb.

The houses are as silent as the couple, a candle in every window to mark the occasion. And a regulation hedge outside every front, pruned and high, so that the entire neighbourhood feels a bit like a maze – need a spool of thread to find your way out, or better yet, a compass.

Apart from anything, the silence is just so unlike them. Usually they get straight to it – the evening post-mortem – the night slit open and the entrails of it slick across the back of the car before they make it home in time for a cup of tea and a drunken fuck in front of the mirror. But tonight, she supposes, is different. Monumental. The milestone finally complete. The months of build-up, maybe even the full two years of their relationship, holding its breath for this: an invite extended to Noah's non-Jewish girlfriend to come for *Chanukah* dinner in the Geller family home.

Aisling's head spins at just the thought of it. The corner of the parcel digs hard into her crotch.

She looks at him to steady herself, the face that never fails to calm her. She sees the gouge-deep eyes; the seasoning of stubble; the impossibly symmetrical features – like one of those children's paintings you fold in half to make a butterfly.

She wishes now that she could kiss him; stop the awkwardness taking hold.

But he concentrates on his driving, his hands stiff around the steering wheel of the Audi S7 Sportback. It is black, lacquered like wet tar; paid for by the investment bank, but then again, if you are going to sell your soul then you might as well guzzle up the perks, the full-fat cream of the leather interior.

The car slides them down Wildwood and onto Meadway, the air electric with a thousand thoughts. At the bottom of the hill they pass death on either side, the Golders Green Crematorium to the left and the Jewish Cemetery to the right. Aisling stares through the shadows at the patchwork of tombstones, entire lives condensed into a marble shorthand. Not that her job is any better, of course – half-page obituaries that leave out anything that matters. Like:

Aisling Creedon. Irish Catholic. Aspiring journalist who moved to London to become a better version of herself.

Or:

Noah Geller. British Jew. Banker and part-time magician who is keeping oddly quiet.

She uncrosses her legs, sweaty from the twenty denier and the close weight of the gift. 'So,' she finally asks. It seems as good a place to start as any. 'Can I open it?'

It wasn't her first time meeting the parents tonight – you didn't get to two years without a single glimpse, even if it was complicated. The pilot run had been for one of Noah's performances – a gritty Camden pub crammed with a troupe of hipsters, and Aisling and the Gellers loitering, pastel-hued, down the back. Hardly your average Magic Show clientele, but they had been united, at least, by that.

The four of them got a drink afterwards around a sticky table; a bowl of American peanuts gone stale.

'My poor nerves,' Aisling had admitted, greedier with her vodka tonic than she probably should have been. 'I was convinced he was going to tell your one the Ace of Clubs!'

While Linda and Robert Geller had stared at her from the other side as if she were speaking in tongues.

So Noah had taken over. 'Oh ye of little faith.' Had rubbed his hand on her denim thigh, smoothing her anxiety down. 'And how about you, Dad?' he had asked then, changing the subject, his very own seek of approval. 'What did you think?'

But Robert only looked down on his coffee cup, a chip in the rim that could savage a lip. 'Look, you...you know what I think, son. But if it makes you happy...'

Aisling smiles now at the memory; how foreign the discomfort with his parents seems. A million miles, especially after tonight.

They pass Golders Green station, a parade of red buses looping around and around the concourse, though the Tube itself looks empty, the Northern line fast asleep. It is the most popular line for suicides, she read somewhere – a career made out of death so only natural that she should know these things. Only, apparently all the Underground stations have now embraced the inevitability of jumpers; pits dug deep beneath the tracks to gather the bodies, open graves for the rats to explore.

She thinks back to her first few months in London, her own tingle every time the train slowed in, the yellow line only a leap away. A chance to leave the loneliness behind – the version of herself she just couldn't seem to make work.

And then the Sunday afternoon in 2011 when she was riding the train to the end of the line and then back again, and then back again, just to avoid the world up above; just to watch the passengers and wonder at their stories – good practice for the obituaries, she had convinced herself. Barely. Until a stranger got on at Leicester Square and sat down beside her; told her he was off to give a performance in Hyde Park where he stood on Speakers' Corner and did magic tricks in silence, protesting in favour of the unsaid.

He made a paper swan appear in her pocket.

She looked at him. *Hello. This is a version I don't normally give.*

A little leap.

'So can I?' Back in the car, her voice is a too-loud thing.

The light from the streetlamps washes up and over Noah, like that game with a hand passing slowly down your face to reveal a different expression every time.

His does not change.

'Noah?'

'What?'

'Can I open it?'

The lump is a book, she suspects, the wrapping paper an iridescent blue so shiny her fingers leave three white smudges that linger for a moment then fade away.

'Well, can—'

'No,' he says, at last. A relief to have an answer. But a firmness to it she doesn't understand.

She hadn't seen the parents since that Camden gig. Made a few comments about it when she was teasing him; a few when she wasn't too.

'What, are you ashamed?'

'Still think they'll disapprove?'

'Coming up to two years now – do you not think it's a bit odd?'

But of course, she knew it was more complex than that. A lot more. And anyway, she reminded herself, two years carried enough weight as it was – most of her friends had already begun the steady decline into house hunts and mortgage rates and maternity leave; wedding invites and babies delivered in their droves – God knows she had no interest in all of that. And even Noah's little sister was six months gone herself, her bump brandished like a medal as she scrutinised Aisling's own stomach from across the dining-room table that night.

Because despite everything, the invitation had finally come.

The chance.

It was six weeks ago he had mentioned it, lying in bed one morning after a gig, the throwaway so quiet she almost missed it.

'So,' he had asked. 'Will you come?'

'What?'

'To Chanukah?'

Twenty minutes later her orgasm had yelled even louder than usual, drowning out the daunting implications. Or maybe the volume was a celebration – turned on by the acceptance, the possibility.

But of what?

They drive into Hampstead Village, the High Street a blaze of festive lights. Despite the hour, a line still stretches from the famous crêpe van – they flock from far and wide; wise men traipsing after a star but no, wrong bloody holiday – she knows better by now. She watches the queue and bites her nail, tasting the start of something sweet. She flicks it to the floor beneath the seat.

The rest of the High Street is deserted, most of the locals staying in tonight to light their candles. Aisling pictures the *Menorah* again, the beautiful thing, its eight arms arched proudly out. And the ninth branch for the *shamash* – the 'servant candle', the one that is used to light the others, or so the ritual decrees.

Or at least, so the Internet told her.

It had just started as a bit of background reading, preparation for the night itself – a feeble attempt to stop her standing out even more than she already would. But there was something about the information that had kept her going, clicking page to page, on and on into the night until her eyes went blurred and black. She read about the rededication of the Second Temple and the Maccabean Revolt; about how there was only enough oil for the *Menorah* in the temple to burn for one night, but how it somehow lasted eight – a miracle of light and love against the odds.

Then a few days ago she and Noah had been sitting on the banks of the Regent's Canal, the Sunday papers spread out across their laps as if mopping up a spill. It was a ritual they had come to observe every week, their fingertips blue and black by the end like love bites gone too hard.

They took it in turns to read to one another, stories traded like gifts back and forth.

'Six-year-old girl gone missing in Kent,' she began. 'Police have found a shoe but nothing else.'

'Don't worry,' Noah had replied, not looking up. 'We'll keep ours locked in chains.'

'Which, our footwear or our children?'

He had laughed in response and she had glanced away, trying to hide her satisfaction. She spotted a pair of swans coasting by on the canal, so perfect they almost looked fake.

He went next: 'New *Merchant of Venice* at the National gets four stars.'

'Want to book?'

'Could try get them through the office?'

'God bless corporate hospitality, eh?'

'No, don't worry, they'll make me slave for them. After all, the line is expressly "a pound of flesh". Although, I suppose your lot would call it a "Euro" instead?'

She had rolled her eyes and checked the swans again – two kitsch, garden ornaments swept away in a flood.

'And there's an article here about *Chanukah*, in case you've any interest?' She had been tentative at first with the line of argument; the casual drop into conversation. 'I suppose it's just kind of ironic that the festival all about rebelling against assimilation and conversion and stuff has become the most secular holiday of the bunch.' Still the feathers paddled by on the water, Tippex-white against the grey. 'And according to this guy Rabbi Hirschfield I found online – quite a witty bastard once he gets going, actually – but according to him the whole thing can be attributed—'

'Aisling, what are you doing?'

Instantly she had stared at the paper in her lap as if she had never seen it before in her life. She checked the water. By now the swans had moved on.

Next she checked Noah, his face still formed into the question; his hair newly cut extra-short. Not that she had ever seen it as long as the photos from his university days, the thick black curls and the flowing Oxford gown, Harry Potter chic. *Sure no wonder you're after pretending to have magic powers!* Even if recently she has started to think that maybe he isn't pretending after all. Maybe, she concedes, in spite of herself, maybe there really is something special going on.

In a way, all the more reason to be careful.

'Pardon me for showing an interest,' she had snapped back at him, smothering the sentiment dead. 'Jesus, I'm bored. Can we get lunch soon? My head's still in bits from those shots.'

So now here in the car, buried in silence, she tries for the same approach – anything to buffer the weight of the moment. Or really, the weight of the present in her lap. 'Are we not there yet? Don't tell me you've got us lost again.'

Belsize Park flashes by, Chalk Farm station up ahead, the distant Camden buzz. The downward slope of the hill makes it feel like they are building speed, the thing a little harder to control.

Of course, she had brought her own gift along with her to the Gellers' house this evening, a bottle of Barkan Classic kosher wine with a bow around the neck. She got it from a website called Booze for Jews where a stranger named Isaac sent her a thank-you email, *shalom*-ing her for her custom, obviously oblivious to her imposter status. Not that she had minded, really – she supposed Booze for Gentiles didn't quite have the same ring.

'This is for you both,' she had said as she stood in the hallway of Linda and Robert's home, each word already drafted and re-drafted in her mind. 'To say thanks a million for having me.' She held the bottle out across the gap, poised in her dry-cleaned black dress and her pinned-up blonde hair – the perfectly preened portrait.

A voice in her head had mocked her for the act. She had glared at it to stop.

But Linda Geller had just tossed the bottle towards one of the helpers without a single word – didn't even check the label – and led Aisling through to the chintz-drenched dining room where the pregnant sister and the brother-in-law were waiting; the unnaturally coiffed grandmother with the lipstick-orange teeth and the barrage of questions from the moment Aisling sat down, a bowl of soup that never reached her lips.

'Yes, Dublin,' she had replied, starting as polite as she could. 'A place called Dalkey. It's near—'

'Eh, yes, Maeve Binchy, that's right.'

'No, I haven't actually read—'

While Noah gripped her hand under the table for support, running his thumb on the soft web of flesh between each finger. Though the tips of his were always rough, callous-hard, as if the magic burned a little every time.

'But I think things are looking up. The Recession—'

'No, not why I left, actually. Got offered a great—'

'Obituaries, yes. As they say, the "dead centre" of the newspaper!'

Next, Noah filled her glass right up to the brim, bargaining for her patience.

'Interesting, yes. Although really it's not—'

'Making a narrative out of life. Something we do every—'

'Ultimately? I'm not sure. Current Affairs has always been—'

Doing a decent impression of a son's current girlfriend whom he has chosen all wrong, but who does seem to be giving all the right answers for now, *nu*?

Eventually, the staff had appeared to clear the chicken soup away. Apparently Linda Geller always got the caterers in for special occasions, needing everything to be just so, no deviations.

Aisling noticed they were mostly foreigners. She tried to catch their eye.

It had been beef then for the main course. Potatoes and peas. A pile of onion rings on the side, a pool of grease to signify that ancient oil lamp – she had read all about this too. But with the change of course the conversation began to move on as well, leaving Aisling in peace. For now. But no, do not talk to me about peace – did you hear about the latest attack? Five dead, I read six, may their memories be blessed, and none of *them* of course well there's a surprise could you pass the piccalilli? And did you read that piece on the Levesen Inquiry in the *Guardian*? Sammy Stogel's son…Blake Grant's younger— And Blake's a nice name, Olivia – what do you think of Blake? But *Mum*, I *told* you, it is bad luck to name him before he is born. Well, tell them, Robert, I had you two chosen before you were even conceived!

So the conversation had zagged onwards. David Cameron to Dinos Chapman; politics to culture to pass the salt but it is bad for you and so what, so is living. Well, did you hear about Bonnie Matthews? No – Cancer? Aliyah? Apparently Moti's brother has started keeping bees. What, in this country? Is he mad? And the new Warhol exhibition at Tate Modern – absolutely awful stuff. His 'Ten Portraits of Jews of the Twentieth Century' – a colder looking bunch you will never see!

Only, the longer they went on, the more they didn't feel cold to Aisling at all, the hurtle warming her up, more beef and more onions and another glass full, 'til she was bold enough to think about joining in, offering her opinions; even, eventually, to think about arguing back.

'But isn't that the whole point with Warhol? Giving value to banality? I mean, I wouldn't take it personally if I were you.'

They looked at her then as if they had forgotten she was even there. She had stared back, refusing to falter, daring a reply. She noticed the grandmother picking at something in her teeth, though she didn't seem able to catch it.

Aisling could tell they were surprised, startled even, by the guts of her chiming in, stepping out from her neat little box. But then they had smiled. 'Well, she does have a point...' Had challenged her even further. 'What about Jasper Johns? Are you familiar with his work?' Had pointed at her glass. 'Another drop?'

And then they had asked other questions too, ones that hadn't been rehearsed; even, eventually, had laughed at her jokes. While Aisling savoured every mouthful, feeling herself flush – not an act any more – all her nerves finally faded and something else there instead, a warmth and a welcome she hadn't known in a long time, maybe even since she had first arrived to this Godforsaken country, yes, maybe this almost felt a bit like—

The word jumps her now, filling in the blank.

'Home.' Noah turns off the ignition with the push of a button.

To their right the outline of her flat sits hunched above, the grimy whitewash of the Islington terrace.

As it cools, the engine clicks a metronome beat.

They sit side by side, each waiting for the other to speak; to exhale at last; to say thank you?

Out on the street, an old man passes by with his dog, a thin pink plastic bag of shit in one hand and a Santa hat perched on his head. There are five days left 'til Christmas.

Without the hum of the engine the silence sits even louder between them, the one that still doesn't make sense. And suddenly the thought occurs to Aisling that maybe she has done something wrong. Convinced she had been a success – that he would be pleased with her, or at least just relieved – but what if she hadn't? What if there was something she had missed? A bit too comfortable, or a presumption too far – something anyway that has Noah frowning now, building his face right up for the fight.

'Aisling—'

'What?' As soon as he speaks she steels herself for defence.

'Just…'

The pulse of the parcel goes quicker in her groin. God, get her out of this fucking dress.

'Just…Let's just save the present until tomorrow, OK? I need to pop to the office but I'll come over straight after, cook us up some brunch, and then we can sit down properly and discuss it all when—'

'What are you talking about *discuss*?' She feigns laughter now as she takes her confusion out on the wrapping paper. 'Jesus, Noah, it's only a present – what's the big fucking deal?' Wrenching it at last and tossing it behind her all over the back of the car, the shreds like sparks from a bright blue firework. And she remembers once telling him about how fireworks are illegal in Ireland; about how you have to drive up North at Halloween to the lads with their crates plonked along the border haggling a wee deal on some screamers and a load of Catherine wheels.

By the time the thing is unwrapped Aisling is out of breath. The newborn book is leather, the back cover torn off and then stuck on again, set like a broken limb. The words on the front, though, are elegant in gold.

'What…what…' Her accent is always stronger when she is breathless, during sex most of all. 'What is this?'

Noah waits. A car drives past; it doesn't have its headlights on. Still he gives no answer.

She lets the query linger – damned if she will be the one to speak – but of course, she already knows what the present is. Exactly. Realises that in a way, she always did – the climax of everything that was set in motion when he made the dinner invitation. Or even when she first sat there on that stranger-wedged Tube, the one with the paper swan.

A scrap of blue has got stuck beneath her barely there nail. She tilts it to catch a light.

Only, if this is the moment she has been waiting for, reading for, then why doesn't it feel how she thought it would? Why is her body suddenly exhausted, wishing it were anywhere else – maybe down by the canal or back on the Underground, the hurtle of the tracks so loud you can't even hear yourself think, only wait for the moment where you glimpse a passing Tube; a reflection in the darkness of another route, another life, that disappears again just as quickly.

'Look, I know it's second hand…' Here in the car, Noah has begun

NINE FOLDS MAKE A PAPER SWAN

to explain. 'And totally out of date. So please don't think you have to…Obviously we will…' She can see how careful he is being with every word, the moment suddenly fragile as glass. 'But according to Mum, it's the only one that was ever published in Ireland, so she thought you…That it might…Anyway, she spent forever trying to track it down. To get you the—'

'Shut up.'

With two words, she sees the colour bleed from his face, the tint of him turned as pale as her.

'What?'

Paler than the whitewash of a dingy one-bed flat on a deserted Islington street.

'I said *shut up*.'

Ghost white. Or even blind white, like a panic setting in. Or like—

'Shut up shut up shut up!'

While below, the gilded letters catch the glow from the street-lamps that has stolen in through the window, to light the whole thing up as it breaks apart.

A VOYAGE OF DISCOVERY –
CONSIDERING A JUDAIC CONVERSION?
by
Rabbi Briscoe
[O'Brien Press]

1. *Right from the Commencement of the Journey, One Must Be Open and Honest About the Myriad of Thoughts that Will Undoubtedly Fill One's Mind.*

'OK,' Aisling begins as she opens the book. 'Let me get this straight.' A change in her already – the sarcasm always so quick off the mark. 'Basically I'm after getting the thumbs up. Passed their interrogations – the Jewish bloody Inquisition – but it turns out it's like, *yes*, we approve, but of course we can't *actually* approve unless—'

'Aisling, come on. That's not fair.'

'No? Because from where I'm sitting—'

'And it's not like you didn't know this was coming.' Once he has said it Noah stares at the gearstick, wondering whether to dare. But he has started now, everything has, a ship that's found land too hard and too soon.

'Well, I mean, you've at least been...playing along...'

'What?'

'Asking questions, doing research...'

'Noah, I'm a journalist – that's what I—'

'...weren't even going to go home for Christmas.'

At this one she has no choice but to stop. She glances at the book. She has opened to the checklist on the very first page – the patronising pointers to start her off.

It had been an early December evening there in her attic sitting room, the pair of them full from Noah's latest recipe-book feast. He sat glaring at a deck of cards while she skimmed an obituary about some American actress who had drowned herself in a lake, a hint of bravery to the story she couldn't quite place.

So instead she spoke: 'Noah, I've been thinking about Christmas.'

Despite the surprise of the words he had stayed fixated on his cards, knowing the attention would only make her self-conscious. Every bit of him, though, had strained to hear, his favourite moments, these, when she let down her guard.

'I just…I still haven't booked my flights, and they've gone up loads…'

He could make half the deck disappear in a flash; make the Kings and Queens pop up outside the window looking in on her confession. Her plea.

'I suppose there's always the ferry, but I get awful sea legs.'

Could make a Heart appear right there in her breast pocket, contrary to what she liked people to believe.

'…really hectic at the paper. And plus, if you've got a few days off work, it just seems a bit of a shame—'

'So then don't go.' Until there it was, the trick she had been struggling with all along. 'Stay with me. You're right,' he said, 'it would be great to have the few days together. You can get your work done and then maybe we could head up to the Lakes or something for New Year's Eve? A proper escape from this place.'

In a way, another kind of bravery.

So she had just done it – or rather, just hadn't done it – hadn't booked her flights. It was a shame to miss the festivities, she knew that, but she told herself it was only a once off; that she really was manic with work. Even if a voice inside kept reminding her that the dead would still be dead when she got back. They had a one-week window to publish celebrity obituaries; up to four weeks for everyone else. When her editor had first explained it she thought it sounded a bit like a 'Month's Mind'. Only, she discovered then that that was just an Irish tradition, the ceremony in the local church one month after the funeral, to stop people moving on that bit too soon – another round of sandwiches and stories down the pub, Guinness-licked and gorgeous on the tongue.

'Ah, but it turns out that was just an elaborate fucking test.' She readjusts herself in the passenger seat now, the seatbelt-chafe taut across her chest. Really, it is the only support she has left. 'And go on, so did everyone in the family have a vote or could certain people veto, Security Council style? Or what is it in Israel – the *Knesset* – but of course, *excuse* me for knowing that.'

'Ash—'

'And how about you, Noah? What did you say to all of this?'

This time she leaves space for him to answer. He looks at her, straight on, his frown holding fast but only just. 'I...I explained...that things were complicated—'

'Oh Jesus, if I hear that word one more bloody...But tell me *why*, Noah? Come on – you're an articulate lad. Oxford fucking educated, in case I hadn't noticed, so explain to me, *why* is it always so complicated? Or would my poor little Irish brain not—'

'For God's sake, Aisling, you know why!' He looks away from the shouted words back down at the book on her thighs. He sees the off-white of the paper and the wrinkle of the leather, almost like the palm of a hand he used to try to read, back in his earlier, eager days, the love line running short.

'Well, go on then. Enlighten me.' And she is daring him now, he knows that – forcing him to say all the things that have remained unsaid.

He fell for the challenge in her right from the start, even if he knew, deep down, it would be the thing to undo them again.

'Because there is something...When the time comes ' He is tentative still, considering, one last chance to double back. 'Just always assumed I would...' Before he realises there is nowhere left to go. 'Aisling, I need...' And that actually, that is sort of amazing. 'Aisling, I...I want to marry someone Jewish.'

2. *Be Sure to Contemplate the Glorious Scale of One's Journey's Final Goal.*

She lets the words replay in her head, or really just one of them. The only one. As surprising as it is expected.

In the distance they hear a siren, the yell of it ripping through the night.

And beneath it, for a moment, she hears another high pitch – a voice that sounds almost like her own, saying yes. *Yes! I mean, I will have to think about it, but…Relished tonight…Felt so welcome, so inspired…*And there would be love in there too, surely? Not infatuation or joking or cutting remarks, just love, pure and simple. *Everything better since…Never been this…*Something, maybe, about belonging? *And I know I never admit it and sometimes I tell you you're strange, like that time you made a paper swan appear while we were having sex as if I had given birth and I panicked and screamed at you to fuck off home when actually I liked it.*

Really?

Yes.

She looks at him now, seeing this new version of herself reflected back in the dark of those eyes, the same black as the London midnight. 'Noah,' she says, barely a whisper. 'Noah, I…'

'Aisling, it's OK, we don't have to…'

While beyond him, out the window, a plane scratches a line through the moon. The plane she decided not to take.

'Noah, I…'

The plane she could never take again.

'Aisling?'

The self she wouldn't be any more.

'I can't—'

And the panic she still cannot ignore.

'Aisling, I'm not—'

'Yes you fucking are.' It is with the last dreg of strength that she picks the book out of her lap and flings it, dead against his forehead.

His whole body flinches, unbreathing. For a moment she thinks he might pass out. But then his hand reaches up to the spot so she opens the door, the ice-cold air gushing in to try to stop the swelling.

3. *One Must Try One's Utmost Not to Flee When It Becomes Too Much. Undeniably It Is an Overwhelming Process, but Thorough Rewards will Ensue Provided One Remains Calm and Committed.*

She pushes herself up and out of the car, headfirst into the night. Through blurred eyes she notices the neighbours must have found some Christmas lights, a string of them thonged up between the railings.

She stabs at the lock until she is in the door and up up up the stairs, all the way to the top-floor flat. It always tickled him, that – the bachelorette in the attic – said that she would grow old and alone and get cats and go crazy and then she told him that in Ireland (never heard of it, *ha ha*) there is a phrase for someone who is crazy – that they have 'rats in the attic'. And he had kissed her then, swallowing the knowledge, telling her that in Hebrew they say *meshuga* – a piece of his world for a piece of hers – holding the shards up to the light to squint at the differences, the connections. Because South Dublin and North London were just the same if you tilted your head, the colloquialisms and the community, the flocks spread out all over the—

She slams the door so hard it makes her chest shake.

She stands in the middle of the darkness.

She hears a muffle of shouts from the flat below, the odd couple she rarely sees. They don't have any children. They've been fighting a lot recently.

4. *One Must Endeavour to Get Some Sleep.*
5. *No Really, Go to Sleep.*

Hours chafe away, closer and closer to hangover. She sits on the wooden floor, her skin itchy with fabric softener and something almost like regret, though it is still too early to know for sure.

Eventually, the growl of the dawn begins from the street. The backwards beep of Sainsbury's trucks. The coo of pigeons. The clatter of luggage wheels late for somewhere, anywhere else.

Slowly, she opens the door of her flat and takes the stairs one at a time. The throb of her head is brutal, the wine-soaked aftertaste. But for the first time in hours her mind is calm again, focused only on the portrait she has been composing through the night: him, waiting there, bruised and snoring against the leather headrest, until she will knock on the window and he will gasp awake with a 'sorry' and that, for now, will be enough – no more overreactions, no more talk – just glad they managed to save it all before it fell away.

In the communal hallway she tiptoes over the scatter of post. The cleaners' cards. The forgotten letters, the corners crisp and white. Like after an argument once when he apologised by running her a bath filled with bubbles and a hundred origami swans that pecked at her body with their little white beaks.

She has kept them in a box beneath her bed ever since, love letters that don't say a word.

She clicks open the latch of the front door and readies herself for the sunlight, the crush of it harsh and bright. But she promises herself that she will stare back into the street, never so happy to see that Audi S7 in all her life, the scratch-free finish and the personalised registration his parents got for his birthday:

NO4H

The naffness spelled out across the bright yellow plate:

N4FF

And a yellow reg back home in Ireland that means you can thump the person next to you whenever you spot one driving by. Because anything British deserves a bashing, apparently – the petty politics of child's play we never quite get past.

   6. *For in the End, This May Be the Most Wonderful, Most Important Decision of One's Life.*

The parking space, though, is empty.

There is no car.

No Noah.

Not even a tiny white swan bent into place, the lines so defined that when you take it apart it can just be put back together again, in nine simple folds, exactly the same as before.

part two | Names...

1911

'What about a man who names his daughter after his wife? And then the next daughter and the next one too so that when they die, he only has to engrave one name on the gravestone to commemorate them all; only has to cry out one word in his dreams?'

Ruth opened her eyes, though she had been a million miles off sleep.

All night she had been too anxious to drop off, her head frizzy on a pillow that was never quite cool enough and her mind skitty on everything the morning would bring – the morning they had all been waiting for.

Eventually, though, she gave up. She made her way to the curtains and drew one aside, just a crack, careful not to let in too much of the day. Behind her, Esther was still asleep, her breaths a slow and even whistle. It seemed the anticipation was going easier on her.

Out the window, the Cork clouds had been rinsed a gaudy shade, somewhere between an orange and a pink. Ruth thought of the rhyme they had learned at school – a shepherd's warning, wasn't that the one? A superstition she hadn't heard before so she didn't know whether to believe. But when she finally looked down to the street she realised the warning had been right, a whole other kind of anxiety waiting below.

Because the birds, it seemed, had dropped out of the sky.

There were hundreds of them, maybe even more; a plague of tattered carcasses scattered across the cobblestones, chests up and beaks apart, their wings matt and still. The wind had obviously been at them too, bluey tufts of feathers caught up in the railings, the bushes, the gutters, the lampposts, all along the terrace of redbricks they had called 'home' for almost ten years now. Or at least, that Ruth had called 'home' whenever her mother wasn't listening.

Their eyes were still open, conker-bright and hard.

The bodies lay undisturbed. Ruth half-expected some cats. But soon the neighbours began to emerge, keen to inspect the inexplicable carnage. There were the Golds and the Epsteins – now a family of five – Leb with his tailor shop, his skinny wife and two snotty little boys. And the new baby Lottie whom Ruth sometimes looked after, a gorgeous thing who slept her way through the entire spectacle.

Ruth checked the bed behind her. Esther gave a sigh but didn't wake.

According to the story in the *Cork Examiner*, the lick of bitter weather over France had scuppered the birds' usual migratory routine. Then the darkness had been so black they couldn't see where they were going, until the gaudy flare of the Cork City lights lured them off course and they thought they had found their way. At last!

Only now they were dead, every one, and nobody knew why.

Ruth stood by the window, her words clinging together as she tried to make sense. What worried her most was that it was some sort of omen for the big day ahead – first the shepherd's warning and now this? All the animals, out to get them.

Inside his head must be a zoo.

Noah's Ark, two by two!

But when she looked again she decided that maybe this was something else entirely – not a sign or an omen, but an inspiration; a chance for a bit of imagination, finally, that would make her Tateh smile. Because come on, she was nearly eighteen years of age – nearly a proper grown-up – so surely even she could manage to shape an idea from a sight as unnatural as this.

She closed her mismatched eyes and heaved a breath, willing herself to focus. First she pictured her compass, the face of it clear and smooth; the points that always kept her calm. Next she pictured her father's face, beaming with pride. And then she focused on the little birdy bodies, the bloated chests and the snaggled claws, not a lick of blood between them as if death had just been on the air, wafted in off the Atlantic to suck their souls away.

Whataboutaflockofbirdswho–

Esther's scream was so shrill next to her they must have heard her out at sea. Their parents came flying in, Mame first, eyes wild with fear then fury. She shook her head and told Ruth she was a brat, that she should have known better, should have just left the curtains well alone.

Hours later on the platform of the Glanmire Road train station, the creatures were still everywhere, piled black like mounds of coal; fuel for the engine's hock.

'From platform three, Bubbeleh, I think it is departing.'

Ruth stayed close behind her Tateh, avoiding the corpses' stares.

'Hurry we must. Miss it we cannot.'

But even in the panic, still she managed a little smile. Because it must have been the nerves that did it, the weight of the day ahead and the strangeness of the morning, but she hadn't heard her father muddle his sentences like that in a very long time.

In a very long time his sentences like that muddled she him had not heard.

To a freak of climate owing, of birds a flock off course to Ireland flew.

She had done it herself when first learning English, her brain refusing to think in anything other than Yiddish so the translation always came out confused. Back to front. Hours in front of the living-room mirror willing her head the other way – the same mirror Esther pouted at daily when she thought no one else could see.

To go, I wish, to America.

'Tickets please!'

Her father fumbled now for the pale blue stubs, too many pockets like a magician's coat. He had purchased the pair over a fortnight ago, as soon as he had received the invitation – the all-important letter requesting his company up in Dublin.

Ruth had read the thing front to back then back to front.

The train conductor watched them now with the usual confusion, maybe even suspicion, though Tateh's beard was trimmed shorter than ever these days – practically the spit of the local lads. He said the old garb had been impractical for his work, and sure, a lot of the other men had started to dress more 'native' too, especially those with jobs in town. Dr Marcus on Grattan Street; Epstein's Tailors on Hanover; business slow to begin with but there was no denying those patterns held their cut, boy.

Soon the conductor gave the nod and they were on, up into

the chaos of the train. Ruth heard the wails of children, begging not to leave: 'Ah why can't we stay in Birdland forever, Mammy, pleeeeease?'

She thought of Lottie Epstein, fast asleep, curled into the shell of her mother's collarbone.

Once the door of their compartment slid shut Ruth dismantled herself onto the seat. She was exhausted. It was only ten o'clock. She didn't remember leaving being so hard. She pressed her olive face into the thumb-smeared window, savouring its cool. And maybe if Tateh didn't need her she could just nap her way to Dublin – close her eyes and forget about the birds and everything that was at stake this evening – the second most important trip of their lives.

'Aileen!'

But now there was another passenger behind her, demanding her attention; yes, always someone else to think about instead.

Aileen Doherty stood framed in the doorway, freckled from head to toe. The spots were everywhere – her eyelids, her earlobes – even the knuckles of her fingers as they held two pale blue tickets aloft.

The fingernails looked oddly naked in comparison.

Ruth could still remember the first time she had seen her class-mate. It had been her and Esther's first day at St Angela's School for Girls, a bizarre morning for so many reasons. The whispers. The stares. The fact that they had never actually seen a nun before in their lives. But in the end it was Aileen's appearance that had surprised the most – Ruth had never known so many freckles were possible. A bit like Tateh's pockmarks, she had decided, only blacker, more absolute. She had wondered if they hurt.

Meanwhile, Mame had said they were just a sign of bad Irish hygiene, which in turn was a product of their alcoholism – drunkards one and all! Even though Ruth secretly enjoyed watching the clumsy ballet of their limbs every night as they stumbled home beneath the stars.

'So tell us, Bubbeleh, is this a friend of yours?' When she finally heard her father's words, the first thing she noticed was they were the right way round again.

Aileen, though, was quick to have them fixed: 'We do be in the same *class*,' she warned as her own father arrived behind, a bumble and then a glare. 'Sure, this is the girl I'm always telling you about, Da. The *Lith-u-a-ni-an*.' She let the syllables drop from her lips one by one, pips from a fruit gone bad.

Lith-u-a-ni-an.

Ni-an-a-u-lith.

The five of them as disgusting whichever way you looked.

There had been other terms flung their way these past few years. 'Bloodsuckers' and 'Moneylenders'. 'Murderers' too. 'Jewtown' the locals called their neighbourhood, though they claimed it was only an endearment; only a bit of *craic* and nothing more. At school it was usually 'Kike' or 'Scab', comments about a funny smell, and then there had been something called a 'Pogrom' that made Mame furious, even though Tateh said she was overreacting; said there had just been a misunderstanding and that everything was fine – better, almost, than ever.

And now he was talking again, back on the train, making jokes as only he could. 'Well, there you are, Bubbeleh – that explains it all!'

Despite his cheer, Ruth didn't look up. She took her crooked finger and pushed it to the side, so far it almost looked straight again. Normal.

'I mean, the birds,' her father went on. 'It makes perfect sense.'

A wry smile beginning to slit across his face. 'Because a shower of brown hailstones there must have been during the night, lethal to avians, but perfectly harmless to humans – only sticking to their skin! And tell me, Sir, do you suppose there is a special soap you could buy to help scrub them off?'

The door slammed so hard behind the Dohertys it didn't even bounce, absolute as it sealed the division tight.

Tateh's laughter was as sweet as a child's. Though when it finally came, Ruth's own was more like a cough, so grateful for the excuse of air.

'And sure,' Tateh carried on, giddy on the notion, 'if The Abbey decides not to put on my play after all, we could always run a Freak Show, nu? Travel the country with our acts – The Incredible Spotted Father and Daughter!'

Ruth shook with laughter at the punch line, letting the relief take her in, even if her mind was determined to protest. Because how could The Abbey not say yes to his play? How could it possibly go wrong?

Those famous last words.

How wrong it could possibly go.

She looked out the window, still shaking, willing the last of her anxieties away. A boy on the platform flapped a handkerchief. A chorus of ads peeled away at the corners like skin.

Fry's Cocoa!

Australia! Canada! Emigrate to Greatness!

But she wasn't going anywhere, she promised now, restored once again. Because this was only a daytrip; only a jaunt up to Dublin and then back home by morning, just in time to tell Aileen Doherty the exciting news that her Tateh had got the thumbs up; that his play was going to be performed on the national stage, all the doubters finally shtum and his family staying put for once and for all – no matter what shower of syllables you tried to drop on them from on high.

Ruth smiled as she felt the engine begin to chug, the track speeding fast towards the North Cork hills. Before she felt something else, something a bit like a scratch; a sting from a bee she hadn't seen.

She reached back to where she found a tiny feather on her neck, a black one that must have got stuck. She crushed it between her fingers; felt the snap of the stem. Then she flicked it away with the rest of the dirt beneath her seat where no one else would ever see.

'Or what about a man who is famous for folding up paper into beautiful shapes? A boat. A flower. A swan. Until one day he tries it on his wife and bends her this way and that, only to break in two every last bone in her body?'

Out the window, the fields lined up one after the other like a queue. In the corners, conspiracies of horses stood gathered, swapping the stories of the day, while around them there were bigger beasts too, great black shapes hulking over the land – the outline of the clouds – God making shadow puppets that loomed for miles before they disappeared behind a wash of gorse.

Ruth sat snug in her seat, fumbling her compass.

The train ricketed along the track, the line up the country like a backbone. Or like how Tateh once told her that instead of knowing a thing off by heart, some languages say that it is 'written on your spine'. So Ruth sighed for that now, longing for Ireland to be written onto hers. Because despite how she called it home; despite how she spoke English and read the papers and knew every scrap of local news, really this was the first time she had seen the country properly – the maps finally come true.

Of course, it was different for Tateh. These days he was travelling most of the time, thanks to his job. Or at least, thanks to the thing that put bread on the table until the playwriting sorted itself out again.

In short, until today.

Because like so many of the neighbours he had decided to become a pedlar – a wandering salesman with a pack on his back flogging bric-a-brac on credit. Geegaws to tart up the boredom. Picture frames. Linens. Religious figurines. 'Never-never' men they were called, though Ruth never-never understood why.

Every Monday morning he would set out across the countryside as part of Jewtown's mass Exodus, and then every Friday evening he would return again just before the sun gave up. Of course, Mame hated it, and not just because he was gone all week, or because he left spare figurines lying around their house ('Tateh, is that sick man on the cross the one my classmates say we killed?'). But because she said it was degrading – he spent the nights in ditches, barns if he was lucky – no place for a man of his grace. Tateh, though, insisted it was perfect. Better than moneylending, and anyway, it gave him time to think, to get to know the country. To be inspired. So after that Mame's complaints sounded closer to jealousy, a lover cast aside for an endless swathe of untrampled fields, the stench of cow-shit and the bloodshot bruise of a sunset over Gortnagross.

Finally, though, he could prove that it had worked; that the epiphany had come. Because here he was, sat on a train to Dublin with the evidence clutched right up to his face.

Ruth had wondered what was keeping him so shtum; why there had been no usual flow of half-hatched ideas, skimming the air like stones on a lake.

What about…

What about…

What about…

To see which ripples took.

She stretched her neck to check which scene of the new play he was reading. Maybe it was the opener, the curtain drawn apart to reveal the beautiful Jewish heroine – a role for Esther if ever Ruth had read one. She supposed it was Tateh's last attempt to try to get his favourite daughter to connect with the land – a gift and an apology all at once.

Or maybe it was the scene where the heroine first meets the Rathnarrow farmer and tells him of her people's plight:

GIRL: *So yes, we were only a few to begin with, but I have heard, Mr Murphy, that our numbers are beginning to grow.*

PADDY: *Ah, but what if there doesn't be any more space for you, Girlie? The island will sink under the weight.*

Ruth smiled. The opening exchange always made her excited – the unlikely friendship and the possibilities yet to come. Only, as she looked at her father now she saw that it wasn't the play he was reading at all. Instead they were a different set of lines – the ones he had received in return – the letter from The Abbey Theatre's patroness, written in her elegant, fountain-pen curl.

Dear Mr Greenberg,

Well, first let me say how charmed I was to receive the manuscript of your lovely play The Fifth Province...

By now Ruth knew the thing like a script itself, whispering it each night as she lay in bed.

...part of the Gaelic Revival, using the Jewish plight as a metaphor for that of the Irish...

And she let the prose play in her head again now, the rhythm finding time with the chug of the track.

...my own new play The Deliverer...

...the betrayal of Moses with the betrayal of Parnell, just when Independence seemed...

...so close and yet...

And soon they were speeding faster on it, downhill towards the end.

Come to Dublin for a chat...

...after the show in the foyer...

...the portrait of Mr Yeats...

On and on 'til it reached all the way to the heartfelt farewell.

With warm regards,

Yours sincerely,

Lady Augusta Gregory.

The first time Tateh read it aloud Mame had left the room. For once, neither daughter had followed.

And it was as if he had written the words himself, the eagerness with which he had looked up then, the letter held forward for approval. 'She...she liked my play?'

First to Ruth – the easiest bet.

Then to Esther – the more satisfying.

And then all the way around to another set of eyes that had

hovered in the doorway; the ones that should and should not have been watching in equal measure.

It was Niamh, the maid.

The servant.

The muse?

So many words, and yet none was quite right.

It was almost four years now since they had hired the local lass full-time. By then, all the other women on the street had had a girl helping out, the communities mingling more and more. So Tateh had insisted Mame deserved the same – they could just about afford it – and plus, they trusted this Niamh girl. She had been their shabbos goy right from the beginning, the one who came in to turn on their lights and fire up their stove every Saturday morning when the Sabbath decreed they weren't allowed to do so themselves.

'Well, boy, *my* God says it's Sunday that I'm to rest, so does that mean ye will be round tomorrow to fix me a pot of tae?'

The memory of the joke made Ruth smile now, leaning in to the window's rising heat.

And she tried to imagine if Niamh had come along today, her red hair yanked up into a knot, her apron smeared with butter and egg; pink sprays of berry blood. She would have kept them entertained, that was for sure, prattling merrily and causing Tateh's eyes to brighten in a way Ruth only saw for one other thing – when they asked him the story behind the Princess of the Bees and he refused, gleefully, to tell.

Because apart from the cooking and cleaning, the gentle little jokes, Niamh had brought something else into their temporary-for-ten-years-now home – stories. A whole new set of them. Just when all the old ones had started to grow stale, along came her endless stream of myths and legends from this native land; warriors and kings who fought and romanced for anyone who wanted to hear.

And Ruth did. Every last word.

'And since we're doing chicken tonight, boy, did you ever hear about a lad called Sweeney?' Niamh would be stood at the kitchen counter, sweat teeming down her forehead as she prepared the evening's stew. 'He was a crazy old lad, put under a curse that turned him half-bird half-man.' Next she would pluck a handful of feathers from the freshly killed fowl. 'So he wandered the whole of Ireland like an eejit, but no matter where he went he always returned to the same place, the Valley of the Mad!' Then she would throw the feathers into the air, the plumage raining down, landing on them like an off-white confetti.

And Ruth would be wired on the telling, sometimes even joining in: 'Sweeney, Sweeney, half-man half-bird!' Tossing a handful skywards and trying the accent out for size. 'How's about that, boy?' Until Esther's cough from the doorway made her leap, the sound as if she had choked on a stray bit of down.

Ruth returned to the train window now, feeling the sting on her cheek where Esther's handprint had landed that night. The dull hum of heat and something about 'a traitor'; about 'staying true to your roots'. Words she had already heard from her mother a hundred times before.

She reached for her compass from her pocket. She closed her eyes, trying to picture the map. They should have passed Tipperary by now, give or take, which meant there would be Kilkenny next – Kilkenny then Carlow and then Kildare. *Kill kill kill.* She wondered if they would notice when they went from one to the other, or even when they crossed the province border into Leinster.

And a while after the bird-man Sweeney and the Valley of the Mad, Niamh had offered Ruth another story, this time about a different place altogether.

'"The Fifth Province" they do be calling it, boy. Do you know it?' She had been darning a hole in one of Mame's frocks, sometimes holding the needle in her mouth so it almost looked as if she were sewing up her lips.

Ruth couldn't help but feel nervous at the prospect.

'Well, they say, boy,' Niamh went on while Ruth stretched the hem for her, nice and tight, 'they say "The Fifth Province" is where all the stories of Ireland live – all the unborn ideas, like. The land, I suppose…the land of the imagination.'

As soon as Ruth heard it, she had let go of the hem; had felt something inside her like a prick or a sting. And then the following Friday when Tateh was just getting home from work she had gone out to meet him in the street. He had smiled, knackered mostly, but surprised too by the unusual welcome. His youngest, oddest child. Before she had handed over the idea – or at least, the bones of it as best she could manage – not her own imagining, but still, it was something.

A bargain for love – the little pleas we make.

By morning, the notion had taken root. Already the women could hear him mumbling under his breath; scribbling into his notebooks. There were bits in Russian for Mame, bits in Yiddish for Esther, bits in English for Ruth, bits in Irish for Niamh – a whole Babel of fresh material he wouldn't let anyone see. Though they could read most of what they needed to on the new gleam in his specs as he wandered in and out of their lives, brighter and brighter each week until one Friday he returned home earlier than usual.

His pack was still on his back as he marched straight up to the Post Office. He handed Mrs Geary an envelope, the front scrawled with a Dublin theatre address and a patroness's name; a lick of stamps and a silent prayer.

The wait was the worst. More sleepless nights – four too-hot heads on four not-quite-cool-enough pillows. Five if you counted Niamh's little cottage out in Caherlag where she lived with her brother, the walls covered in holy pictures and figurines she purchased from an anonymous travelling salesman on credit.

Until finally, the reply had come. The miracle.

And now they were here.

'Bubbeleh, do you see?'

Out the window, the River Liffey looked almost solid, a road for swans to walk down. Along the quays the throngs of people made it seem as if the whole capital had gathered specially to welcome them.

Kingsbridge Station, the sky-high roof overhead.

Once the engine had stopped Tateh stood up; gathered his pile of papers to him.

'You will be wonderful,' Ruth tried, forcing herself back into her role – the only reason she had been allowed to come along in the first place. Nearly a woman now, so she had to learn her duty.

'Thank you, Bubbeleh.'

'No really.' She placed a hand on her father's wrist. 'Wonderful.' She was surprised by the looseness of the flesh.

'Well, as says Miss Niamh, let us hope I am the knees of the bees.'

Though as Ruth watched him make his way down the concourse, spouting words no one else could understand, she knew he was only ever thinking of the Bees' Princess instead.

GIRL: *Mr Murphy, there is something I have been wanting to ask you.*

PADDY: *Fire ahead so, love.*

GIRL: *It is these Provinces, Mr Murphy. These regions that Ireland is split into – four of them, I am believing.*

PADDY: *Ah yes a'course a'course. Ulster, Munster, Leinster and Connaught.*

GIRL: *North, South, East and West.*

PADDY: *Well…yes, I suppose, in a manner of speaking.*

GIRL: *But what I cannot understand is why there are only four of them? Because if the Gaelic…the Irish word for Province is 'cúige', 'fifth', then does that mean…Is there another one, Mr Murphy, hiding somewhere else? A fifth province?*

(It takes a moment but his eyes widen. And then he smiles.)

PADDY: *Well, truth be told, Girlie, it is a good question you do be asking – fierce good altogether. Let me…Well, come here to me now and let me tell you a story…*

'So, Mr Greenberg, how did you find it?' There was no hello, no warning at all, she just appeared, every buxom inch of her, smiling a wry smile as if Tateh and she were old friends from long long ago, maybe even lovers.

The heap of her would have crushed him flat.

'I do hope it was to your liking?' Her questions bounced along the lowlit tiles of The Abbey Theatre foyer where the last of the evening's audience buttoned their coats, swapped favourite scenes and canvassed suggestions for a quick post-show sup.

'O'Mahony's round the corner?'

'Christ, the thirst on me.'

'Sure it's serious work, all that talk of Independence.'

The theatre's stained-glass doors had first flung open in 1904, all in the hope of 'rewriting the Irish identity'; of using culture in the fight for freedom. The plan was to draw on the artistic expertise of the gormless-looking men and women whose portraits now lined the dusky hallway; the perfume-and-cigar air. Here before them, though, Lady Gregory looked anything but gormless.

She wore a stiff black dress with a scooped-out neckline, her bosom hoisted up to meet her wrinkled, sun-toughened neck.

For some reason Ruth thought of horses; the thick, slow lashes.

Not that it mattered, but Ruth herself had found the play magical; had spent the last hour happily watching Moses and his men, or Parnell and his, or whichever Messiah you wanted to suck out of the allegory. Either way, they were fighting hard for a land to call their own.

The Chosen People!

A Nation Once Again!

But even despite the rouse of the thing, Ruth had to admit she had let her attention wander just a little; had spent the last hour also just gazing around her, soaking up the surroundings. The semi-circle balcony scooped deep and wide like a patroness's neckline; the ornate lumps of stuccowork crusted up around the balustrade; the shining faces of the rows below as they stared up at the altar, utterly transfixed by the Word. And in a way, she thought, it was almost like a Saturday morning at Shul where she sat peering down from the women's gallery, trying her best to follow the Rabbi's lessons. Because there would always be a quiz from Mame on the walk home, so no choice but to get full marks – to please her mother the only way she knew how.

Of course, Mame was supposed to have come along to Dublin tonight; to be here to clutch her husband's fingers as they finally rewrote the family fate. But in the end, she had had to host a meeting instead – the usual get-together for her beloved organisation – in fact, these days, the only fate she really seemed to care about.

The Zionist Women's Group (Cork Branch).

They gathered once a week to discuss the return to the Promised Land, each session a ritual of lists and tea and *a Jacob's biscuit? Oh God no – this isn't a party, dear, this is history, thousands of years of it.* The women would babble away for hours, discussing emigration plans, irrigation initiatives, the Jewish National Fund. The latter was going well at least, every Jewtown home now with a blue and white collection box sat proudly on their mantelpiece, gathering spare change to support those who had already answered the call and returned to the Holy Land.

A penny a day is the JNF way.

A penny a week is what we seek.

Every Sunday Mame handed Ruth her pocket money and watched as she dropped it straight into the little slot. A dull clang. A rare nod of approval.

Meanwhile, just outside the city centre, the Zionists had also purchased a patch of land so that the men could start to learn some of the skills the Promised Land would require – farming techniques; the sowing and the reaping – all the simple but vital basics. They took it very seriously, a piousness to every rake, despite the climate's refusal to cooperate (*not much chance of oranges with this endless rain, nu?*), and despite how Niamh always had Ruth in stitches as she described the farce of it as she walked by en route to work: 'So this morning, right, I see this local lad going: "Right well, today we will be discussing the procedure known as 'bailing'." To which one of your lot replies: "Oh, to us do not even talk – on enough sinking ships we have been to last a lifetime!"'

So yes, most of the time Ruth could just see the humour of the whole affair, a perpetual pantomime only a mile away or crammed into her living room while she sat on the upstairs landing looking down. Needless to say, Esther was allowed to join the women in their gatherings. Needless to say, those days Niamh was told not to come to work.

But then just last week Ruth had walked past her parents' bedroom and discovered that the thing was starting to come a bit too close. Her mother's best red dress had been laid out on the bed, a pair of earrings gilding the pillow. 'Going out are we, Mame?' she had asked in a singsong Yiddish, still the only tongue her mother would answer.

But Mame didn't look up; didn't reply. Until: 'To the New Jerusalem. Our home at last.' Doting on the frock with a mother's love. 'And this is what Our God will see me wearing, the very first time my foot lands on Promised soil.' And right then, the humour of the thing had choked, stuffed down into the satin shoes which sat at the foot of the bed. Ruth leaned closer to check. They were Mame's wedding shoes – she hadn't even known they had come to Ireland.

She wondered now if Tateh did either.

Back in the foyer, though, her Tateh was clearing his throat. Still he clutched the pile of papers to his chest, a bit like he had been wounded and the bundle was soaking up his blood – a staunch of words to stop the gush.

'So if we could begin...' he tried, eager to get things back on track. 'If we could discuss, perhaps...the play?'

Because no, Ruth told herself now, shaking all thoughts of her mother away. Because it didn't need to be a leaving outfit any more – why not an outfit for an opening night? An Abbey Theatre première, the playwright's wife glowing by his side? Ruth wondered if she could get a new frock herself, to wear to the big event. Maybe she could even bring Niamh along with her – she was her friend by now, wasn't she? Her only one, yes, but wasn't that better than none?

'But of course, Mr Greenberg,' Lady Gregory eventually replied, the gentle lisp of her words gliding down through the foyer. 'Do tell me your thoughts. For I am simply *dying* of curiosity to hear.'

So Tateh began, at last, a speech he must have been preparing for weeks – or really, for an entire decade – each line recited over and over to the stone walls he passed across the countryside, not a single lick of glue or mortar to hold the shards of rock together.

An act of trust, calcified over time.

'Well, ever since to this wondrous island my family and I have come, an idea I have been looking for that is something…something special.' He paused. Still his sentences puckered in the middle. But that was all right; to be expected. 'Until I heard about this place "The Fifth Province", you know it? This phrase your countrymen have. The realm of the imagination.'

Ruth leaned into the idea now, feeling a blush of pride. She knew she didn't deserve it, really – that it was Niamh's doing most of all – but still she let it linger for a moment.

'So then I wondered…' Tateh added, his smile letting rip. 'I wondered what would happen if…well, if this place were real.'

And so he was away, explaining it all, plundering the ragbag of snippets he had managed to pick up over the years on the road. Bits of myth. Bits of rumour. Bits of inspirations stashed into his tattered backpack in between the poke of candlesticks and the indecent sheer of stockings; the wink of naughty farmwives as they stretched them out along their arms to check for a ladder or a snag.

And he blushed himself as he poured out his stories, his Irish ones and his Jewish ones – just the same, really – all the connections he had found. While Lady Gregory listened on, eyebrows cocked in fascination. Admiration. Maybe even seeing a connection of her own. Because Niamh had told Ruth all about the patroness – about how she was a bit of an outsider herself. A woman. A Protestant. An upper-class. A youngest daughter who married a man with a Big House who evicted his tenants during the Famine – the poor things sent off to starve!

But after his death, Niamh said, Lady Gregory had written a new past for herself; had learned the local language and collected the local folklore and then shoved it up on stage – oh, she knew about belonging, all right; about adapting. So it was no wonder she was stood here now, hanging off every word this genius had to say, his Fifth Province and his Promised Land and his second chance at last.

'Now, let's just hold your horses there for a minute, Mr Greenberg!'

Ruth started. She glanced up at the patroness, the thick, slow lashes reared back in surprise.

She looked at Tateh. His were too.

Lady Gregory smiled at the silence, though only with her mouth, the peck of her tongue strangely girlish when she lisped. 'Now, all this is very good. Very good indeed. But I was wondering if I could ask you, Mr Greenberg, to return *specifically* to the play.'

Ruth waited. She stole a glance at the portraits on the wall, locked away in their frames. There was Wilde and Bernard Shaw; a lad called

Synge she knew you were supposed to pronounce funny. And then there was Willie Yeats himself, thinking of Lake Isles and Innisfree.

'So did you like it?'

'So did you like it?'

Slowly, Ruth closed her mismatched eyes. And slowly, she opened them again, the green one and the brown – the colours at odds with each other as much as her father and this woman.

'Mr Greenberg, I hope you're not…*My* play. *The Deliverer.*'

Two things you could compare all you wanted to, but that didn't mean they would ever be the same.

'The reason I invited you here tonight…To see what you thought. To get an…*authentic* opinion, so to speak.'

Even though Tateh himself would not get to speak another word.

The patroness beamed on now, her words falling quicker as she ushered the ghost-white figures towards the door. 'Well, I hope you have had a pleasant day? And do make sure your lot back in Cork pay us a visit, won't you – it is always such a delight to have a few *foreigners* in the gallery. A bit of *variety*, so to speak. I spent some time in Egypt myself, don't you know?'

Egypt.

Foreigners.

Lith-u-a-ni-an.

Ruth felt the syllables jam into her throat as she stepped back through the stained-glass door.

Outside, the air was pure damp, as if there had been rain. In the distance, they heard a tram bell ringing; a dirge from a pub on the corner of Abbey Street winding down for the night. Ruth listened. It was one of Niamh's tunes, an ancient air she liked to sing while making soda bread.

Beside her, Tateh stood, seeing and hearing these things too. Or maybe seeing his wife's face, hours from now, awaiting his return. There was embarrassment in it, yes, but also something else in the eyes – the tiniest lack of surprise, like she already knew the mistake he had made.

Without warning, he flung his arms wide, a diver about to jump. Or a maestro taking an elaborate bow, soaking up the douse of the applause. Ruth watched as the pages flew free from his grip, floating down alleyways, cartwheeling into gutters, stringing themselves up on poles, lampposts, cables. Others drowned in puddles, too deep, the ink running off in a matter of minutes, translating the words to smudge. But even in the blackness the sheets still glowed bright white, gaudy beneath the moon, the flap of them almost like the sound of a thousand wings.

(*She stands on an overturned potato crate before the crowd.*)
GIRL: *I am here today to tell you that I have found a place where we can go. All of us.*
(*A ripple of whispers; of disbelieving eyes.*)
GIRL: *The Fifth Province it is called, and I have been told we can make it our home, and send to our families elsewhere and tell them to come too. Scattered we will be no more, for this island holds the place we have been searching for. The land which God once Promised!*
(*While Joe Murphy watches on from the sidelines before tipping his hat and kicking his horse to walk on.*)

CURTAIN

May

Every night as I lay in the scut of my Montague House bed, I tried to picture my mother's face. Not as I had seen it last, soggy with tears the day she gave into my father's demands and left me here alone. Or even white with terror up on the Shul balcony the day of my Bar Mitzvah – the day I stopped speaking and this whole mess began. But just Ima, smiling, fresh from the shower so that her lovely blonde hair was free from its headscarf, her skin mottled a pinkish hue from the water's heat.

Each night I savoured the image, the single thing that kept me going these days. Only, the longer I stared at it the less it looked like my Ima at all, the face distorted with time and doubt and fear until really, it was nothing more than an approximation, an estimate. Like a thesaurus for people, abstracted so many times 'til the original just doesn't make sense.

I love you.

I strongly like you.

I, *strongly similar to you.*

I, *with large muscles…*

So close to being lost altogether.

*

'SCROTUM!'

From outside the window I could hear Tourettes Tony shrieking at the Scrabble board.

'SCROTUM! SCROTUM! SCROTUM!'

It would be a decent eleven pointer, in fairness to the lad; could even change the 'O' for an 'E' and do 'RECTUMS' instead, better and cruder yet. But I suspected Tony didn't actually have the letters for either word, or even the blanks.

It was four o'clock on an anaemic-looking Tuesday afternoon, which at Montague House meant Games Hour, the weekly bit of craic amidst the gloom. The sessions were closely supervised to ensure no one tried to shove a dice up their arse, or slit their wrists with an Ace of Hearts – better again, a Joker, if they were feeling particularly ironic – but while the rest of them acted the bollocks with counters and boards, I was down on my knees and hands in the muck, crawling beneath the protrusion of the Common Room bay window, praying to God I wouldn't be seen.

I had never really been the outdoorsy type – my hands much too far away to coordinate with my eyes – so the sweat of the crawl alone was a killer. But with the added terror of being caught, my chest was relentless – needed a few blanks of my own to calm the bloody thing down.

I paused to pant. The stones were digging into my kneecaps, a vicious impale like a gnashy set of teeth. But I carried on despite myself, dragging my body under the ledge, my face so close to the dirt my nose might scrape a rut that looked like the trail of a snail. Or no, I spurred myself now, why not like the trail of an IRA officer penetrating a British base? Or an Israeli soldier invading Sinai back in '56? Or like an un-Bar Mitzvah-ed mute off to meet an old

Jewish cripple for Tuesday afternoon story time?

I rolled my eyes but they saw only mud. I remembered Alf once told me it was better to be buried on your front, to make sure you were a gonner, like.

Of course, Alf himself never seemed to bother with any of this cloak-and-dagger shite; always just wheeled into our meetings from round the front of the House, casual as you like, as if the whole thing were above board. To be honest, I half-suspected Sister Frances just sneaked him out then covered up his tracks, the pretty nun still caught on some daft bit of softness for the grouch.

We had managed a couple of get-togethers a week, out here in a forgotten part of the garden – about all that was feasible, given the constant vigilance of the place. Apart from Games Hour there were the ongoing sessions with Doctor Lally ('Maybe your voice box is in a sort of a coma, lad?'); the Priest's Visit (an obese prick named Father Dwyer who wouldn't so much as acknowledge my existence); the weekly Shower Hour (''Scuse me, but why is your langer missing a bit at the top?'); the Nits Check (a new one they had chucked in as an excuse to shave off our skulls so we all looked the same). And apart from the hectic schedule, there was the added restriction that Alf refused to meet on Friday evenings or Saturdays, always surprisingly strict in that regard. 'It's the Sabbath, you gobshite. *Thou shalt not create* – didn't you pay attention in Cheder at all?'

Even though I wanted to point out that actually, I didn't create a thing out here, only transcribed the words exactly as I heard them – my side of the unlikely bargain.

The secret garden was most likely the remains of the Montagues' old potting shed. When I arrived I wiped the clumps off my knees and began to yank at the rocks in the corner until, finally, I had uncovered the thing I needed.

The jotter was the same as the ones we had had at school. A dull, piss-yellow colour; a sketch of a Martello Tower on the front as if to encourage every gobshite in the country to become the next James bloody Joyce. And actually, I thought, didn't he once have a wank over a retard himself?

I opened the book and took out the pen that had been wedged in against the spine. The ink was already running low – Alf would have to nick us another one soon. Or how about getting one of those quills like that Rabbi Loew lad we learned about in Cheder? Apparently he would just dip the nib of it in ink, close his eyes, and let the words come down from above; scrawl out predictions about the massacre of the Jews until, unbelievably, the things came true.

And maybe if I had that quill I could do the opposite now – write down what I saw and somehow make it untrue again – and then speak.

And get out of here.

And see my Ima.

'Jaysus, Shmendrick, you look more like a convict every day with that bleedin' hairdo!' Alf rolled himself in with a growl and a spit. 'Fucker of a day, isn't it?'

I looked at him and nodded. Charmed.

His regulation shirt had been buttoned the wrong way up, his slacks at least two sizes too big so that his legstumps were absolutely swimming in them. Or maybe it should have been drowning. From what I could gauge the flesh ran out just at the knee, which was kind of ironic given my own slacks had been lopped off exactly there, my shins permanently exposed to the world.

'But come here to me, like,' he said now, straight to the business of the thing. 'This can't be a long one, all right? Apparently Monica the Mutt is on the war path today so we'd better leave a clatter of time for getting back to tea.'

Dutifully, I began to flick through the jotter's pages, looking for the next blank.

'Come on, come on.' Alf had wheeled himself in so close I could feel his breath on my forearm, drying the mud into cracks. 'Where were we?'

Until it appeared, the last line I had written. I tilted the Martello Tower so he could see:

> *From the first time I saw her I plied her with questions,*
> *needing to know every bit.*

It had been four days ago, that smear of poetry. Four days and how many years? How many lifetimes?

But Alf wasn't waiting to find out. 'Yeah, that's right, Shmendrick, absolutely plied her with questions. I just wanted…well Jaysus, I just felt this *need*, like, to know her; to have every last piece.'

With one palm beneath the jotter I clenched my fingers round the pen. Muck dropped from my nails, little pips like a fall of extra punctuation. Or really, like a *dot dot dot* for everything I knew was about to come.

The story itself was just a love story, once you got to grips with it, though that was easier said than done. At first Alf's memories had come out arseways, a gnarly mess almost impossible to follow, but by now I had found the shape of the thing at least; the bones.

It had all started on Clanbrassil Street in 1941. As he put it, 'an unlikely place for love'. But a woman had been standing there – middle-aged like himself – handing out flyers to recruit some people to come and dig turf from a bog. Apparently the country had been absolutely ravaged by fuel shortages courtesy of the War going on in Europe. Or the 'Emergency' as the locals preferred to call it – happy to ignore the thing as best they could.

Until they needed fuel; needed volunteers to come and dig turf from a bog.

'I was bloody raging when she handed me the leaflet,' Alf had told me, a force in his voice that left little doubt. 'As if I gave a shite about an empty coal bucket when there were already these rumours coming from beyond – nasty stuff, like, we didn't know whether to believe. But there was something…Ach, I don't know, Shmendrick, there was something about her that made me feel I should go. Made me feel…'

So off he had gone, down to County Offaly. And this time round, he had taken me with him.

He had told me about the bus full of volunteers that travelled that day, a hotchpotch of do-gooders and low-lifers alike; told me about the black stretch of bog where they were set to work, the air rich with the iron-stench of the earth's innards. And he told me about how they had clicked instantly, himself and herself, working side by side in the trenches of peat.

'She dug while I stacked, one after the other. And she had a fine way with the spade, let me tell you, Shmendrick. Not exactly spring chickens the pair of us, but we made decent progress so we did, going deeper and deeper into the dirt.'

While Alf went deeper and deeper too, losing himself in the telling of the tale.

'The fold of her shoulder blades was something else. Like a pair of wings tucked in...'

'The frizz off her hair was only gorgeous, wiring skewways out of her skull...'

I wrote it as it came, though in the beginning I couldn't quite believe what I was hearing; couldn't believe the way this fucker changed when he spoke of her – the wet in his eye, the child in his face – a different man entirely from the one I spent my time inside the House avoiding.

'Still I bombarded her with me questions, gagging for more and more...'

And then after a while I realised it wasn't just the teller I didn't recognise, but also the words themselves. Because to be honest, I had never heard love quite like it; never known it could exist between a man and a woman. No, I thought that kind of infatuation was reserved only for mothers and sons; for Imas and Shems.

'And you know, Shmendrick, she had gorgeous eyes, but they were both different colours?'

At this, I looked up from my page.

The day was already fading around us, a decent gust getting up that set the weeds to dance. It looked a bit like Alf's hands, the flickering that wouldn't go away.

'I had never heard of it before,' Alf went on, elaborating the unexpected image. 'Never even known it was possible, but it's true – she had one green eye and one brown one. Smashing stuff, like.'

For a moment I wished I had two different-coloured pens, to make the writing match.

By the end of each session Alf tended to be knackered, his memory a muscle overused, but before we headed back he would shut his own eyes and hold out his hands for the book. I would pass it over, then watch as he clasped it to his chest and rocked from side to side.

I stared at the ground. It almost felt like I was intruding on a moment.

And when he handed it back the jotter would still be warm as I stashed it beneath the bricks of the ruined shed, piling them high before I moved away, slowly. Though I always went in reverse; always careful not to turn my back; a reverence and a respect to the words.

Once inside Montague House again, it was business as usual. As merciless. To be honest, if anything Alf had become even more cruel than before, using the humiliation to cover up any whiff of our cahoots:

'Ugly little squirt never known a bit of skirt.'

'You know he pisses the bed every night?'

While Sister Monica smiled on in sinister approval. 'Would you look at that – the kike turning on the kike.'

But by now I could understand, just about, that Alf's bullying was only for show – a default bitterness he played to the crowd – whereas back in the safety of our bedroom he left me alone, barely even said a word, both of us still buzzing on the latest batch of the tale.

In the comfort of that silence I could have sworn something different had begun to form between us, a fresh reek on the pantry air.

So for a while, the new bond was almost enough – the unfurl of the story and the secret routine brightening the dull of the days.

'We slept on the shitstraw of the farmer's barn...'

'Me nails were stuffed fat with the dirt...'

'Did you know the phrase "left-footer" comes from a type of spade?'

Every instalment was a new distraction, a bit of unlikely warmth to keep me going, like the fuzz that had started growing back on the top of my slappy little head. Only, in the end it didn't seem to matter, because no matter how hard I tried I still couldn't manage to stop thinking about her. My Ima. Or more precisely, I could almost trick my mind into other things – divert it down to other bogs – whereas my body refused to have any of it, the separation turning physical now as well.

My bowels were in bits, a rainbow of squirts every time I grazed the toilet bowl. My appetite was annihilated. Not that I wasn't hungry – my gut would growl something ferocious all day – but by the time dinner came I couldn't seem to do it; couldn't bring myself to lift the spoon and gorge on the grey. So instead I would find myself just sitting there in the canteen, hunching over my plate, remembering.

I knew you were special from the moment I was pregnant...

The echo of her voice would fill me, the gorgeous countryside lilt. I knew she had grown up on a farm, though she never really liked to talk about it.

The other women all craved cheese when they were expecting, or some-times even pickles. Or Mary O'Kelly making sandwiches out of coal, the dirty little biddy...

I remembered it now word for word, one of her favourite boasts, massaging both our egos with her spindly little hands.

But me, oh no, I was different – I was after getting language cravings! Word pangs! Every time I heard one I would have to find a rhyme. Time. Crime. Mime. Craving. Raving. Misbehaving. And I knew then, pet, that you would be a different kind of baby. A very special kind.

Back in Montague House I stared down at my dinner.

Sinner.

Winner.

Getting thinner.

I stirred my soup. The skin on the top puckered like an elbow.

Other times I would remember the year I had gone through a strict phase of only eating my food in alphabetical order:

Apples.

Bread.

Custard.

Dumplings.

Or sometimes only in an order that meant something:

Lettuce.

Onions.

Veal.

Eggs.

Spelled out on a plate that only she and I understood. We would giggle like gobshites, gone on it for hours, until Abba would bang his fist down on the table and scream at us to stop.

'Kike!' Sister Monica bellowed now across the canteen. 'Eat your fecking grub.'

Or there was this one time, a year after my Bar Mitzvah, when I caught my mother crying in the kitchen. She was doubled over the counter halfway between the dairy utensil cupboard and the meat utensil cupboard (because of course, the two aren't supposed to mix – something about the life force between an Ima and a child). I was right beside her before she even realised, and then she got all flustered, blaming her tears on the onions, so to be funny I took out a flashcard and wrote: *THANKS SHALLOT*, to try and make her smile. But it only seemed to make her blub even harder, the joke somehow lost in the telling.

I think that was the first time I realised just how much I had given up.

A few days later, Alf and I were back in the secret garden, squatdeep in the story and the muck. There was a taste of damp off the air around us, like when the boys in school used to make me lick the library books until the ink came off on my tongue. 'Open up, freak!' they would shout, holding my face to the page. 'Get some words back into you!'

Remembering it now, the stains on my gob must have looked a bit like one of those gammy inkblot patterns Doctor Lally kept shoving at me these days, asking me what I saw; how I felt; what the fuck was fucking wrong.

I stood up straight, though I always felt too tall next to Alf's chair.

Slouching back, I tried my best to focus on his words, his tale the only thing that might bring me a bit of cheer. By now the week of bog-digging was finished, so all the volunteers were on the bus again, headed back to Dublin. She was sat in beside him, her and her two different-coloured eyes, though she didn't say a thing.

I pictured the image afresh – the strange mismatch – one green and one brown.

'When they dropped us off we strolled to her bedsit, there on Clanbrassil Street.'

I shuffled my position and lowered the pen to the page. A glut of ink congealed at the nib like it might form a scab.

'She made tea, but she had no milk in the gaff since she'd

been away all week, so we took it the old way instead. Honey and lemon, like. And you know, I hadn't had it that way in years and it tasted…well, it tasted of the Old Country.'

Alf ran his hand over his scalp as if to press down on his brain and make it slow.

'We chatted about everything and nothing. The success of the dig. The weather for the week. Of course, I was still a mad one for the questions, wanting to find out more and more about her, but she was a great one for telling tales instead – distracting me with stories, like. Sometimes they were Irish ones, sometimes Jewish ones – variations, of course, on the same fecking theme – but tonight she started on the one about the Golem. You know it, Shmendrick? The one with the magic spoon that makes the man out of clay?'

I knew the one, all right – the unlikeliest of miracles – so I nodded in agreement, the closest thing to a conversation we could ever share.

'And she was just about to reach the climax, where the lad comes to life to revenge the downtrodden Jews, when suddenly it hit me, shite-ton of bricks stuff we're talking, but suddenly I realised…sure wasn't I after falling in *love* with her?'

In the silence a flicker of awkwardness passed through me. I clicked my neck left and right and left.

'So I took her cup and I placed it down and I…well, Jaysus, I kissed her – a proper smacker! Then I kissed her again and again until I led her to the bed where she let me make love to her – for hours, like – the sweetest fecking thing I had ever tasted.'

Alf had begun to tremble now with the excitement, a shake like his hands but going all over his body. While my own body only stiffened the more I heard, a foot gouged deep into the filth.

'And with every minute I knew for certain that she was the real thing, like – the *one*. So in me head I started to tell meself another story – the one about the beggar who can throw his voice so he yahoos to a couple of birds who have been blown apart so as to bring them back together. Have you heard it, Shmendrick? Have you?'

I shook my head. No, I hadn't heard.

'So I repeated it to meself, over and over; matched it to the rhythm of our love. Because someone once told me that the sex and the type of a child you have depends on the story you're telling while you make it. Did you know that, Shmendrick? Did you?'

Still he bombarded me with questions, new ones from every angle, which only bred even more, like: *What tales did Ima tell for me?*

And: *Did she learn them on the farm?*

And: *How about the one tale that I could never tell?*

'Because you see, I had always wanted a babby. A legacy, like, for after I was gone. And even though we were a bit over the hill, I knew there was still a chance we could make it happen; that me love for this lass could be enough to make the miracle come true, our very own root down into the earth that would grow and grow forever more!' As he finished, Alf flung his arms so hard he nearly clobbered me in the crotch.

I flinched away. A legacy of bruises.

In the silence, Alf kept his arms held out, crucified in the sickly light. His chest panted, his body thrilled by the memory, while I just stood, imperfectly still. And waited.

And I promise I wanted to share in his enthusiasm; to be infected by his joy. To be honest, there was just something weirdly lovely about seeing the wanker so elated – the biggest miracle of the entire thing.

But it didn't matter what I wanted, because I just couldn't remember the knack of it. How to smile. How the hell to feel. No, not now – it seemed I missed her too much. I missed the stories she used to tell me every night before bed; missed how she would sometimes write them out and leave them under my pillow, her spelling always terrible. Or how she would sometimes change the names of all the characters to Shem, so that it was only me in her world and no one else.

Shem and the Ark.

Shem and the Whale.

Shem at the altar where his daddy obeys God's will and sacrifices him to—

Dingaling!

The bell for tea rang my heart out of my throat, down to the dirt below. I watched as Alf dropped his arms and headed off, his wheels crushing the dark-red organ into the muck. And as I hid the jotter and crawled back towards the House I could have sworn I could still feel the thing beating, left bleeding there behind where no one would ever find it.

That night I couldn't sleep. I lay in bed, the Braille of the springs keeping me awake – a message I couldn't for the life of me make out. I rolled over. My scalp was belting with an itch.

After a while I tried to picture my mother's face as usual – the single thing that ever brought me a bit of peace. I closed my eyes; kept my hands down my pants for warmth. Only, for some reason tonight it seemed a bit harder to persuade her to come.

I knew Alf's spiel this afternoon had thrown me, but I didn't really understand why; couldn't figure out why it had left me so awkward, why I couldn't just be happy for his love. At the very least, I knew I should have been able to see something kindred in the force his affection – God knows I had an obsession of my very own!

I rolled over and tried again, my mind digging deeper like a spade, everything focused on bringing my Ima back to me. Because I knew that if I could just catch a glimpse of her smile then I would be grand, the silence of sleep at last.

I waited; dug my hands a little deeper too.

But when she finally arrived she was smiling, yes, her teeth white as mints and sweet enough to lick. It was the frame around her, though, that wasn't right at all.

Because it seemed Alf's story was after digging up something else, another memory – another version of my Ima that I had spent the last five years trying to bury away, but which was suddenly back again. And now as then it was clear that I had no choice but to watch the mess unfold, no matter how ugly or how hard it hurt.

It was a Wednesday afternoon and thirteen-year-old Shem had mitched off from school for the first time in his life. He had been working on a map for weeks now, a route home to his Ima where all the streets followed one after the other in alphabetical order. It was a circuitous path, to be sure – all around the houses stuff – but he was high as a fucking kite on it. A then B then C then D. Each one spelled out in his head as he stomped along left then right then left then right then left, *dropping Scrabble tiles behind him like a Hansel and Gretel trail. Until eventually he came to G and turned up the Glenvar Road and saw a woman standing there – a figure he recognised straight away without a beat or blink.*

In the darkness now the pain began to spread, my body reacting to the memory; a writhe off me I couldn't manage to keep still.

She was on the front doorstep of a house that Shem had never seen before. Her hair was out of its headscarf, spilled down her back, a long, golden spew. And her fingers were locked with the fingers of a stranger – the tightest grip Shem had ever seen.

My limbs started to twist, jagging off the bed, my bones making funny shapes. I shut my eyes even tighter, but it didn't matter – the thing had taken hold.

Shem looked at the stranger, touching his Ima; a pale lad in a woolly jumper; a rosy cheek and a look on his face that meant only one thing. Love. And before the truth of his mother's affair could fully seep in, Shem turned around and ran, never once looking back, all the way home to where his Abba would be waiting to go through the final preparations for tomorrow, the Torah portion and the prayer shawl starched white and the trousers freshly pressed upon the—

'Shmendrick!'

The slap on my cheek felt almost cold at first. And then it was not. A vicious scald.

I opened my eyes and saw that Glenvar Road was gone. My limbs flopped out of their contortions with the relief. But then they saw Alf instead, sitting up in the bed next to me, holding one shaky hand in the other. 'Shmendrick, what are you…I think you were having a…Shmendrick, there's something I need to tell you.'

Still my cheek pulsed warm and stingy, reeling from the force of the touch, though it was his words that startled the most. Because it was weeks since he had spoken here in the pantry – a comfortable silence, yes, but a silence all the same – yet suddenly he was saying he needed to break it, which meant that something was very wrong.

'Shmendrick, we need to talk.'

I lifted my head from the pillow, away from the memory, the effort of it knackering as I went.

'Look, I'm after…I didn't know how to tell you…but I'm after getting you a phone call.'

A string of spit clung from the fabric of the sheets all the way to the chap of my lip.

'Sister Frances,' Alf explained. 'I had a chat after dinner, and she…arra, she said that maybe she could…Anyway, I know…I know I said I would help get you out of this place…' His words were rushing now, bombarding me with something I couldn't yet make out. Though amidst the confusion, I thought I could spot a hint of impatience, a hint of anger too. 'But this will have to do for the moment, all right?' Maybe even a hint of guilt. 'All right, Shmendrick, do you hear me? Tomorrow afternoon?'

But it didn't matter, because the following day, just like he promised, I heard only her.

The pretty nun led me down to the front hallway while all the others were out on Yard Hour, sneezing hayfever and dead-skin dust; allergic, like, to life. I could tell Frances was petrified, beetle-eyes going nuts to be sure the coast was clear, but finally we reached the console table by the front door where the telephone sat black-lacquered in all its glory. It was one of the old-fashioned kind, a long thin handle and two eggcups at either end, the hollow of it cold against your ear.

I noticed the letters 'AH' etched into the base, the same graffiti I had spied all over the gaff.

'Right, you've got ten minutes,' the nun explained, craning down the corridor again, the sinews in her neck pulled taut like an instrument. 'No more or I'll be dead.'

But how could I tell her that actually, ten was plenty? That really, ten was everything? Ten minutes of my Ima as she answered

119

the call: 'Hello, Máire Sweeney', then heard the silence and then, instinctively, felt me there – a split second and then the fall.

The same, I had always thought, as love.

'Well, what a nice surprise, pet. I'd been wondering when we would hear from you!' Instantly, she began to ramble, her country lilt banishing all ugly memories away. She told me about the neighbourhood gossip that was doing the rounds; about the new Audrey Hepburn picture she wanted to see; about the pile of books she had just borrowed from the local library. And all the while I pressed her to me, tracing my finger along the curve of the mouthpiece then tangling it in the loop-the-loop cord – the life force between an Ima and a child.

'I hope you're eating...*Borscht*...your mammy, eh?'

The reception was bloody terrible, splinters on the line. The interference of all the things that weren't being said. But still I drank it up, the nectar of her, savouring every drop.

'*Abba*'s in...Sends his...'

Though of course, he didn't come to the phone himself. 'Why would I...' I heard him growl in the background. '...a *dead* handset?' The 'd' word walloped nice and hard.

But I didn't care about him now, only her, here with me; the pair of us stationary at either end of the line.

'*Aliyah* ambassadors...The Kleins heading Friday...can you imagine...a *kibbutz*?!'

I pulled the phone back from my ear just an inch, her laughter just a tone too loud.

In the month before I left there had been a lot of talk about Aliyah, all right; about members of the community moving 'home' to Israel. By now it was a full decade since the country had officially been born, Mazel on her Tov, so more and more Jews had begun to flock East. And meanwhile with Ireland's economy going down the Swanee, sure everyone here was leaving too, for loads of families it was a double incentive – two migrating birds, one fresh-start stone.

'Shem? Shem, hurry up please, it's time.'

But as Sister Frances took the black lump from my hand, I could feel my own fresh start rising over me. Because even the sound of my mother's voice had reminded me, all over again, just why my sacrifice was worth it; just why I was stuck in here, keeping shtum, keeping her safe.

I promised I would stay positive from now on – no more nightmares; no more ugly memories – just as good as gold until I found my way out.

The nun hurried me back to the yard; the pigeon-grey of the day. Edna Flaherty was doing shuttle-runs down to the boundary fence and then back again, and then back again, wrangling his hands like he was washing them under some invisible tap. Apparently Eoin Moore had been stung by a bee, flapping his fingers like a spastic or like a mock impression of Alf.

In the corner of the yard I saw him, seeing me.

He raised his eyebrows, just a bit. I raised mine back, just the same.

That night I guzzled my dinner, scraping the bowl, a bang of onion behind every bite. And a swarm of silent words rising out of the mush that had the sweetest taste of all.

Tough.

Enough.

True love.

Saturday

Her fingers jitter on the track pad so that the little arrow on the screen jitters too, stuttering over every click.

Cl-cl-cl-cl-click.

Outside, she hears London, clearing its throat. It is only ten a.m.

From? London Stansted.

To? Dublin T1.

Dates? Immediately.

Return? Yes.

Are you sure?

She places her hands on her lap, trying to make them still. But she hates them for the way they feel empty, as if, somehow, they miss the weight of the book; the heft of everything that has suddenly been lost.

The first time she brought him here to the flat he had looked at her and laughed, genuinely surprised that her offer of a late-night cup of tea turned out to be real, not just some ruse to get him upstairs. He had watched from the sidelines of her half-unpacked kitchen as she filled the kettle, too tipsy to lift the lid so she aimed the water straight down the spout instead, magicking the white crusts of limescale away.

SECURITY CHECK.
  Type the words shown above into the box.
  She glares at the screen, resenting this demand for answers. For clarity. She sees a wonky 'L' slant into a too-thick 'O'; mangled letters like a ransom note cut out of magazine scraps.
  I-CANT-BELIEVE-THIS-IS-HAPPENING.
  GET-ME-ON-A-FUCKING-PLANE.

'Would you like the London Eye one,' she had asked him next. 'Or the "Caf-fiend" one I stole from work?' Still only two mugs in the whole place, squat in an empty brown cupboard with hinges that squeaked as if in pain.
  '"Caf-fiend", please.'
  She took two Barry's teabags from the box, the last of her stash from home.
  'And are your colleagues aware you're a thief?' he asked.
  'Probably,' she said. '"Pikey Irish" and all that.'
  'Ha, I know the feeling. "Scabby Jew".'
  'Fine for us to say, but if anyone else…'
  'Exactly.'
  An unlikely foreplay; the room thick with lust, prejudice and the kettle's rising breath.

A window pops up now for Dublin hotels; a slew of five-star reviews. A banner ad for The Gathering – the big national reunion the government's been trying to push – anything to generate a bit of tourism; a bit of much-needed cash. She pictures her childhood bedroom. The bay window. The double bed. Old newspaper clippings stacked in alphabetical files. And the giant poster of Nelson Mandela on the wall where the boybands and heartthrobs should have been.

So maybe, she realises, a hint of disgust; maybe she has always just loved to prove a point.

Thirty minutes later his mouth had tasted of wine and the green-top milk she had grabbed from the corner shop, the one with the prices scrawled out on neon stars, a confectionery disco. But it tasted good, the sweet, oddly wholesome tang as Noah padded his lips against hers. Though there was no tongue – not even a bit – it didn't seem to be the English way.

Title? Ms.

 Last Name? Creedon.

 First Name? Aisling.

'And how would one pronounce that?' The perpetual question.

Well, it's 'Ais' like rash/smash/lashed out.

And 'ling' like ring/cling/Aer Ling-us, but they were too pricey for a last-minute flight hence the Ryanair Inquisition; the onslaught of questions, she supposes, a bit like last night.

He was on top of her next, surprisingly light, gentle yet urgent too. The sofa corner was rougher with her, jutting into her nape – no cushions yet, no softness to the place at all, because really, where was the bother when it was only ever her up there, alone?

Baggage? Oh the irony.

Travel Insurance? Don't Cover Me.

SMS confirmation?

But no, he hasn't called. Hasn't even sent a text. Just made his demands then drove away without a hint of remorse – the nerve of him she cannot actually believe. Though she supposes it just shows that they were always doomed; always the same roadblock lurking up ahead and no real way round.

He had knelt down then, skidding the storage boxes out of the way; trailed callous-tipped fingers up her thighs and down her skirt then peeled off her pants – red lace, too obvious – but she didn't care about that now, only hooked her heels around his shoulders and let her head roll drunkenly back, a damp grey crack in the ceiling and then stars.

Card number? Yes.

Verified by Visa? Yes.

Security Check and are you sure you're sure? Of course! And anyway, even if she wasn't, there has been no sign of an apology; no plea for forgiveness, so it seems the decision has been made either way.

Yes?

I—

Yes?

I—

Yes!

Afterwards, they lay sprawled amongst the boxes, two bodies fallen from the sky.

'Did you ever make a fort when you were a kid?'

'Does the Pope shit in the woods?'

'Cowboys and Indians?'

'Protestants and Catholics.'

'Ha! You Irish and your conflict.'

'Like you lot can talk.'

'I'm sorry for your Troubles.'

'Fuck you.'

'What, again?'

She can't even see the laptop any more, blinded by her rage at this memory that seems to have hocked itself up from nowhere. She feels a tingle between her legs, still the same itchy twenty denier from last night. She hasn't yet managed to change.

He was the first person she had let in here to the flat. Before him it was only the Skype faces distorted and delayed across the Irish Sea, or her brother all the way from Australia, a smear up onto her screen. She pictures the conversations like badly dubbed television, the words and the lips out of sync with each other. Or like drunken encounters, slurred and confused – lazy sentiments repeated over and over again:

'I'm doing grand, thanks.'

'What?'

'I'm *grand*.'

Shouting it so many times until she almost believed.

She had been marooned in that sea of cardboard for three months by the time Noah waded in to join her. She just hadn't found the time slash energy slash incentive to unpack, to make roots.

If anything, she had found the impermanence of it oddly comforting.

The boxes themselves had come smuggled in the boot of a friend's car – Aileen, a girl from school who, along with one thousand other Emerald Isle deserters per week, had taken the boat across the sea to find herself a brand new, Crunch-free beginning.

You could swim it if you were desperate enough, and God knows some of them were.

Aileen and her freckles were moving in with four other girls down in Clapham where the rest of the London-Irish seemed to have converged, familiar faces swarming the High Street; all the regional newspapers for sale in the stands by the Tube. The *Limerick Leader.* The *Roscommon Herald.* A special shelf in the local Sainsbury's that stocked the soda bread they needed to survive.

And can I pay for that in Euro please, boy?

Aisling had managed a total of two weeks down there – a single fortnight on the girls' moulting couch, before she had sprinted North to the overpriced Islington attic dive, up where the air was stranger but clearer, trying to figure out where exactly the line lay between community and claustrophobia; the cosiness of a home away from home and the terrifying sense that she had taken this leap and traded countries for…for what?

For this?

She prints off her boarding pass and folds it quickly like a secret. She reclaims her body from the little black dress, breaking the zip she yanks so hard.

After a shower she takes the dusty carry-on from under her bed and chucks in a few essentials. Toothbrush. Charger. A pair of runners, as if she will have the energy to jog, or even the incentive now.

She drags the case down the hallway, lame with one wheel broken. She checks her phone, but still there is nothing, only his face as a screensaver which she changes to black, a symbolism that only takes a click. She throws on her coat and her scarf and stamps towards the door, the tuft of the welcome mat bald from two years of comings and goings; of drunken stumbles and tiptoe kisses with no tongue and, as it turns out, no bloody point.

HOME SWEET HOME.

She stomps her foot on the 'SWEET' with all the rage she can muster; rage for everything he was asking, but also just for how easily he gave up – more pathetic than anything else. Only, for some reason the conviction doesn't seem to take, faltering a bit as another memory rises up from the mat, the home so sweet they had to write it twice.

It was Noah who bought it for her, a few weeks after their meeting amongst the boxes. There had been a series of them since, a curious ritual building up – maybe even something like an intimacy – though surely it was too soon to tell. But eventually he had declared war on the chaos of her apartment and kidnapped her into his Audi S7, up the North Circular Road ('we have one of these in Dublin too, you know?') to the blue and yellow kingdom of Ikea.

They spent hours trudging through the gaudy maze, the fully furnished rooms like theatre sets – a version of reality that could or could not be.

'How about a BORGSJÖÖ?'

'A HUSVIK?'

'A BROMÖLLA?'

'A KVART?'

'Sounds like something you'd have to apologise for.'

Awkward jokes to compensate for the domestic sort-of-bliss.

Until it was time for the reassuringly unromantic meatball lunch, the pile of grey-brown tumours submerged in the grey-brown gravy mulch.

'So what,' she said as she sat down with her tray, 'you'd rather go hungry than eat here?' As defiant as she was embarrassed that he had refused lunch, leaving her to queue while he found a table.

'No,' he smiled. 'I usually love reconstituted balls. It's just that I…I'm fasting.' He looked at her searchingly, to see if she understood. 'Today is Yom Kippur.'

She panicked, mid-bite, then defaulted to another joke. 'A YOM KIPPÜR? What's that, some kind of light fitting?'

He looked down at her tray.

Her mouth hummed with the fuzz of meat fat.

'It's a festival,' he said eventually, tucking back a curled sideburn that wasn't even there. 'The Day of Atonement. More for my parents' sake than my own, but basically it means no eating for twenty-five hours. In fact, technically no having fun at all.'

She glanced around the canteen. 'Noah, you should have…' She suddenly felt so out of place. 'There is no way I would have dragged you here if I—'

'Don't worry about it.' He smiled. 'In fact, if anything it actually works out, given Ikea is pretty much my idea of punishment.' He had looked at her then, hungry and smirking, a dust of her blusher on the chest of his shirt like she could see the pink of his heart. And out of nowhere he had leaned across the table and kissed her, tongue and all, sliding it against the gravy slick of hers.

Afterwards, he had driven her back and helped her lug all the stuff up to her home sweet home. 'I'm sorry – I would stay and assemble it for you,' he said. 'But I promised I would break the fast with my family.'

'Don't worry,' she said. 'I keep telling you I don't need you.'

Only, she never actually got round to putting the flat packs together that evening. Instead she spent hours on the Internet reading up on the history of the Day of Atonement – the thousands-of-years rituals, still alive – ignoring the grumbles in her gut as she skipped dinner, the meatballs enough to keep it going until morning when she woke amongst more boxes than ever before as if they had been breeding through the night.

She steps out onto the landing now and shuts the door, slamming it in the face of that loved-up version of herself, the one she still can't believe she let herself become. She trundles down the three flights of stairs, her case bouncing behind like a ton-weight shadow, to the communal entrance hall with its confetti of post. She kicks the letters, vicious with them; flicks up the laminated skid of a pizza leaflet. And then by the door she kicks something solid too, something that might just be real.

She looks down, expecting it to be a phonebook. There always seems to be a new edition, another list of the numbers and names of all the bodies clogging this heifer of a city – the one where she had finally felt she belonged, but which she now needs, so furiously, to flee.

His handwriting, though, is too distinct. Too Oxford sharp. The letters of her name etched deep as scars.

The year after Ikea, 2012, she had been much better prepared for the festival, probably even more clued-in this time than him.

'You know you're not allowed to wear perfume?'

'Leather shoes?'

'That ten days ago on *Rosh Hashanah* you were supposed to cast off all your sins by throwing a load of breadcrumbs into "a body of moving water with live fish"? Bit of a bizarre one that, if you ask me – like feeding the ducks but much crueller – making them ingest all your fuck-ups. Like that rumour when you were a kid that feeding rice to pigeons would make them explode.'

He had tried to shut her up by seducing her in her now-beautified snug of a living room, but:

'Oh no you don't.'

'Oh sorry,' he said. 'Are you—'

'No, it's you, you eejit. It's *Yom Kippur*.' She said it slowly, loving the repeated pout of the last syllable on her lips – the secret language she was starting to learn.

'And?'

'And...no sex.'

'What?'

'I know, I know. You're probably feeling vulnerable after dwelling on all your sins, but you're not allowed, mister. Not today.'

His eyes had waited, then flashed the colour of someone else's. 'Bloody hell, Aisling, what are you playing at?'

As he exploded in anger she had thought of that pigeon again; of feathers falling out of the sky. Before she had lashed back in spades, resenting the implication – his hunger versus her indignation – one of their most fundamental fights yet.

Though nothing, of course, compared to this.

She stands in the hallway, staring down at the book-shaped lump. She knows she can't just leave it out here in the open. And there is no time to trek back up to her flat – Jesus, at this rate she will miss the plane altogether; will just have to hide in the airport for the holidays instead, relishing the no-man's-land of it. Like taking the Tube to the end of the line and then back again, and then back again, just because she has nothing better to do in this city, no one else who will stand so close and too much pride to ask.

Until a stranger said hello. The same stranger, she tells herself, that must have returned; must have stood on her doorstep and posted the package, the bruise on his forehead blooming up and the choice placed back in her hands.

Outside, the ice air crystallises the wet of her ponytail. The extra bulge in the front pocket unbalances the case. She feels it veering, tripping over cracks, the whole thing so close to toppling entirely.

Stansted Airport is a purgatory. A punishment. She ghostwalks her way between Royal Baby-emblazoned teapots and the reek of All-Day Breakfasts. She doesn't meet any eyes. But as she goes, she leaves a Hansel and Gretel trail behind her – biting her nails and spitting them to the floor – just on the off-chance somebody might be following after all.

With the weight of the book in the overhead locker she is sure they won't make it off the ground. But then they do. They rise.

She looks out the window, the wings skimming the upward air; a plane so light it could be made out of paper. In the seat in front, a head falls and re-falls into sleep. Across the aisle a woman peels an orange for her son, the rind giving off a white spray of dust. To her right a man breathes heavily, attempting the Scrabble puzzle in his newspaper. And despite herself, Aisling spots that it is not just any paper, it is hers. A pathetic coup, she knows, but lately she cannot help it – as if she were the owner or even the editor of the thing, not just some young aspirational tucked down in the desk affectionately known as 'the morgue'.

They once sat by the Hampstead Heath pond eating fish and chips when she noticed her cod was wrapped in a page of it.

'Just imagine when it is your Current Affairs articles they serve batter on,' Noah had teased. 'That's when you'll know you've really made it.'

'Or imagine you had to eat chips off your lover's obituary?'

'Clag up their life with ketchup.'

'A bloody death.'

She closes her eyes. Cruising at eighteen thousand feet yet still it finds her, the banter that is only theirs. She breathes in the vinegar and salt. The back of her throat is dry.

But then she smells oranges instead. She opens her eyes; the young boy plops segment after segment straight onto his tongue. She retraces the hefty outline of her neighbour, the gold chain dangling the stub of a cross. He isn't wearing a wedding ring, she notices; his nails are oddly white. And against everything else she forces her mind to try to piece the snippets together; to take a guess at his story – her default distraction – because where some people picture strangers naked, Aisling Creedon (*temporary obituarist*) pictures them dead, remembered in peace.

FATHER OF THREE WHO PUT MALE MANICURES ON THE MAP.

PROFESSOR OF THEOLOGY WHO OPENED GOD-FRIENDLY BURGER CHAIN.

It always starts with the bullish opening paragraph, to set the tone, announce the facts, before the languid, three-paragraph arc from beginning to tragic but undoubtedly noble end, converting the mess of a thing we call life into one perfectly logical narrative. Half a page, maybe a picture; copy on the editor's desk by three for tweaks and typesetting and off to print before a pint round the corner to toast the day's deceased.

Of course, there is nothing remarkable about the process, this much at least she knows. Because we do it to ourselves all the time – turn our lives into a story – anything to try to keep the chaos of the self in check. Like:

Once upon a time there was an emigrant flying home for Christmas because that was part of who she was, and she wasn't going to change for anyone, no matter the kick of doubt.

Or:

Once upon a time there was an emigrant flying home for Christmas because she had to tell her family that her other half had invited her to do something she had secretly been—

'Drinks or snacks? Any drinks or snacks?' The air hostess brings her back with a jerk, startling both versions away. She overpays for a cup of metallic-tasting tea; winces it down in hot, hasty gulps.

So they cruise, barely a bump in the sky. After a while the pilot comes on to say hello, chatty like he is just bored up there, lonely for some company.

But the further they go the more Aisling can feel the reality of the decision looming over, no matter how many distractions she tries out for size. Because she knows that soon, something will have to die, her future or her past – her old self or her new.

#RIP.

One of the most popular hashtags on Twitter this year, she read – the digital way to grieve. A bit like the new website back home. RIP.ic. Updated every day to list the recently departed. Though for the older generation death is still done by analogue – little tales at the back of *The Irish Times*. Births, Marriages & Deaths. The whole life cycle bundled together on a single page so that every morning people like her parents can read it over breakfast, always recognising at least one of the names-in-lights.

'And you know,' he told her once, 'the *JC* does the same.'

'What?'

'The *Jewish Chronicle*. We call it Bingo in our house – if you know one name from each category. A baby, a bride and a body.'

A voice that just won't go mute.

She finds the window again, surprised by the clarity of the view. The sea below looks as if it isn't moving, set solid like you could just walk the rest of the way. Apparently the Rail and Sail do a decent deal on the crossing – the train from London up to Holyhead and then the ferry over the ocean; a fully stocked bar so that by the time you are back in Mammy's arms you can barely speak let alone wish her a Happy Christmas; blame the toss of the tide for your vomit, which she strangely enjoys cleaning up, needed again at last.

Aisling squeezes her cup. The stubs of her nails dent little smiles into the cardboard.

It has been a while since she was home all right. Or at least, so her friends are forever reminding her:

'Why so long?'

'Come to Gráinne's engagement party?'

'Kitty's baby shower?'

But there is always an excuse. The newspaper. The Tube Strike. The Jewish Magician (or the 'Sexy Yid', as they like to call him, somehow thinking it is OK) – always busy with her new life, trying to become a better version that will make them all so proud.

Well, how about this? she dares to think now, denting a little harder. *I'm going Yid myself! Changing for the man I love – what about that for better, eh?*

As if in warning, the seatbelt sign pings on. She looks up; sees the little red light. And she thinks of the locker above it, the one that holds her case that holds the envelope that holds the black leather book, Russian Dolls that make her feel dizzy. She needs a drink. Or really, she just needs to stay up here a little longer, somewhere in between, sipping tea and breathing oranges until she decides where it is she actually wants to land – who it is she actually wants to become.

But then they descend.

The lad beside her blesses himself, another stubby cross. She mimics the gesture, an ancient habit. The clouds are rough as they shove the aircraft through, raindrops on the window as if on cue and then the view below.

Dublin.

Her Dublin.

Quicker than she'd even remembered it.

They land with an almighty thump, dents in the runway like the dig of nails into a cup. The cringe of the on-time fanfare sounds out over the announcement system. Disarm and crosscheck. Forward and shortly the rear doors. A garbled Christmas greeting from the air hostess in an accent that makes Aisling wonder whether the poor girl will make it home herself for the big day. Because it is the only time of year that people go back to where they came from, before a hand reaches down and shakes the world like a snowglobe, scattering everyone again – a thrilling, melancholy flurry.

The arrivals hall is full of smiles; a sea of A4 signs.

WELCOME HOME!

MUMMY.

HAPPY XMAS PAT.

They remind her of a homeless man she once saw on the Tube holding a square of cardboard that was completely blank.

The taxi slides down Parnell Street, past Polish supermarkets and phalanxes of umbrellas. Every second lamppost brandishes an advert for The Abbey Theatre's Christmas show.

'My God,' her mother shrieks when she opens the front door. 'Aisling! But I thought—'

'Yes,' she says. 'It's me.'

Until finally, she lets herself collapse.

Home.

The thick folds of relief come cashmere-smooth, her first touch in too many hours. The smell of perfume under smoke. The impale of earring on cheek. Her mother holds on with an unusual force, as if somehow she knows not to let go, only to wheel her daughter in through the beige of the hallway towards the AGA-swelter of the kitchen; to sit her down and put the kettle on.

'Dad at work?'

'Where else.'

'And Séan? I thought he...'

'Tomorrow. Now darling, tea or stronger?'

And despite herself, Aisling almost smiles; sees the tasteful tinsel in the window and the warmth of the holiday she knows she could never give up, no matter who was asking.

'Tea, I think. Thank you.'

Though after the first pot of Barry's her mother insists on taking her suitcase upstairs, struggling with the heft of the load. 'Christ, child, what on earth have you got inside?'

And Aisling feels a draught then, as thin and cold as doubt, coming from underneath the door.

part three | And he called...

1921

'What about a man who courted his woman via pigeon mail, so he called the chef the night before their wedding to ask if he can cook the bird and serve it at the reception, to allow the guests to ingest the effort of their love? To tear the brown, gamey flesh and hook the wishbone with their little fingers and pull either side 'til it snaps?'

The Cork sky was a faint almost-blue. Ribbons of white cloud spooled downwards, unravelling all the way until you would half-expect to find a pile of them gathered on the ground or caught in one of the church spires poking up across the city.

It was the day before Passover, and Ruth was down on her hands and knees in the middle of the yard. To her left in the muck sat a bucket filled with kitchen knives; to her right an empty one. She picked up the first blade and held it to the light. A little tilt to see. Before she plunged it, deep into the soil; pulled back and then stabbed again, over and over, hacking at Ireland as if the poor thing hadn't endured enough violence lately to last a bloody lifetime.

Ruth paused, panting with the effort. She felt the hairs at the bottom of her spine smooth moist, a swirl of patterns like the print of a finger or a thumb.

All week it had been like this, working lives aside, the entire neighbourhood hell-bent on getting everything prepared for tomorrow's Passover feast. The local kosher shop, Shalom Stores, had imported most of the ingredients over from Manchester – massive crates of the stuff, weighing the ships down – though even still there didn't seem to be enough to go around, the neighbours bartering with one another or taking the train up to Dublin for that last batch of horseradish or else the whole holiday would be ruined. *Ruined!*

Back at home, Ruth had been relentless with the effort. Boiling the eggs; sorting the Matzoh crackers; stabbing the knives into the ground ten times each to make sure they were purified, just as the ritual decreed. And as ever, she was happy to help out – of course she was – her role in life, to be sure. But this year she couldn't deny the burden felt just a little different. A little heavier.

She picked up another knife and clenched. The whites of her nails were already clogged black and full.

Niamh had always worked overtime in the run-up to the festivals, extra hours and extra days. Apart from the cleaning and tidying she had done the main whack of the cooking; had mastered all the special dishes, finding such craic in the strange holiday routines she had never heard before:

'So what, we do it ten times, boy?'

'In ten different places.'

'And what if we end up accidentally decapitating a worm?'

'Oh no. Then we must start again.'

Ruth paused at the memory of her friend's laughter. She felt it in her chest, a little hack of its own.

It was nearly six months now since Niamh had said goodbye. One hundred and seventy days, to be exact. It had come from nowhere, but as soon as she was out the door the rumours hadn't taken long to mill – that Mame had finally given her the boot; had finally acted on a long-held jealousy.

'Well, it is no coincidence that the Ratman has not put on a single play since the help arrived.'

'I hear he's had his hands *full*, all right.'

'And not with his Princess of the Bees...'

And Ruth had even fantasised about some version of the gossip herself. Niamh, Tateh and her, the family that might have been – the other origins we construct, better versions in our dreams. But the truth of it was far more cruel, because Niamh's brother had been an IRA man in the recent War of Independence, his limbs blown off by the Brits – freedom, it turned out, came at a price – so now his sister had to stay put in their countryside home and care for him instead.

Ruth checked the next blade for nicks, imperfections. She squinted so hard it made her eyes sting.

In the beginning, she had written letters to Niamh, to keep her company in that faraway cottage – they were friends by now, weren't they, so wasn't that what friends did? She wrote about the local gossip she had overheard; about the horrors she had read in the *Cork Examiner*, the War still doing its worst – she asked Niamh when she thought it would end? When the Brits would set them free? And then she also asked if Niamh would mind sending back a few stories in return, because the place was starting to feel empty without them, without her, a sort of dampness creeping in as the days went on.

In the end, no letter of reply had ever come. Not a single word, boy.

Ruth turned the blade to its side and spotted a dent at the tip.

She dropped it back into the bucket with a clang. It would have to stay there now, away from all the others, unclean and untouched.

The following night the candles made a pair of yellow spotlights on the table – centre-stage, awaiting the actors' arrival – while the rest of the room lay in shadows, so dark that you might not even notice the emptiness of the place. By now most of the furniture had been given away, either to one of Mame's JNF fundraising sales or shipped directly East to Palestine to decorate the homes of those who had already made that splendid, Promised journey.

Ruth looked at herself in the oval mirror on the wall, one of the few luxuries to have survived. The face it framed was an adult's face now – twenty-eight years turned wide and round, the curls wrenched into a bun so that the skin beside her mismatched eyes was pulled tight into surprise. And in the half-light, she could have almost been…pretty. Maybe. If only God had been able to decide, green or brown – belonging to one or the other – instead of leaving her botched up somewhere in between.

Across the room the table was filled and ready to go. The candles. The flowers. The copies of the Haggadah story, all set out between the four place settings.

NorthSouthEastWest.

Though the wood on one of the chairs had faded in a different pattern to the rest, since the sunlight always caught it in the same position these days, unmoved and unused.

Ruth looked at it. The scars of another loss.

'Oh for goodness sake.' Mame raged in from the kitchen, her body shrunken, though her features were still at their most striking when they glared. 'What time do you…he's late! The meat will be dry as a bone!' She had been hiding in the kitchen since sunrise – of all the tasks, she had insisted on doing the actual cooking for once, basting the lamb until the knuckle shone like a gem.

Mame caught her daughter's eye, then looked away; focused instead up the stairs towards the man they both needed – in a way, the only link between them any more. 'For God's sake, Moshe, would you *please* come and join your family at—'

Until finally they heard it, a voice crying out in the wilderness. 'Ah, but what if there doesn't be any more space for you, Girlie? The island will sink under the weight.'

The sound of the questions made Ruth flinch, even if their familiarity couldn't help but bring comfort too – the words she knew so well, whether she liked it or not.

ACT TWO, SCENE ONE. A FARMER'S YARD.

He had been working on the script for over ten years now – not quite the Haggadah, but still a very old story at this stage.

'Moshe. Where have you *been*?'

'But it is these Provinces, Mr Murphy,' Tateh squeaked on, treading carefully down the stairs. 'These regions that Ireland is split into – four of them, I am believing.' He skipped the last step and kissed Mame on the cheek, then Ruth too, never once breaking the rhythm of the monologue. 'And I have been told we can make it our home, and send to our families elsewhere and tell them to come too.' He patted the top of the spare chair before, finally, he reached his own. 'Ach, Girlie, and what a delightful Seder table we have here before us!' He smiled his best smile at the punch line, the pockmarks on his cheek shoved high with delight.

The women looked at one another again, this time linked by something else. Was it fear? Ruth wondered as she sat, laying her napkin across her lap. Or maybe, she thought, maybe it was shame?

In the beginning it had been a strength not a weakness, her father's cheer; his grinning in the face of…everything. For weeks after Lady Gregory's rejection he had been unreachable, practically mute, but soon his bounce had returned, convinced that his beloved play just needed a few small tweaks before it got the thumbs up; before their lives were totally transformed. Every month a fresh draft of *The Fifth Province* was sent up to Dublin, the envelope covered with enough stamps to take it halfway around the world, just in case. And at first, the patroness had written back, a few lines of politeness. Excuses.

I have been busy taking Playboy of the Western World *to America.*

The Easter Rising – Dublin is in chaos. But at least Independence is drawing near. This time we cannot lose!

Until soon, the replies were the thing that got lost; awkward eyes from the postman and Mrs Geary at the Post Office, unable to meet the playwright's weekly enquiry.

'And what about the land of unsent mail?' Tateh had speculated, the way only he could. 'A realm filled with all the things we wish we had said?'

Ruth sighed. She wondered if that was where all her letters from Niamh had ended up too.

And even now, ten years on, still Tateh's conviction hadn't faltered – if anything, it had only grown – so that whenever the neighbours dared to ask he told them that yes, *The Fifth Province* was about to sweep the nation, The Abbey's finest debut yet! But then again, if they asked him anything these days he gave a beaming answer. That his peddling work was going well; that his daughter had lots of friends.

That the family was better than ever, not struggling a bit.

Ruth stared down at the white of her napkin. She had cleaned her fingernails, but still they looked grey against the cotton.

All along, she had tried to follow her father's optimism. She had been raised on it, sure – why stop now? And even when something inside him had started to slip, a manic flash, still she would wave him off each Monday morning and truly believe that he would earn a little more this week; that he would get the play right this time and everything would be grand.

Recently it had been pencils the only thing he seemed to be able to sell. The irony of a playwright who has been writing the same thing for over ten years making his pittance by flogging cheap pencils.

If anything, it sounded like one of his crazy ideas in itself.

But then even on the weekends, back at home, he spent his days out wandering too, venturing far beyond the Boundary Markers they were meant to stay within on the Sabbath. He claimed he just liked to go for a stroll down to O'Leary's pub, to improve his ear for the regional lilt – he had realised that that was the thing holding back the play. But then one afternoon Ruth had been wandering the docklands herself, sneaking to the letterbox to post more pleas to Niamh, when she saw him, down by the cove.

He was alone, though he spoke and laughed aloud. 'Scattered we will be no more...*Girlie speaks a little louder.*' He thrashed his arms through the air like they were punches or wings. 'For this island holds the place we have been searching...No no no, the place we have been *searching* for, this island *holds*...yes, better, much better.' He rubbed his hands together like a magician, then ripped off his clothes and sprinted into the freeze of the Atlantic, his body ghost white against the current and—

147

'Right, shall we begin?'

Ruth looked up, back from the sea to where they sat, all three of them here at the kitchen table.

Slowly she nodded at her mother's request and picked up her faded Haggadah pamphlet. The pages smelled damp, stiff from wherever they had been buried for the last twelve months – almost, but never wholly forgotten. She looked at her parents, the smile and the frown. She looked at the empty chair and the silent kitchen.

And then, despite everything, she joined them as they read:

Blessed are You, God, our God, King of the universe, who creates the fruit of the vine...

Blessed are You, God, our God, King of the universe, who has chosen us from among all people...

Blessed are You, God, our God, King of the universe, who has raised us above all tongues...

'Ach, it always takes so long to get going,' Tateh chimed in. 'You see, Austėja. I am not the only one who overwrites!'

The women sipped their wine, pursed lips to rims.

When his laughter had run out they carried on.

But after a while the lips began to relax, the reading loosening them up. Because there was no need to worry about saying the wrong thing – or worse, sitting there in silence – when the words were right in front of them, telling them what to say.

If he had given us the Torah, it would have been enough...

Ruth reached for the wine to top up their glasses, to will the moment on.

If he had led us to Mount Sinai, it would have been enough...

She liked this bit especially, the repetition like a momentum driving forward.

If he had split the sea for us, it would have been enough...

'And what if the Atlantic had split for our Esther, Girlie? Maybe she could be all right after all?'

At her father's words, Ruth placed the wine back on the table.

By now it was a full nine years since that other departure from the house; that other boat that never made it to America.

Esther had bought her ticket without a single hint – even after the announcement she refused to confess where she had managed to procure such a sum.

ONE WAY the document said. *CORK TO NYC.*

The final chapter of the journey after all.

At first Mame's face had flared livid, incandescent in its rage, then had collapsed just as quickly again. 'But what about the Homeland?' she begged. 'If we are going to leave, Esther, it should be there.'

While Tateh only smiled same-old smiles: 'But we are happy here, my darling. So nearly ready is *The Fifth Province.*'

And somewhere in the background, Ruth had seized the moment, a rare chance to try to impress: 'Well, Niamh did say it is the largest ship the world has ever seen. It was built by the White Star Line up in Belfast, and then Cork is the last port, so really it is an all-Irish affair!' She was pleased with how she had put it, the last bit especially. She wondered if she would ever be described as 'all-Irish' herself?

But Esther continued on as if her sister hadn't even opened her mouth. Not now and not ever. 'I will stay with Uncle Dovid and get a job on Broadway – I am nearly twenty-one, after all. And of course, with the movies starting up...'

Oh yes, Niamh had told her about them too!

But no, Ruth decided, no point in trying again; please them more by shutting up.

'And just think, Tateh,' the beauty went on, saving the best 'til last. 'As soon as I am famous I will be able to convince some famous director to put on your show. How Lady Gregory will eat her hat then, eh?'

As soon as Ruth had seen the look in her father's eyes, she knew that Esther would be on that boat; that they would stand amidst the wailing carnival of Queenstown Port waving her off, back and forth until their arms lost all their feelings, the rest of the mammies saying prayers as if over the dead, almost as if they knew.

It was an hour before the dot on the horizon dropped away completely. Another week before the bad news washed up.

Mame cleared their plates and disappeared into the kitchen, refusing all offers of help. She made no noise as she went. She stayed away that bit too long.

When she finally returned with the main course, though, the plates that she carried were piled high. Ruth and Tateh made a fuss, heaping their compliments in return:

'It looks delicious.'

'What about a feast so tasty that—'

'Just eat.'

But it really was good, too much for three but they were not complaining, drowned in a sea of gravy, the scald of it so hot you might burn your tongue off, or better yet, your grief. Ruth passed around the potatoes, her very favourite – dripped with butter, which made them even nicer – then the carrots and peas, each mouthful speckled bright. And after a while, the eating began to soften them again, the most ancient comfort of all. An extra comfort for Ruth especially, since it was just such a treat to be served dinner like this any more. Because it was her job to do all the cooking now; to recreate Niamh's recipes as best she could; to recall the ingredients and the tricks that went into every one. And sometimes she even tried to re-tell Niamh's stories while she worked, plucking the chickens or stirring the slick of stews, knowing the food would taste better if she could just remember the tales the right way round.

She sliced open her third spud with her knife. She checked for flecks of black against the white.

And maybe it was all the cooking that meant her body had started to fill out a bit, her dresses finding curves she hadn't known before – in a way, the very opposite of Mame's shrinking – as if she were compensating. She smiled. She would have to get Leb Epstein to tailor her a new frock. Though in truth, she had barely even noticed the change herself until she had heard the women's whispers up in the balcony at Shul, a fresh batch of gossip aimed her family's way.

A tiny part of her had almost felt pride for the attention.

The whispers, however, dealt mostly with shame; said that she was letting herself go – twenty-eight now and still single. 'Nu, isn't she running out of time?' While others said it wasn't *natural*, the friendship she had had with that *local* girl; the interest she seemed to take in *native* matters. And that maybe, God help them, but maybe…it had been the wrong sister on that ship?

Ruth lost her smile now and closed her eyes. She felt another stretch in her hand-me-down dress, this time for the thump of her chest.

'And don't forget we must pour some wine for Elijah. It is time for the Prophet's Cup.'

At the sound of her mother's voice Ruth took a breath. She opened her eyes, adjusting them back to the room. The candles. The oval mirror. The almost-nothing else.

'Well, what is the hold up?'

'Yes yes, Girlie. Go open the door for when the prophet comes.'

Slowly, Ruth stood, tilting with the bulk of her hips. It was too early – they weren't finished their dinners yet. Her stomach grumbled. Her dinner would go cold.

But of course, she had to remember that she was happy now to please her father's whims; to do precisely as she was told. Because the women could whisper all they wanted, but these past few days had reminded her all over again just how much she was needed here – a different kind of girlhood dream for a very different type of girl, realised at last.

She glanced back at her parents; the splash of gravy on her father's beard; the knuckle-jag of her mother's collar. She smiled.

Because with Esther gone, and now Niamh as well, Ruth knew that they would be scuppered if they lost her too; that actually, they relied on her more than ever before. So in a way, she asked herself, as she crossed the room and reached for the handle, but in a way wasn't that almost the same as love? Or at least, the closest she might come?

She yanked the door across the swollen step, the lip of it fattened from last night's rain. She returned to her seat and crossed her legs; poured a glass of wine and placed it out in case the prophet decided to join them.

She noticed the candles were running low, the wax drips brittle like fingers.

They were supposed to say the prayer, but none of them spoke, each one staring at the doorway in silence; each hoping for a different soul to step inside.

Elijah?

Esther?

Niamh?

The breeze from the street reached the table, sucking the last of the steam from their half-eaten plates.

Lady Gregory?

Uncle Dovid?

The man I married?

The draught of air that tasted of nothing but sea.

Soon, they had had enough, leaning back into their chairs and picking up their Haggadah pamphlets one last time.

Next year in Jerusalem!

Next year in Jerusalem!

Next year in Jerusalem!

All three of them read the final blessing – the same phrase as every year – though of course Mame was the only one amongst them who really wished it true.

Ruth turned to her mother now, a little bird in her emerald dress. The nubbin of candlelight had turned her softer, a different woman than at the start of the meal – the Princess of the Bees with her wine-stained lips, staring across at the Ratman with his flushed little pocks. And Ruth smiled at the thought, because even now the pair of them remained united by that story, the one she would never get to hear. It made her glad to know they still had that at least.

She took another drink, feeling it sweet on her tongue; a swoon between her temples. No doubt there would be headaches in the morning. But as she watched her parents watching one another, it wasn't just her head that felt lighter. Because the rest of her felt it too, a little fist unfurling from its perpetual scrunch and a chance that maybe next year didn't have to be Jerusalem, but something else; something better.

The year her father's play was accepted.

The year her mother stopped her mourning.

The year their family came together again, no maid and no friends, but each of them as one.

North

South

East—

'Right, time for a stroll!' Out of nowhere, Tateh's announcement stood them up. The chairs screeched like animals in pain.

She checked the door. It was already waiting for him, ajar.

He said he needed to stretch his legs; to get some air after such a beautiful feed. 'And don't forget, Girlies,' he cried as he bounded away, 'next year in the Fifth Province!' before he slammed the door behind him with a bang that shocked the place still.

The women waited, allowing the air to readjust to the absence – a loss they felt so much more than they should. And then they began to clear, working in silence, scrubbing the place all over again, though the weariness upon them felt more good than bad.

'You have had a busy week,' Mame said as she rinsed the plates. 'You have worked very hard.'

Ruth looked at her mother, carefully; at the closest to a thank you she could ever bring herself to come.

'And Ruthie,' she added then. 'Do you think…' She paused, as if choosing the right words. 'Are you sure he will be…' Her eyes flickered towards the doorway and beyond, seeing but not quite.

Before they returned again to the water, the unasked question rising up like a bubble between them, higher and higher through the air until it burst.

'And what about a blind man who travels the earth telling myths and legends to kings and queens, until one day he arrives at a palace where a beautiful maiden starts to tell him a story instead? It is a story about a blind man who travels the earth telling myths and legends to kings and queens...And upon hearing this, the blind man falls down dead on the spot, his heart ripped through by the ecstasy of knowing that his dream has finally come true. For now it will be others who tell tales about him, and in this way he will live forever.'

From the moment Ruth opened her eyes, she knew.

The room was lit up, honey-bright, even if it still felt too soon to be day. She slid from the bed, the floor gasping cold beneath her feet. She tiptoed the landing to the door of her parents' room and peered in on the snoring heap of her mother, the left arm thrown across the empty flat of blankets stretching for something or someone it couldn't quite reach.

Ruth went downstairs and outside without a pause, no bother with a jumper or a pair of shoes, the little shards of ground pricking up into the pads of her heels.

She made her way through the maze of alleyways; spotted a cat on a ledge, deep asleep. She turned her head left and right, but already she knew exactly where she would find him.

Her fingers tingled for a go of her compass.

When the cove came into sight she called for him. 'Tateh?' The word so much smaller out in the air, gobbled by the shingle's crunch.

'Tateh?' But no, maybe she shouldn't wake him yet – God only knew how long he had stayed up last night walking, rehearsing, digesting; telling the sea his latest tricks.

She stopped when her shadow was just short of his, the two silhouettes about to butt heads. The paleness of his torso glared, the girlish pink of the nipples and the giant hollow in the middle like a heart scooped out. His feet were bare, his glasses off, but he had kept his trousers on, the brown soaked a darker, earthier shade.

'Tateh?'

When she noticed the bulge in his pockets she reached down to pick one out. The limestone fitted snug in her palm. She recognised it – the same kind of rock as the country walls he walked alongside every day. She rolled it in her hand; felt it smooth across her skin. She noticed a fleck of green running through the grey that looked like a flaw. A rupture.

And as she made her way back through the Cork silence she remembered Niamh once telling her how in Irish beekeeping lore it is said that, after a death, you must 'tell the bees' – go out to the hut and drape it with a black cloth; then inform them of the loss. Because otherwise they will be hurt by the neglect. Frantic. Maybe even abandon the hive altogether.

'How do I look?' Mame arched her back to the fall of her red dress, the waist cinched tight before the stiff frill to the floor. It was a dated fashion, but of course, it was years since she had set the frock aside, waiting for that special day – her first step on Palestinian soil.

Today the cream shoes would step on Curraghkippane soil instead, the muck staining the sheer of the satin black.

It had been a busy week. Another one. Maybe even more so than the Passover build-up since this time the locals also seemed keen to play their parts, nervous tweeds clustered on the doorstep, curiosity and condolences in equal measure.

'Used to buy me Babby Jesus figurines off him, boy.'

'And if you'll pardon me asking, but is it true that a Jewman does be buried standing up?'

Of course, it wasn't true – the Burial Society placed his body in shrouds, lying down, the flesh washed and the fingernails cut short. Meanwhile, Ruth had a cut of her own to show that she was in mourning – a little rip there in her left sleeve as is fitting for someone who has lost a parent, to symbolise the tear in her heart. She noticed Mame had opted to wear a black ribbon instead. The frock would not be harmed.

Once the preparations were complete they led the body out to the horse and hearse and the procession with Ruth and her mother at the head, just the two of them now, *NorthEast*. It was a giant plot, too huge to ever be filled, even with all the bodies that were sent by train from the surrounding counties – as the locals sniggered, 'wandering even after their death'.

Each headstone was covered with pebbles, weights to hold down the scraps of paper scribbled with prayers and offering notes. Ruth looked away. She was glad tradition meant it was a year before anyone would leave stones for her father.

Later, back at the house, the room was stuffed with people, the table buried in stews and treats the neighbours had brought – all the smells of somewhere far away. Even though she wasn't supposed to, Ruth felt that she should offer them around; see if anyone needed a drink, a chair. But she seemed barely able to stand herself, legs rocking like they had done after being at sea, *EastWest, EastWest*.

She had to clutch the banister for support as she accepted the invocations that she may grieve no more and avoided the sentimental eyes, more attention than she knew what to do with.

Just when the farewells had begun, there was a knock on the door, a latecomer across the threshold.

She said she was only sticking her head in, like, to pay her respects. To tell Ruth and Mame that she was so very very sorry.

Ruth's heart wished it had the strength to swell.

And her body too, to leave the banister behind and go to her; to hug her and beg her not to leave again. Even if Niamh's face somehow looked a little different now, the eyes raw, the lids drooped like someone had pulled on them for too long.

But she would always be a great one for a smile. 'Ah now, lads, this isn't what he would have wanted!' Her announcement came as a singsong across the knackered fug of the room. 'If you don't mind me saying, but in our custom a night like this is for tales. Stories, like, about the dearly departed – sounds right up his street, wouldn't you say?' Before anyone even had the breath to reply she had begun, hunched on the arm of a chair, prattling out a gem from years ago. It was back when she was only their shabbos goy, popping in to light their stove of a Saturday morning – back when they were only here for a while until they moved on to a place, supposedly, called 'home'.

'And I does be fiddling with the matches, right,' Niamh explained, cosied up to them all with her shock of sunset-red hair, 'when suddenly your man turns to me and says: "Miss Niamh, there is a question I am having." That strange back-to-front English he used to speak, arseways altogether. So I says: "Go on," and he says: "Down in the village I was yesterday when I heard someone ask the butcher: 'How is she cutting?' and then someone else tell the barber he was 'on the pig's back'. And I have been trying to figure it out but your people...they seem very confused with their professions and their words!'"

The room traded glances while she spoke, but by the time the punch line came they had no choice. Their laughter bounced off the ceiling to the floorboards above, buffeting into the cracks.

Ruth felt a twinge of pride for her friend, then another kind of twinge for her foolishness.

Leb Ebstein spoke next, his neck host to more jowls than ever these days. 'Well, it was me and Moshe, may his memory be blessed, who went to the Housing Office when we first arrived. But on the way back on the tram a lad takes one look at our garb and asks: "Where are ye boys from?" And Moshe replies: "Kh'hob shoyn fargsen" – that is, for those of you who don't..."I have forgotten". Because I think his head is in a right spin at this point, trying to take it all in. But then the lad replies: "Well, *Séan Ferguson*, pleasure to meet you, boy, and welcome to Cork." Shook his hand and everything! And so I called him *Séan* from that day forward. His Irish alter ego!'

There was a unanimous smile this time, as contagious as a yawn. They had to speak over one another to decide whose turn it was to go next.

And the more that was told the more the room reclined, easy on the tales. Stories about the deceased but also *by* the deceased, favourite ideas recalled. Like the one he had about the women knitting, or the couple and the pigeon, or his Fifth Province business, nu – I always wondered where he conjured that one from?

Ruth looked to Niamh. The pink face gave a slow, generous nod.

Eventually it was Mame's turn. As she stood she flattened the frills of her dress; adjusted the ribbon on her chest. It looked a bit like a debutante's corsage. And it took a moment for Ruth to hear what her mother was actually saying, because it almost sounded like she was using English; making sure that everyone in the room could understand. 'Well, the first…the first time I met Moshe was at the theatre. Ironic, no? A play in a theatre in Vilnius.'

Ruth clutched the banister even harder. Her body longed for the landing up above – the vantage point for the little listening girl.

'I had read some reviews and, being the curious thing I once was, if you can believe it, lied to my parents and sneaked off to the show. Alone.'

Ruth watched the moving lips, transfixed by the confidence with which they shaped the foreign words; the unknown past.

'It was a play in seven acts, with an intermission between each one, and during the first break Moshe came up and introduced himself. He was a scrawny man with his shirt untucked, but being on my own I had no choice but to say hello. Of course, I tried to be as rude as possible, but during the second intermission he was over again. A few words, mostly about the performance, but then during the third one he made me laugh. A stupid thing, I can't even remember, but it was too late after that, and during the fourth he offered me a glass of something sweet.'

The voice grew louder with the list. Ruth checked them off with a twitch of fingers behind her back.

'…fifth and sixth were filled with more jokes – he had a great one about a pigeon and a swan…But it was the seventh, after the show, that convinced me.' Mame paused for a breath now, a chestful, sucking in the air for the climax. 'He walked me home to my parents' house. It was a warm night and the stars were out, but of course, already he could tell that I was not the type of girl to be moved by such things. And when we finally reached my gate and we were just about to say goodbye he...he tried to kiss me.'

There was another pause, all of them poised together now, united there at that gate.

'But how could I? I knew that my father would have noticed me missing, and that he could maybe see us through the window. I could only imagine the punishment – he was not a kind man. But for some reason I grabbed Moshe's bony hand and led him round the back of our house to the barn, into the darkness out of sight, where yes, I admit, I let him kiss me.'

Ruth felt a little triumph for her father now, brave with this imperious young woman. She scanned the room. Leaning in, each face looked like a better version of itself.

'I had had other kisses, I am willing to admit, but this one was...different. The smell of straw and animals was all around, but our mouths could taste only each other, until we backed our way up against the wall so hard that we heard a loud bang. A smash. And then a buzz.'

It started low, but Ruth could already hear the sound inside her – a warning hum for what was about to come.

'It was a beehive,' Mame continued. 'So of course, I screamed. I had always been terrified of the things. And I ran outside, crying frantically; heard the back door of my house opening and my father storming out and booming in his deep, threatening way. But Moshe knew that if my father saw him I would be done for. Courting strangers? Even speaking to a man? Nu, what kind of good Jewish girl does this? So instead Moshe waited in the shadows until

I reassured my father that I had just got a fright – had seen a fox – and led him back inside.'

By now Ruth's skin had grown sweltering hot, her dress clinging tighter than ever.

'In the darkness of the barn the bees did their worst. They swarmed, they stung, over and over, every bit of him – the doctors said he could have died. Should have died. Nearly lost the sight in one of his eyes, which is why he always had to wear those hideous glasses.' Mame swallowed the last word, her first hint of emotion all night. 'And ever since then he called me his Princess of the Bees. May…may his memory be blessed.'

A wall of hush lingered in the room. Not one of them moved. Instead they just hovered there in the darkness of a North Lithuanian shed with a beautiful young girl and an earnest young boy, stupid with love; a woman they had never quite liked and a man they had never quite understood. But suddenly the light had caught them differently, just two characters in a story, right back at the beginning – a story that had finally been told.

As Ruth realised that now, everything really was lost.

June

'Jaysus, she has a fine rump on her all the same, eh?' Alf kept his whispers low, trying his very best, though his wheelchair had started to rattle with the thrust of his laughter. 'Virgin me arse – I'd say she had her fair share of shtuppings in her time, all right!'

I smiled back at him from where I sat. At the joke, yes, but also at the whole scenario, still struggling to fully get my head around it. Because here I was, huddled on the floor of the corridor at one o'clock in the morning opposite a legless grouch while he made filthy jokes beneath a gigantic statue of the Blessed Virgin, a crown of lit-up stars mangled into her pious little head.

'Moany Mary, nu?'

It was almost a week since Alf had suggested relocating our sessions from the secret garden. He said we needed something more regular, something other than a snatched half an hour here and there. 'Why not make it a nightly job, eh Shmendrick?' A credit, I suppose, to how well the story was going. How well we were.

That said, when he first led me to the new spot I was still half-convinced he was taking the proverbial – two sons of Israel, crouched at the foot of the mother of the New Testament – talk about ironic! But it wasn't her Testament we were interested in, or her Beloved

Son, only that the flicker of her nocturnal headwear spat out just enough light to write by, and that her position in Montague House was just far enough away from the nuns' dormitory to be safe for whispers; for the scratch of pen on yellow jotter page.

And so, simple as that, our Night Lessons began.

We followed on from exactly where we had left off before – Alf and his lover, back from the bog, lying naked and intermangled in her Clanbrassil Street bedsit – the same ecstasy that had left me so out of sorts. But it was different now, because ever since I had spoken to my Ima on the phone I had remembered, all over again, the reason I was doing this – that I was in here because of her – the only incentive I would ever need, so no more complaining. And anyway, I reminded myself, sure hadn't I agreed to help Alf with his story precisely because he had promised to get me out of here again? To get me back to her? And for that, I would have sat under any bloody statue; would have mangled the crown into my own skull until it ruptured a nasty gash.

So no, I just had to bide my time; just had to keep on writing.

And there was also a sort of familiarity to the process itself I was beginning to recognise. Because it reminded me of other sessions I had had through the years – different truth-sharings that had come to pass. Like the lads in Cheder who had bullied me to bits about my newfound silence:

'Hush little baby...'

'A willy up the bum makes a bold boy shtum!'

But then after a while they had all sought me out, one by one, and asked if they could confess. It was a ritual our faith didn't offer, a chance to spew their crimes aloud, off their chest and onto mine instead, knowing I could never pass them on.

Like David Greenwood after he pilfered from his daddy's wallet.

Or Michael Steiner who set the cat on fire and blamed his retard little sister.

Or Jacob Bloom who shifted a gentile outside the Blackrock Parish hop, a grope of her lacy pink bra that gave me a stiffy just to hear.

At the time I could hardly believe it, these boys I'd known for years suddenly entrusting me with such gems! Such dirt! And yet, part of me also wanted to remind them that even if I had been able to talk, I wouldn't have blabbed. Because didn't they remember what Rabbi Hart had taught us in Cheder when we were younger? About the dangers of spreading slander and speaking ill? Because I remembered, all right. In fact, the spiel had never quite let go of me since, not then and certainly not now as I sat here in the scrotum shrivelling corridor of Montague House.

'Lashon Ha-ra,' the Rabbi had announced, the syllables booming through the half-empty classroom. 'The evil tongue is the scourge of the human race – the worst crime a Jew can ever commit.' His superlatives made their way over the barely listening heads to where I had started getting angsty down the back. 'It is a crime equal to Murder. To Idol Worship. Even to Adultery – a wife betrays her husband, so a person can betray their God with their words.'

At the time it had sent me panicking, unable to believe just how disastrous one wrong speech could be – why the feck hadn't they warned us sooner? What if I'd let my tongue already slip? Though remembering it now, the Rabbi's last example couldn't help but make me smile. *A wife betrays her husband.* Yet another undelicious irony, given everything that had come to pass.

So Alf went on telling me his words, his secrets, a routine that meandered us nicely through June. He would go forward with the story, but also backwards too, circling over the same trampled ground to give me a little more each time – another skullful of details to flesh the thing out.

Like the sandwiches the farmer had made for their lunch on the bog, 'the cheese so fresh you could still taste the rennet'.

Or the country walls that jagged away in the distance, all the bricks slotted together 'like jigsaw bits'.

Or the stories his woman liked to tell him to kill time while they dug. My favourite was the one about the man and the woman who court via pigeon mail, until the woman falls in love with the pigeon instead. Yes, that one made me smile for the rest of the night.

And Alf was so clear with every detail, painstaking with it, like, which was funny, because at other times he started to say that he thought his mind was beginning to slip. 'Arra, I can feel it, Shmendrick,' he whispered once, out of nowhere or nothing at all. 'It's…it's beginning to go.'

Part of me wanted to ask where precisely he thought it was off to, and what type of sambos they served for tea down there?

That night as he spoke of her, though, the memory was perfect – a poetry to every line. Even when, finally, it was time to reveal how the story had ended; how the whole thing had cracked in two.

'So I was lying asleep next to her in the bed, happy as a pig in shit.'

We were running short on space so I had started writing in the margins of some of the pages we had already used. It reminded me a bit of the Talmud – the Rabbis' words laid side by side.

'I was bare-bollock naked and dreaming away, but also conscious the whole time that my waking world was pretty terrific too. Pretty fucking terrific. But the next thing I know I'm not dreaming any more, and me whole world is after ending. Because just like that I heard the fucking BANG!'

The shout was so unexpected my body flinched, my wrist scratching a line of ink across the page. Almost, it turned out, as if it knew what was coming next.

'The bomb woke me, but I couldn't see a thing. There was smoke everywhere, thick as paint. And the smell? Christ! Until me eyes adjusted and I realised then that she...Jaysus, Shmendrick, she was...gone.'

I was very young when my father first told me about that World War II bomb, one of the few to have landed on Irish soil. But as luck would (or wouldn't) have it, it had fallen on Clanbrassil Street, right in the heart of Dublin's Little Jerusalem, and for many the coincidence was just too ugly to manage.

'We knew it was the Nazis,' Alf dictated now, spitting the suspicion loud and clear. 'Knew they must have found out where we lived and aimed straight for us. Bullseye!'

With one hand I wrote while with the other I began to scratch, discovering a scab on my knee.

'The Krauts swore it was just a mistake – a glitch in the radar, meant for London instead – sure what business would they have with little neutral Dublin?'

When the crust chipped off I began to peel, the give of it a bit like an orange skin.

'But really it didn't matter, because either way the blast had split the gaff in two – literally straight down the middle. A line through the bed with me snoring away on one side, happy as fucking Larry, while the other side was just...just...'

And even though it hurt, I kept going, using nails and all, because

167

already my mind was skipping ahead to what exactly this meant – that if the house really had exploded, did that mean that she was…? That she had…?

'And Shmendrick,' Alf groaned, as if it were his knee now trickling. 'I swear I looked for her for hours. Raked through the rubble. The fire brigade all slow and methodical with their search in case the foundations were fucked as well, but Jaysus, I didn't give a shite about that – didn't give a shite about anything except finding her there in the debris. There were beams everywhere, snapped in two like a shipwreck. And the dust!' he wailed. 'Billows of the stuff. Me skin completely covered. So that when I finally saw meself in a mirror that night I didn't even recognise the freak staring back at me. A bog man, like. A proper bloody Golem.'

I looked at him, half his face lit up by the Virgin's light, the other half in shadow – half here and half all the way back there.

'I searched for hours,' he sighed, slower now, the effort of it defeating him once again. 'From six in the morning 'til it was pitch black, but I found nothing. Not a trace. Not a hair off her gorgeous head or a lash off her lovely eyes – the green one,' he paused, faltering in between. 'Or the brown.'

By the time he had finished I could feel it myself, the utter weight of the loss. I closed my eyes and hung my head; pictured the devastation. The smoke. The rubble. The tears. The redbrick terrace ripped in two.

When we returned to our beds the blood from my knee dripped across the sheets. I let it flow, a pathetic solidarity.

For the following days it stayed with me, the image of that halved-out house. The borderline between brick and nothingness; between bliss and tragedy. Of course, even without Alf mentioning it, it seemed a given that we would leave it a couple of days before our next session – God knows he didn't appear to be in the mood for hurtling on.

I tried to catch his eye across the canteen, but it didn't work. He didn't see.

So the memory lingered, the pair of us united now by something other than love – a chance occurrence that had torn everything apart. I shook my head. They had shaved it again. My ears looked like they had been stuck on. But after a while, the melancholy of the story actually began to feel a bit out of place, because for some reason the rest of the House had a different air going on – an atmosphere that, unbelievably, had started to swell.

June had arrived, summer at last and a decent enough spate of weather, I supposed – bluey skies and the sun splitting the stones, or at least, so the saying went. The World Cup had kicked off in Sweden, and even though Ireland hadn't made the cut, it still gave the radio's chatter something worth listening for. England had only managed a 2-all draw with the Soviets. I wished I could've seen the gobshites' heads hung in shame. But regardless of the elements, or the soccer overseas, there seemed to be something else that was after giving the place a bit of a lift – an excitement that had suddenly caught on like a plague, or a dose of the shits, until eventually I managed to catch a glimpse of the reason why.

At first, when the posters went up around the corridor I thought they must be fake, some sort of prank, Sister Monica always a demon for new ways to torment. But when the rumours bubbled over I realised that it was actually true; that suddenly it was just a matter of days before the outside world was coming in, here between the mould-slick of these very four walls.

16th June. The Montague House Visitors' Day.

My pants were nearly doused for the thrill of it.

The effect of my mother's absence had remained just as intense, shittier than any sort of dose you could imagine. Of course, I had managed to remind myself why our separation was necessary, for the moment at least, but that didn't mean I didn't still crave her, even just the air around her.

Her goldy hair that was paler than any I had seen in my life.

Her big-small lips that spoke with an accent so different from Abba's.

But now it seemed the countdown to all those things had officially begun, *left then right then left then right then left*, because she was on her way – no longer just some image in my head – the prospect of it bringing out a brightness in me I barely recognised.

Of course, I did feel a bit guilty at how easily Alf's disaster managed to fall from my mind, the rubble and dust blown away on the wind. Next time I saw him in the canteen I didn't go looking for his eyes. But I couldn't help it, because actually, the more I thought about it, the more I had begun to realise something else as well – that it wasn't just the promise of my mother physically *being* here that had me giddy, but the promise of what would happen next; what exactly she would do on 16th June as soon as we were back together again:

1. *Give me a kiss.*
2. *Take a final look at this hellhole.*
3. *Bring me home.*

To be honest, it was the loveliest list I'd ever made.

As the days went on, I let myself imagine it a little more – the rescue mission come at last. Sometimes she apologised for the last few weeks; sometimes she cried; sometimes she begged for forgiveness, so vehemently I half-wondered if she had actually figured out the truth of what I'd seen. And sometimes I added other bits too, like in one version where Ima marched right up to Sister Monica and gave her a box in the face, blood glooping from her broken nose like ugly, reddy slugs. But in all these different versions, the bloody and the not, the grand finale was the same – that my Ima would lead me out the front door, hand me my flashcards, and officially set me free.

Even in the car home I knew I would have a million things to scrawl:

I missed you.
Can you cook me borscht?
Did you hear the one about the man and the woman who
court via pigeon mail?

Because see – I had learned now that not all love needed speech to survive.

On the buzz of the notion, time flew by, the whole of Montague House wired up. Even Tourettes Tony seemed only able to shout out happy things, like 'LOVELY CUNT' and 'ANGEL TITS' – a better kind of smut. Until without warning the week had seen itself off and it was my very last night in the place, and, I supposed, my very last session with Alf.

It wasn't one of our longer ones – ever since the bomb the energy in him had been quicker to sap. Twice this week he had even forgotten, mid-spiel, what it was he had been saying.

It took me a moment to realise he wasn't taking the piss.

So no, I decided that maybe it was for the best that we had reached the end of things – a natural conclusion or some shite like that. And sure, his side of the bargain had been rendered null and void by now, given I was on the way out anyway. Talk about jammy for him! Even if a part of me did still feel a pang at the prospect of goodbye.

Back in the room I stashed the jotter away while Alf lumbered himself out of his chair, the usual wretched sigh. Instead of bed, though, I made my way to the wardrobe, squinting through the darkness for what lay inside – the handful of items they entrusted us with in this Godforsaken place.

My spare woollen jumper, moth-devoured.

Two pairs of regulation slacks, slashed short at the knees – the same as all my trousers ever were. Because apparently my Abba's Abba had had a rule that men were only allowed to wear full-length trousers once their Bar Mitzvah ceremony was complete – yet another tradition to mark that special day. So ever since mine, Abba had made sure my shins remained permanently exposed, hail, rain or snow.

Hail Mary, full of gr(eat trousers).

Once I had placed the clothes in a pile on my bed I wondered what else I should take with me – a souvenir from this life to the next. I thought about the tumour of soap from the shower room, the pubic pattern indenting the skin. Or my first scrap of paper – the one Alf had, somehow, discovered – the one he had used to haggle for this. For everything. And then I thought of the jotter itself and whether I should try and take that instead.

I had already started to wonder what exactly Alf wanted to do with the story, now that we had got it down – all the different versions, crammed into the margins. He had mentioned something about 'legacy' all right, about the roots we leave behind, so I supposed that maybe once I was home again I could try and take it off to a publishers? Split the royalties and buy his ransom from this place? Or better yet, maybe buy him a gaff not far from me where I could go and visit for a cuppa; bring my cards along and have a proper chat – real friends at last! Only, I did wonder if we would miss the Virgin Mary, the stare of her looking down; the orange crown and the wry smile at the unlikeliest exchange.

'Shmendrick, are you off?'

At the sound of him, my wondering went stiff.

I waited, frozen in the darkness. A guilty air, even if there was no reason for it really.

'Your Ima,' Alf continued, asking questions though he stated them like facts. 'She's coming tomorrow, isn't she. To get you out.'

Slowly I began to turn, trying to angle myself towards his face, even if I could barely make him out in the black. I thought I heard a noise. The rats, probably, listening in on the final words.

'Well, I'm glad that...I promise I did try and find a...it was just...' But there was something in his voice now that made my limbs fall soft. 'And just promise me, Shmendrick, you won't let...It's yours now, Shem, OK? You're my...'

And for everything Alf said, and everything he didn't – an apology or a request, I wasn't sure which – but in the midst of his gibberish there was only one word I heard. Not 'Shmendrick' like it usually was; not 'lad' or 'freak' or 'wanker', just Shem. My name, my real name, uttered at last.

I felt my pulse go in my neck and then down into my gut, butterflies on the move. Though actually, I'd always suspected they were moths instead, nibbling holes into your innards; singeing their wings against the bulb of your heart.

And for the first time in our entire friendship I wished that I could answer Alf, properly like – to reply to his garbled speech; to tell him how much I…And that I would of course…Just a few lines – sure, it would hardly even count.

But of course I couldn't. Not now and not ever. Not me.

And I remembered then how when I was a kid I went through a phase of talking in 'nots'. It had just been another tick – another habit to add to the list – but this time everything had to be a negative not a positive. So hungry was '*not* satiated'; exhausted was '*not* alert'; happy, '*not* melancholy', as if there was nothing on the spectrum between the two.

My Ima, as with most things I did as a boy, was instantly smitten with the fad, eager to play along: 'You are *not* average', 'I do *not*…' but love was one of the hardest to translate. Because '*not* hating' someone wasn't the same. '*Not* caring' maybe? '*Not* knowing your own reflection unless they are the ones holding up the mirror'?

Of course, Abba had despised the whole thing – had gone totally nuts. Which was ironic really, given how minor it was compared to everything to come. But he demanded to know who was to blame for such a preposterous routine.

My mother tried so hard to stifle a smile as she answered him. 'I don't know, pet. *Not* me!'

We had laughed for hours, beyond giddy, while between breaths she told me it was a bit like having the outline of a son cut out of a giant piece of paper – the gap left behind, instead of the solid shape itself. And at the time I found the image hilarious, but in the years after it kept returning, just below my ribcage – an empty space of air where I should have been. My darling mother and her eccentric '*not* son'.

I thought of it now, here in the smallest hours of the night. I listened to the silence, to the sigh of my '*not* enemy'. And I realised, despite everything that lay ahead, the holes we would leave in one another's lives.

'Well, isn't this only grand now?' Ima asked. 'Gorgeous altogether?'

I looked at her and then around her, assuming it was a joke. But in fairness, she wasn't entirely wrong. The nuns must have been up through the night with the preparations, hefty falls of bleach-white lace starched out along the canteen tables. Seat cushions. Doilies. Ugly little vases rammed with weeds from the yard – all props for the staging of this grand, gorgeous farce.

16th June. The Montague House Visitors' Day.

According to Sister Monica's spiel that morning it was a chance for us to see our families again. But also – and more importantly – a chance for our families to take a fresh glimpse at the charming surroundings which were so instrumental in aiding us on the road to recovery, day by flower-filled day.

Needless to say the annual invoice would be sent out next week. The annual increase. The nuns thanked each visitor in advance of their generosity – no doubt their place in Heaven would be secure, doilies and all.

For me, though, the pomp and circumshite didn't matter a hill of beans – they could keep their bleach and their spray; the sniff that would send your head to the sky – because for me this was it, sitting there on the other side of the table. Heaven.

I smiled at her for the millionth time. I felt the blush all the way to my freshly shaved skull.

It was two and a half months now since I had seen my mother. Almost the life cycle of a drone bee, which we once learned in Geography class – ten weeks of nothing but fertilising the Queen. The other lads had all gone wild at the prospect: 'What? Ten weeks of pure riding?'

Ten fucking weeks.

She wore a purple hat I didn't recognise, the swirl of a Celtic brooch snagged in on the side, and a matching pout of colour on her lips, the big one and the small.

I wondered if she had been to see her fancy man, or if she would go later after dropping me home.

The thought made me blush again. We waited in silence, breathing other people's conversations. Out of nowhere, I thought of Alf.

'So, do you know who's after dying?' Ima finally trilled, the ultimate Irish opener.

The victim in question was Archie Rose, may his memory be blessed, the Baggot Street dentist with the missing eye who dropped dead last Thursday night. I couldn't remember much about him, only that he never wore his glass eye so the hole would just be there, hovering over your face while he prodded your teeth. To be honest, it always felt like such an intrusion staring into another man's skull.

'There was a big enough turnout at the cemetery,' Ima reported, relaxing now with the information. 'His mother's people down from Belfast. Only they did say they had to be careful with their accents. Trouble brewing and all that.' Her hands were placed one on top of the other at the edge of the table like a pair of polite lovers.

I flicked one of mine up to fix my '*not* hair', then wedged it back safe beneath my arse.

'And Mr Jackson was asking after you. And Mrs Feeney from the library, do you remember her? Says she still thinks of when you used to come in, the best-behaved garcún. How you would just sit there and soak up the quiet.'

It was strange to hear another voice that wasn't Alf's as it spooled away, ticking off subjects she pretended were spontaneous but that had probably been prepared for weeks.

'And do you know who's after getting married? You'll never believe. God I've missed these little chats!'

We had always been close, my Ima and me, right from the very start. Even when I was a child she would climb into my bed every morning and ask what I had seen in my dreams, then swear she had seen the very same – even our fantasies, knitted into one.

But despite our bond, our intimacy, there had always been the sense she was keeping something from me. A perpetual niggle. And I swear I wasn't just saying that now I knew the truth! But the problem is that adults tend to underestimate just how much a child can notice; how much they can sense all the things that aren't being said. Like the twitch in her whenever I asked about her childhood down on the farm – no siblings, her parents both six feet under – not a single photo of them anywhere and *do you miss them, Ima, do you?*

'Leave it, boy,' my father would hiss – he caught me every time 'I'm warning you.' Until I decided it was such a sensitive subject it must've been something to do with the Shoah, even though I thought the Nazis hadn't really made it to Ireland – a bomb over Clanbrassil Street but nothing much else.

Then one time I remembered I had even tried to read my Ima's diary; had carried a chair in from the kitchen and climbed up to the top shelf, there where I had seen her stash it away. It was a leathery thing, with metally letters on the front, always kept off limits which is how I knew what it was. But I had managed to convince myself that she wouldn't mind me having a gander – we were so close, surely there was nothing I couldn't know? Surely our bond meant only honesty?

But Abba was on me again, just in time, his wallop so hard I flew from the chair and split my lip on the corner of the bed. The flesh exploded, a deluge of blood as he grabbed the book and raged out of the gaff, driving like a man possessed.

The silences a family is made up of, to try and protect one another; the silences which shove us apart.

So to be honest, when I finally discovered the truth about Ima's affair it was almost a relief. An answer. Because despite the initial shock, there was something about it that just made sense and explained away the gaps. Like how she would go to Mikveh every month, even though none of the other boys' mothers ever bothered. I had thought she was just weirdly devout, but now I understood – the perfect cover-up! Or like that little silver angel necklace she kept down the back of her jewellery box – it must have been a present from her lover – see, at last the clues meant something!

'And how about yourself, love? Any...any improvement?'

I looked at her now. Her smile. Her pale eyebrows raised high.

Of course, I knew it was odd that I hadn't been more upset by the infidelity. A singe of betrayal all right, maybe even a bit of jealousy. But after a while the relief of it had just overwhelmed, the truth found out at last, and the knowledge that she had at least discovered some way to be happy – some solace that even my father couldn't reach.

Meanwhile, in the weeks after my Bar Mitzvah, Abba himself just tried to pretend everything was grand – just another stupid phase I was going through.

'Shabbat shalom,' he would say to me on a Friday night, the spasm of the candles between us. 'Shabbat shalom.' A little louder – a demand for a reply. 'SHABBAT SHALOM!' Until he smashed the candlesticks to the floor and the flames puffed out, a burnt stench that poisoned the air and didn't pass.

After that, Friday night dinners just sort of…dried up. Abba and Ima were barely able to look at one another, let alone share a meal. And then it wasn't long before we stopped being invited to other families' dinners too. It seemed the whole community had taken a united stance on my condition. Shem Sweeney, the Little Jerusalem scapegoat. Because not only had my Bar Mitzvah ceremony been a complete and utter disaster but, apparently, a personal slight against each and every female in the neighbourhood, now one mensch more likely to have to emigrate to find a suitable husband.

At least it would be an effective way to get us all to Israel, I thought – make one sex keep shtum and then the other will have no choice. They should try it at those Aliyah meetings, Zionism simply for want of a conversational partner.

No, no improvement, I wanted to tell Ima now. But I like your hat. And are you wearing your angel necklace underneath your frock?

Then a few months after my *not*-Bar Mitzvah I had had the funniest thought. Because actually, I realised that I had seen your man before. Ima's lover. And I didn't just mean that afternoon on the

Glenvar Road when I had caught them, but also, once I looked back on it, another time too.

The pair of us had been strolling down Grafton Street one December Sunday heading to Bewley's Café for tea and a sticky bun (only we had renamed it a 'Bicky Stun' given I was going through my strictest alphabetarian phase). The buskers were wailing their usual wail. The wind was pissed off. The Switzer's Stores windows were all gauded up in festive tack. But then we bumped into this man with a big face and two ruddy cheeks; a woolly jumper and a look of utter shock.

I thought he was just some crazy lad, trying to start a fight, or maybe a homeless guy having a beg. But he and Ima just stood there, staring at each other, locked on either side of a borderline I couldn't see. Until she gasped: 'Gerry, I'm sorry'; practically yanked my wrist out of its socket, hauling me down the cobblestones towards Molly Malone and away while he just stood there, calling after: 'Máire, wait! Máire, please!'

'And *Abba* sends his love, of course.' We were back to my own father now. Her husband. 'Told me to wish you *Tsu gezunt.*'

I rolled my eyes at the Yiddish words. 'Good health'. As if I just had a dose of the flu; as if my sinuses were just too congested to speak.

But that was Abba all right – only ever interested in his religion. Or more importantly, in all the damage I had apparently managed to do to it. 'The pair of you de-Jewing us entirely!' he would say, a venom I didn't understand. Because for feck's sake, why couldn't he see? Why didn't he realise that the very act of me sealing my lips about what I had witnessed was precisely a Jewish bloody gesture – no Lashon Ha-ra! Even the Talmud tells of some poor lad who lets the cat out of the bag after twenty-two years and is *still* expelled from his house of study. So no, this was going to be a long-term commitment, whether I liked it or not.

'He's been taking me to a lot of those *Aliyah* meetings at *Shul*.' Still my mother kept going, oblivious to my rant. 'You know…it really does sound so beautiful out there, pet. The orange groves. The Eastern sunshine.'

But I couldn't listen. Because actually, the more I thought about it the more I realised that God Himself had kept fairly mute on a load of stuff through the ages. Wouldn't answer our questions; wouldn't reveal His face, while we waited, and believed, in the silence. So then who better than us, a Jewish family, to shape ourselves around an absence?

An unseen God.

A destroyed temple.

A son who cannot speak.

I leaned forward in my chair; caught a waft of Ima's lemony perfume.

An old man who lives for a woman who was blown to dust seventeen years ago.

A boy who has given up everything for his mother because he loves her so bloody much.

'Shem, there's something I need to tell you.'

This time, it was my name that brought me back. No sign of 'pet' or 'darling'. Not even a sign of 'love'.

I had wondered how long she would spend building up to the big announcement, the real reason we were here. But I supposed she was just nervous – sure, it was massive news – a *drumroll please* and a *cough cough cough* that she was finally taking me home. Or better yet, that she was taking me away somewhere where it could just be me and her and nobody else. How about a County Offaly bog, I thought now? Or a scutty little bedsit on Clanbrassil Street where we could just tell stories and eat cheese sandwiches all day long?

'Shem, it's your father.'

Instantly, though, I knew something was off.

'He...he has booked. Our tickets,' she said. 'For August.'

She gave the truth piece by piece, like it was all she could manage.

'To Israel.'

The words alphabetical and everything, as if that would somehow soften the blow.

'Shem, can you hear me?'

August.

Israel.

Shem?

As I listened I tapped my fingers against the air; felt the void as it closed in either side, *left then right then left then right then left.*

'Shem, he says...he says if you're not...if you don't...'

My eyes defaulted to the window where Father Dwyer was out in the yard, his jowls stuffed into his dog collar and his arms linked with a pair of men. They looked so alike they had to be brothers, though one was dressed in regulation attire and the other was not.

'But just...just say you're getting better, love?'

The lives we lead, the lives we might have led.

'Because if you do then it's fine, pet, you can come along. But if you don't speak up...'

The secrets we might have made.

'Shem, he wants us to go without you.'

Finally my eyes jolted back. To her. A smudge of purple had

migrated to her tooth. It looked like a fleck of beetroot, as if she had been eating borscht – my father's favourite, as well as mine. Sometimes he ate so much his lips turned lipstick-pink, like he was having an affair of his own.

The next thing I knew, the nuns had pulled the plug. Ima had to stand on tiptoes to kiss me goodbye, the purple staining my cheek this time instead. I pictured it like a bruise, a wound I had no idea how to heal.

And as I watched her walk away for some reason I remembered how she once smuggled me a candy cane on Christmas morning, so that I wouldn't feel left out. 'They used to be my favourite,' she said as she undid the wrapper. I must have heard her wrong. I sucked for hours, the sickly sweetness coating my gums, my body stiff for the sound of Abba's footsteps.

So I wondered now if a family could ever really exist without these lies, these secrets to keep it alive. Or if, in the end, that was the definition of love.

Sunday

Aisling wishes she had brought the book with her to the church. It would have been incongruous, yes, absolutely, but it is the first time she has been apart from the thing in twenty-four hours and her whole body registers the absence, her hair still matted from sleeping with the flat of it beneath her pillow.

She has been awake since seven, though she was restless all night. The heavy fug of the electric blanket. The strangeness of the silence. Because on nights when she and Noah slept apart he would always make sure to Skype her and leave the laptop on the bedside table next to him; the rhythm of his breath as they nodded off, side by almost side. So by the time her father came looking for company this morning she surprised him by saying yes, any excuse to get out of the house.

He sits beside her now in the pew, the solid wedge of him dressed in his usual Ralph Lauren uniform: shirt, chinos, dress shoes. All the little horses, cantering across his limbs. In a better mood she would remind him it is supposed to be a day of rest. And she half-remembers they used to have a joke about horses and the priest, still the same grey-green stick-man then as today, his voice frantic like a commentator down from the pulpit, sprinting his way through the service:

And coming up the outside we have the Holy Spirit but begob the Lad himself is making a fine comeback, twenty furlongs to the home stretch and it's winner all right! Winner all right!

He always had them wrapped up by five past one at the latest, over the road for pints and a roast or home for the dirty fry up, Clonakilty Pudding and all – the blood and spice that repeated on you for the rest of the day.

'The Lord be with you.'

'And also with you.'

'And with your spirit.'

Aisling listens to the South Dublin accents around her. They are nasal, strangely Americanised; half of them garbling one response while the other half garbles another. She read that they brought in a new translation of the Mass a while ago, the old Latin having been deemed inaccurate. But it seems a lot of people just haven't bothered to adjust, sticking to the old script instead, as if a few words here and there can really alter a faith.

'Thanks be to God.'

She shuffles on the bench, the wood varnished stiff and cold. She stares at the plaque on the armrest, dedicated to the memory of one *Frank O'Meara, Beloved.*

And she wonders a bit about translation now, about what is lost in the process. Thousands of years and a handful of tongues and do the words still mean the same thing? Or close enough?

She touches the metallic indents of the stranger's name, the shortest obituary in the world.

And then what about translating people – reconfiguring them in terms you can better understand? Like changing some aspect of yourself to suit the person you happen to love? Only, by the end of it you might not even be the same person any more – the one they fell for in the first place. No, you might have become someone else altogether.

She checks around, as if the other congregants can hear the ramblings in her head. But they pay her no attention, not even much to the priest himself, too busy making shopping lists in their own heads and *Is there rugby on today?* and *There's your one from down the road after getting a new haircut – mutton as lamb, wouldn't you say?* Worse again, she remembers how her teenage self would use this time to scope for members of the opposite sex. The local disco the following Friday: *Eh, I think you go to the same church as me?*

Bless me, Father, for I have sinned.

She looks up at the altar. The colossal advent candles sit ganged up and glowing. The crib is crammed with life-size figurines and an empty manger, big enough that she could just lie down now and close her eyes, make a blanket out of the velvet curtains from the confession booths lined up along the side.

She made her First Confession here all right – her First Confession and her Holy Communion and then her Confirmation too. Not out of any great decision, but just because that is what you do in this country, the ritual you find yourself following before you grow up and move to London and don't step foot in another church again; don't pay it all another thought.

So really, it isn't the new religion that would have her worried, but the religiousness at all. A few token nods are one thing, she thinks, but an actual conversion? An active leap?

She breathes in, floor polish and radiator-tang. A silence descends. They stand up to greet the Gospel, like students when a headmaster enters a room.

And in a way, she thinks, going a little further now, giving air to the thoughts that have been at her since she woke, but in a way it feels disrespectful to the faith to just take it on, just like that; to suddenly pretend you're after having some big epiphany, simply because you find the traditions kind of fascinating; because you like the family aspect; love the idea of a culture that actually encourages you to ask questions and challenge everything it says.

This time, it is the collection basket that interjects. She nearly drops it. Her father hands her a two Euro coin – another token nod – before he adds a crisp blue twenty of his own – a bit much, but of course, he knows people will be scrutinising so he doesn't really have a choice.

From the corners of her eyes now, Aisling scrutinises him too. The thick fingers are clasped in supplication, sausage-fat. Her father's fingers, yes, but also the politician's fingers, praying for re-election next time round; a party restructure. Or maybe just for no more persecution out in the street – no more gobs of spit and blame from the voters who still can't quite believe it all went quite so bloody wrong.

Your fault! You wankers!

Expenses to the eyeballs while I can't even feed me bloody children!

But at least he believes in what he's praying for, she thinks now, her top lip pulled back so that she can gnaw at a nail. Whereas Noah isn't even particularly religious – rarely ever goes to *Shul*; says he doesn't know what happens next; bacon sandwiches when he's hungover – bet the book doesn't advocate that!

But the mention of the book catches her short. Her jaw slackens, her hands suddenly remembering their emptiness. While the priest's words come looking for her, down from the mic: 'In the

Gospel today we hear of the two hearts each of us possesses. The split sense of self of which the scripture speaks.'

Aisling bows her head and thinks Amen, both sides of her growing weak. Above, a figurine of Jesus hangs, bleeding from every limb. While the Virgin Mary watches on, her eyes full of calm, an easy flow to her blue, porcelain folds.

After the Mass, the priest shakes their hands in the sunlit porch like a host at the end of a party.

At the car-park gate the Romanian beggar wears a Leinster rugby jersey, adjusting his image to the parishioners' tastes. Her father guides the Merc past him without opening the window or even slowing down. 'It's a coup we've never been sent one of those Nigerian priests,' he thinks aloud. 'The accents are supposed to be a divil – have you ever heard the likes?'

Aisling, though, is barely listening, too focused now on getting home again and straight up to her room. To the book. She doesn't want to open it – no, she isn't ready for that yet – she just needs to feel it, to take the weight. The surprising strain on her wrists like in a child's game of 'Mercy'.

Only, when they make it home they discover there has been another arrival. And despite herself, Aisling feels a little lift in her chest.

'Séany!' Her father moves first, grabbing his son in a tackle. 'Welcome home.' Thumping him on the back the way men do, as if burping one another – infants once again.

Aisling watches them, careful not to breathe. She sees the blue eyes peek up and over the embrace, bright even after the longest haul. 'Ash, what are you...I thought you couldn't—'

'You thought wrong.' She moves now, unwrapping the endless

coil of her scarf. A bees' nest of knots has formed halfway down her hair.

'Just couldn't bear to miss me, I suppose?'

'Ha, hardly!'

Until they are standing opposite one another, brother and sister, mocking already. He is two years older, though they could easily be twins. Or even 'Irish twins', that ancient phrase for siblings less than twelve months apart. But these are a full twenty-six and recently a few thousand miles too, just for good measure. Irish-London-Australian twins.

Aisling tucks a strand of blonde grease behind her ear. He wears a hoodie she bought him for a birthday years back. She notices the sleeves are saggy over his fingers, as if his body has shrunk in transit.

'Well, it's good to see you.' Séan reaches towards her. 'Even if you do look like shit.' Defaulting to the dig, yet she is surprised all the same that he caved first.

She presses herself into the cavern of his hood, inhaling the unfamiliar smell. But she supposes it has been years now, quite literally, whereas Skype chats reek only of cheap wine and microwave dinners, the brown rind around the carton edges like a tide line on a sea wall.

'No Magic Man with you, no?'

Aisling pulls away, scanning his face to see how much it knows – the face people say is so like her own. It is heart-shaped. Handsome. Though the skin is much darker these days; the eyelashes bleached – all the beautiful blemishes of a new life the other side of the globe.

'What?'

They were always close growing up; competitive too in equal doses. She was the winner academically, but with the age advantage he was always onto more interesting things by the time anybody noticed – coaching rugby in Zimbabwe or gallivanting off to Australia, twelve months of bar work before the requisite stint picking bananas to earn his visa extension until he settled down and found a proper job and now it is impossible to imagine him ever moving back.

Another loss, Aisling thinks to herself; another separation.

They always kept different friends out of principle, not that his didn't make sure to try it on with her, just to piss him off. At first she would blink away their advances – it wasn't worth the betrayal – but then it was university and they had a falling out so she arranged to meet a different one each evening of the week; to do what she thought another kind of girl would do, not the little sister any more.

On Monday she fucked Martin.

Tuesday, Cillian.

Next JP.

Rory.

O'Dwyer.

Saturday, Chris.

And on Sunday she made up with Séan again, a mixture of smugness and shame pricking her legs as they draped across his lap on the couch. Especially when he took her nail-chewed hand in his and told her he was moving away.

'It's just so important to get out of here and have a fresh start,' he had announced, philosophical for himself. 'To make yourself up again as you go along.'

To take the swan and fold it another way. A cleaner, better shape?

'No,' she finally replies, back in the hallway, as straight as she can manage. 'No Magic Man.' Holding her brother's gaze a second too long, as if to prove something. Before they follow in a line towards the AGA-broiled kitchen, the Creedon clan reunited at last. In the heat Séan takes off his jumper and hands it over, the ghost of some old routine, while Aisling puts it on and buries herself in it as deep as she can go.

That night the beef is blackened, the blood bled out long ago. The dining table is vast, far too big for just the four of them, but after all, they are celebrating. Around them the wallpaper is jade green, a bit dingier than she remembers, and up near the ceiling a strip has started to unpeel – another layer underneath and then another again, all the past incarnations; rip them off like skin until there is no wall left at all.

The feast, though, is an abundance. Her mother doles out wads of roast potatoes, iridescent in their goose-fat sheen. Aisling watches the older woman, giddy on white wine and reunion – the vices she needs to survive. She used to be an air hostess, back in another life, hospitality above the clouds. Until she gave it all up for an aspiring politician and a South Dublin semi; dinner parties on tap and enough Waterford Crystal to twinkle an army. But then eventually, the Crystal crowd went bust, the decanter drained, and champion housewifing was slowly replaced by quiz-show marathons and *Come Dine with Me* on repeat, so that when her husband's party failed to be elected for the first time in fifteen years she had nothing better to offer him than a recipe for Philadelphia soufflé and a stream of facts from that afternoon's rerun of *Who Wants to Be a Millionaire?*

When Aisling passed the spare room earlier she noticed the bed unmade. Used. And for some reason she thought of Séan first before she realised.

Another secret. The different lies we tell for love.

She pictures the book hiding underneath her pillow. The indecision tucked away where no one can find it.

'Aisling?'

Before she is caught.

'What?'

'Would you like another slice of beef?'

She looks at her plate, her heart beating extra blood. She shakes her head and takes a long, sickly sip of red.

'Are you all right, honey?' her mother asks. 'You've been quiet?'

'Pining for loverboy?' Séan cracks in, stiffening her body once more.

But when she doesn't reply her mother moves on, turning to the Prodigal Son himself. 'Would you like some mustard, darling? Or I can do more gravy – I know it's your favourite.' Aisling watches her, easier with her boy, yes. But also more needy – never quite relaxed. Because that is the secret of the emigrant child – that the further you go the more power you have, the bigger the return you might one day just decide not to make. 'And do you cook much in Sydney, pet? JP and Eamonn any use in the kitchen?'

'Ah, Geraldine, sure you know Eamonn Duffy has come back.' Her husband has bounded in now, a hint of scorn in his tone. 'In fact, I met his uncle in the club the other day – he says Eamonn's after moving up North?'

'That's it,' their son agrees. 'Seems to be happy enough.'

His father looks smug like he has got a question right. 'Only did I hear he's after marrying a Presbyterian?'

'Christ, how did the parents take that?'

Aisling's knife slips on the plate.

'No, it's true,' Séan says, ignoring the squeak of the china. 'He's finally settling down. Gave up the accountancy and now drives some kind of bus around Derry, bringing the tourists to all the Troubles hotspots. The murals. The bullet holes. The Palestinian flags. "Conflict Tourism" he says it's called, though some people think it's a bit—'

'Ah, but sure any tourism is good tourism these days,' their father cuts in, defaulting, as ever, to his politician's nod. 'Sure, the country is only desperate for it. And actually, there's another scheme in the pipeline not too far from here.'

'Oh?'

'Yeah, that house in Rathmines where one of the World War II bombs fell. You know, up there where all the Jew lads used to live?'

This time Aisling has to shut her eyes.

'The terrace like, split down the middle.'

She swallows, tasting the gravy rinse of her mouth. She needs to brush her teeth.

'Well, they're planning to add a big wall of glass down the side of the house, then to build an education centre, to lure the tourists good and proper...'

But in the blackness behind her eyelids, Aisling finds she can almost picture that old redbrick – only one half of the whole left behind. She visited it on a school trip, years ago; told Noah about it once too. And she also told him about the old story that sometimes went along with the place – that a couple had been lying there when the bomb fell, so that their bed was split right down the middle.

'...and trust *them* to find a rake of funding at a time like this, eh?'

A perfect heartbreak line.

Thankfully, it isn't long before the men move on, switching

the focus away. There is the rugby season. The NAMA debt. The Gypsies on the move (*I think you're supposed to call them Travellers now. Oh whatever, same same*). Easy banter back and forth, back and forth, languid with the flow of it. Like two lads Aisling saw one freezing Saturday afternoon in Hyde Park, knocking a sliotar back and forth, back and forth, the *donk* of their hurling sticks nearly lost in the mist.

When, finally, it is time for dessert, her mother goes out to the utility room and reappears with the Christmas Day trifle. 'What's a few days early, eh? Especially for a celebration like this?'

Aisling takes a bite, the familiarity cloying on her gums; the boozy sponge and the gelatinous squeeze of the fruit. Only, between mouthfuls she begins to realise there is something else there too – another taste that won't seem to go. A different dinner and a different ritual, just two nights ago, niggling at her now to compare and contrast.

'And did your mother tell you about the hoo-ha over the Quinns' granddaughter?'

Two versions of belonging, held up to the light.

'So their daughter is after shacking up with this atheist lad, right? And they just had a baby, but decided not to baptise him.'

Different sides of her, both crucial in their own way.

'So last weekend when no one was around Janey Quinn dunked the little pet into the kitchen sink and said a few prayers, to make sure he wasn't ending up in limbo.'

Only now the decision must be made – which side of her won't be invited back.

'But because he didn't realise, the following day Daithí Quinn did exactly the same – tipped the wee one over the sink...'

Her choice stacked up in her bedroom with the gaffer tape like a gagged mouth that needs to speak.

'…so the lucky thing is after getting a double dip!'

'Noah has asked me to convert to Judaism for him.'

As soon as it comes, the laughter for the anecdote dies a death.

They stare at her, their spoons held aloft. Her father. Her brother. Her mother.

Aisling lifts a finger to bite a nail, the rim bloodshot like an eye.

She doesn't know how long they sit there, staring, a family of mutes, the sickly slime of jelly on their teeth. After a while, Aisling finds herself thinking about that couple from the bomb again. She wonders if the man ever found his lover, underneath the rubble, or if he is still looking for her even now; wandering Ireland and refusing to accept that they have really been blown apart.

'Aisling? When did this—'

'Oh love. We had no—'

'Pub?'

Slowly, she moves her eyes to her brother. Already he has stood up, his head cocked towards the door, away from their parents' stumbles.

So she rises, following him out into the freezing night, the suburb streets weaving down and away like a maze they might never escape.

When they step inside, O'Gormon's is pure swelter. The place has been renovated since the last time she was here, a more sophisticated model. Roaring fire. Reek of turf. Blackboard specials, an impossible eighteen Euro.

Everyone knows everyone.

Everyone is drunk.

Everyone except for her.

They shove their way through the half-cut light, trying for the bar, but the sea of Christmas jumpers is dense; the wall of *Jaysus, Creedon, is that you? We heard you'd married a kangaroo!* The various snippets of the annual rant in all its different forms, like how lucky they are to have escaped, but how bloody amazing it is to be home – The Gathering indeed – nostalgia and disdain all slurred into one, the emigrant's beautiful paradox.

Séan orders the first round just in time for 'Fairytale of New York' by the Pogues to belt out over the speakers, as if the raptures couldn't grow any more rapturous. Aisling has to hold her vodka in the air like an offering to the Gods to avoid the thrust of the elbows; the Céilí dance, part-merriment part-violence.

As it happens, she got to do the obituary for Shane McGowan himself, lead singer of the Pogues. They call it an 'advance' or a 'pre-dead', written and stashed away so that when he finally boots the bucket, all they need to do is add the when/where/how of the end – the mouldy cherry on the top. It turns out he grew up down in Tipperary, but then deferred to London – a literature scholarship to Westminster School, no less. Only he was expelled then for bold behaviour – bold, pikey Irish behaviour – and decided to write songs about bums and lost dreams instead.

'Jesus, all the old heads.' It takes Séan a full five minutes to join her at the table in the corner, resisting the pleas to stay social.

They should have gone somewhere quieter, Aisling thinks. They shouldn't have come at all.

'And did you see the state of Joe Mac?' he goes on. 'I heard from Facebook he's after getting engaged, but Christ, you wouldn't know it from the cut of him.'

She nods, though she doesn't answer; takes a mouthful of her drink. Facebook profiles. LinkedIn. Dating apps and sites. All just the same as obituaries, really – the glowingly inaccurate portraits of the people we would like to be.

'And do mine, do mine,' Noah had once begged her.

'Fine.' She had smiled, wondering just how cruel she could get away with. 'How about: "Banking bigshot turned illusionist, desperate for love. Skills: Killer risotto chef and origami master. Weaknesses: Does whatever his mammy says."'

His laugh was wild but his reply tame, knowing by now her skin was never quite as thick as she made out. '"Irish bombshell, tentatively seeking. Whose steely determination breaks hearts and touches lives."'

'Tea-totaller,' she had joked, guarding herself against the sentiment.

'Likes long walks in the rain.'

'Ha! My arse.'

'Oh yes, of course, and how could I fail to mention the perfect arse?'

'Well, strictly speaking it wouldn't be the first time you've decided to switch religions.'

It takes a full moment to register Séan's voice. Or at least, the Australian version. And then another to realise what he has said – the acknowledgement come at last.

'What?'

'Do you not remember? You were about five at the time. Said you wanted to become a Protestant because you were going up North to try and solve the "Doubles". That's what you called them – the "Doubles". As if the problem was just something to do with the number two.'

She stares at the vodka as if she will find the memory there, but she can manage nothing – a portrait of another girl entirely. She listens.

The gathered voices bellow something about an NYPD choir; a place called Galway Bay.

'Well, if it's any use,' Séan says next, producing a packet of Tayto crisps –nostalgia's sake and nothing else – God knows they have eaten enough, 'but Mum and Dad won't mind, if that's what you're worried about.'

Aisling rolls her eyes, inhaling cheese and onion.

'No, I mean it,' he says, chewing fast. 'They seem to have liked your man the few times they've met him. Never made much fuss about him being—'

'So then what about the Quinns' fucking granddaughter?' The snap is louder than she means it to be, which only makes her more annoyed. She looks away to behind the bar where the waitress is stealing a gulp from a dented two-litre bottle of TK red lemonade.

'What?'

The bob of the Adam's apple is violent, a hard-fought battle with the fizz.

'I mean...' she says. 'Can't you just see them, like, with me and Noah's poor baby?' She tries to stay calm, but her voice is rising. 'Dunking him in the kitchen sink when no one is around, to baptise him on the sly? Give him a nice saint's name, just to be sure, his snipped little willy and all.' She glares at her brother, wondering when was the last time he slept – probably continents ago.

But all of a sudden he is gone, doubled up with laughter. She is not long after. Whether it is the mental image or the tension, neither is sure, only that their laughs are noisy over the fiddle's instrumental, a crack in her throat and a dimple in his chin she had forgotten about when he smiles too hard.

Their shoulders shake for longer than they might.

'And Aisling?' Séan asks, his voice still high-pitched. 'How long has Dad been sleeping in the spare room?'

Until they stutter still.

'I don't know.'

'I'm a bit—'

'I know,' she says. 'I know, Séan. Me too.'

The song fades out. The bar is silent, a heave of elation and exhaustion before they have to do the whole thing all over again.

Aisling looks the other way. This time she sees a couple standing in the corner, the girl's hand in the boy's back pocket, stealing his soul.

'Well look,' Séan sighs, his most serious-sounding yet. 'I know it's a big decision.' He finishes his drink to be sure. 'But I'd just…take my time if I were you – just talk it through with Noah and—'

'Well, that's the thing.' She ignores the stab of the name. 'We've…we've broken up.'

'Oh. So *that's* why you ended up coming—'

'Yeah,' she admits, all other excuses long gone. 'That's why I came home. We were supposed to spend Christmas together – or December the twenty-fifth, whatever – but I think…well, if we don't…I think I've decided that's the end.'

She looks down. Her beer mat has gone soft and torn in two.

And she knows, really, that there is no rush, the ultimatum as much in her head as anything. But she also knows that if she is ever going to make a decision then she needs the cut-off point – Jesus, they have wasted enough time on this already – no point dragging the thing out. Plus, that is how she has always functioned, on deadlines.

And lifelines?

'And tell me, Ash.' Séan takes on the last of the crisps. 'Is he the one?'

She shoves the cardboard pieces back together again. If only she had a strip of gaffer tape to make it right. 'What?'

The couple is closer now, the boy nibbling the girl's neck, a cluster of stars tattooed down the length of her nape.

'You know – the one. Is he?'

And Noah once suggested that they got a tattoo themselves, the pair of them, right across their knuckles. He said they should find a phrase that only made sense when they held hands – all the letters, slotting into place.

T

H

I

S

I

S

H

O

M

E

'Well, it depends...' she replies, the ghost of a smile as she dips her finger into the crumbs, the foil of the pack like blue wrapping paper. 'Did I mention about the book?'

*

The bedroom is barely lit by the antique lamp. The Journalism MA sits framed on the wall, next to Mandela's eyes – the poster poignant now he has finally passed away. Down the back of the door hangs a map of the world, a slit at Antarctica so the handle can poke through, a strange beast rising up from beneath the glaciers.

'OK, well, I'll leave you to it, so.' Séan stands in the middle of the room, remembering in glances. 'Let me know if there's anything else you need.' He turns to go, clumsy with his step – one pint too many and the rest – but then he stops and lingers at the map, tracing the epic span he has to cross again in just one week's time.

Aisling wonders what she could say to make him stay.

His footsteps disappear down the stairs before the muffled shriek of the television comes to life. Three a.m. programming, though his body clock probably doesn't know any better.

She waits a minute longer, straining. The silence of a family at night. Somehow the most together it will ever be.

She sits for a while with the book in her lap. She dozes then wakes almost immediately. The push on her belly makes her need to pee. She cannot for the life of her get up. So instead she decides to open it; to tense her hands, one beneath the bulk of it and the other to hold the cover down, the leather so dark you'd think it would rub off on your skin.

1. *Right from the Commencement of the Journey, One Must Be Open and Honest About the Myriad of Thoughts That Will Undoubtedly Fill One's Mind.*

She stares at the first in the checklist – the preparation for everything that lies ahead. She feels herself waver, her and this other self, the one she may or may not become.

But eventually she reads on, for better or for worse. Because maybe it is the buzz of the evening, or her good-for-nothing-or-possibly-everything brother, but if she has any hope of finding an answer then she supposes she may as well know it all first, every last word – the bones and the basics and the right questions to ask – the pages held together if only just. And whenever she thinks about stopping she pictures her parents next door in their two separate bedrooms, their two separate beds, facing the other way. She wonders if they bothered to cut their electric blanket down the middle too.

part four | In the desert...

1931

'What about the one with the farmer in the desert?' Ruth almost shouted the question, loud enough so that it could be heard over the wheeze of the almost-mother who lay below on the hospital bed, her lungs declaring war on the agony between her legs.

'Or maybe the legend of Oisín and Princess Niamh? And the land of *Tír na nÓg*?' Ruth sopped a cloth across the woman's forehead, glancing at the splatter of blood up the wall.

It always looked more like they were in the business of killing here, instead of the opposite.

'Well, her name was Niamh,' she went on, no time to wait for an answer. She saw the first glimpse of skull begin to show. 'Niamh of the Golden Hair.' The cranial bones spread out across the anterior fontanelle. 'And his was Oisín, son of Fionn— Now just keep pushing, Mrs Klein, we're nearly there—'

But in between panting, it seemed the patient had other ideas. 'No!' she cried, toes flexed skeletal with the force of it. 'The story,' she said. 'Don't you dare stop the story!'

As she crouched down, Ruth tried her best to hide her smile, her palms stretched wide and ready for anything.

It had become her signature addition, this telling of tales – the reason the expectant mothers requested her, specifically, to do the honours. Of course, the vast majority of them also tended to share her religion, faces she recognised from around her new Dublin neighbourhood, but she liked to think it was more than just that.

Apparently her father was a great man for the stories too.

A bit odd that she's so up on all the native ones, nu?

Ah, but from what I hear there was oddness in the family. Sure have you seen the state of those eyes?

'So *Tír na nÓg*,' Ruth went on, then translated: 'The Land of the Young. It was a gorgeous place in the far far West, off the edge of any map. But there, nobody ever grew old, or knew sickness or pain, only beauty and most of all youth.'

The skull slipped out a little further, almost an eye. Ruth spotted the tips of ears.

'And the poet Oisín was invited by the beautiful Princess Niamh to come and live with her in— Deep breaths now, Mrs Klein. Remember *in-out, in-out*, like we—'

'Keep going! I said keep going!'

It had started with a few of Tateh's forgotten ideas, something to distract the mothers-to-be. Then after a while, Ruth had added a couple of Niamh's stories too, and then a few bits she had gathered herself over the years – books and rumours and things overheard – all the little Irish snippets. So now when the big day finally arrived she felt as much of a responsibility bringing another child safely into this world as she did bringing it specifically into this country, this tapestry of tales.

'So Niamh took Oisín atop her magical horse— That's it, pushing, pushing— Who could gallop atop the Atlantic— You've got to—'

'The story! Give me the story.'

'Until, eventually— That's it...Eventually they reached...that blessed, sacred...'

'AH!'

They let the baby's cries finish the myth for them, the gurgle like a gobful of sea.

Ruth held the tiny fidget of flesh in her hands while Maura, her assistant, called the father inside. She handed him the scissors, slippery fingers that could barely believe let alone cut.

Ruth remembered she once heard someone say umbilical cords were a bit like phone lines, linking us all together.

'A boy,' she announced now as she wiped the child clean. 'A beautiful baby boy.' Smearing away red mucus of his old world and exposing his perfect skin to the shiver of this one instead.

It took hours every night to scrub away the rings of pink from underneath her nails.

She handed the tiny creature over to his parents; saw the first sinews of love reach out to meet him, as pure as they would ever be. And she could have stayed all day, watching them – a jealousy and a joy – the moments she only ever saw from the outside, looking fondly in. But once Mr and Mrs Klein had signed the birth certificate (*Nataniel Joshua; 7 lbs 7 oz*) Ruth wished the family well and left them alone. She never liked to linger too long, despite how their eyes suddenly pleaded in terror as she walked away, out into the squeak of the corridor, the feel of it so empty compared to the delivery room circus.

Tír na nÓg. The Land of Eternal Youth.

She smiled. She hadn't told that one in a while.

She scuttled away from the room, her shoes giddy on linoleum skids. She dodged the traffic of wheelchairs and beds, the smell of raw meat and the sound of cries from lungs as small as pebbles. She took the marble staircase down to the hospital's entrance hall, the mahogany banister steady beneath hands that still buzzed with the touch of new skin, so supple you'd think your fingers would leave dents in it.

The foyer was lavish in tiles and chandeliers; pregnant women and bag-eyed men. Ruth smiled at them all, longing to just sit them down and fix them a round of tea. A couple of biccies. But she couldn't linger just yet, because she still had to cross to the back staircase and descend again – one more step before the birth was truly complete. If anything, she thought, as she scraped her key into the basement lock, her favourite step of all.

It was three years now since she had moved to Dublin; nearly two since she had joined The Rotunda. Originally it had been called the Dublin Lying-In Hospital, as if the women just checked in for a couple of extra hours in bed. But as a maternity hospital it was the first of its kind in Europe, and, as of 1926, it held the rare distinction of having a Jewish man for its Master. Bethel Solomons was an Irish rugby legend turned gynaecologist, his giant paws guiding those babies' heads with the same tenderness as they had guided those leather balls. Though Ruth had heard they used to make them out of pigs' bladders, so she wondered if his parents had made him wear gloves while he played, to keep the victories pure.

His cousin was a friend of Leb Epstein's, so when Ruth relocated to the capital a meeting had been set up. She had been terrified, awake through the night staring at her compass – surely she was too old to be starting all over again? But Dr Solomons had promised that if she managed to complete the Midwifery course at Trinity

College then there would be a job here waiting for her, a fresh start in her fresh city, wrapped up in a dicky-bow smile.

In the end the struggle had been almighty, but she had made it; had delivered a whole new little life.

Her feet slapped against the concrete steps. The basement darkness was bone-cold, the shadows scattered with disused equipment and dribbling pipes gone *gombeen* with the bleakness. Ruth bowed her head as she passed the first section, the metallic trays for the poor little bodies who hadn't quite made it, may their memories be blessed. They lay wrapped and chilled for the undertakers to lift away. It only took the strain of a single arm to carry the weights.

She kept going, all the way to the end where the rows of filing cabinets stood tall, drawers knackered beneath the hefty burden of all the names and details of every human being who had begun their existence – their very own story – here in these draughty corridors.

A noise from behind sent her crossways. She had already complained about the rats.

Her drawer was the second one down, third unit from the end. She reached for the cold metal handle and tilted her head to where the necessary folder would sit, a tab that poked upwards with the small letter K for Klein.

Nataniel Joshua. 7lbs 7oz.

Still his screeches rang in her ears, the throaty things more animal than human.

When she opened the drawer, it was a smell not a sound that hit her first. The wet ash had a metallic reek, alkaline and harsh. It sent her retching. Once. Twice. Doubling over to grab her gut. Until eventually she managed to straighten up and look.

The metal sides of the drawer were coated in char, a crust like rust gone black, while below, the soggy mess looked as dark as soil or peat. But it wasn't either – it was the cremated remains of her folders. Her babies.

Her Irish-Jewish babies.

She coaxed herself to stay calm. To breathe. She reached for the drawer above hers, to prove the taste in her mouth wrong. But Mary Kelly's batch sat neat in their brown paper rows, the tabs from A to Z, while down below, Deirdre Fanning's were grand as well – totally out of order, the letters all over the place like a bombsite or a bout of dyslexia, but what mattered was that they were safe and Ruth's were not. No, it seemed Ruth's were the only ones that had been destroyed; the only ones that had been Chosen.

When she slammed it shut the unit shuddered hard, almost as if it understood. Some flecks of black coughed out and fell to the ground. She wondered if the rats would eat them up.

The funny looks had been one thing, all right; the murmurs in the canteen; the headlines that had started to appear in all the magazines:

IRELAND FOR THE IRISH!

A JEWRIDDEN RACE!

Though they tended to be tucked away down the margins – easy to pretend she just couldn't see.

Then there had been the pelt of rashers on Dr Solomons's car – some cleaning staff over a lack of pay rise, he had told her. 'Nothing to worry about, my dear!' But the sense of something wider, something uglier, had begun to fester, threatening to pounce, until this afternoon down in the basement morgue she couldn't swallow it back any more; couldn't just put on a brave, mismatched face and laugh off the jokes; see the good that her father had taught her, so blindly, to see.

She smoothed down her blood-smattered smock, nice and flat. She would need to do a wash when she got home. And then, without fuss, she decided to escape.

Outside the traffic din was deafening, the cars all racing towards O'Connell Street, the Liffey's borderline. The air was quick and unfriendly as she went, through the car park past the giant marble colonnade with the roof curved smooth into a dome. It was the 'rotunda' – the city's very own pregnant belly – only it didn't even belong to the maternity hospital any more, not since they had sold it off last year – to a theatre company of all things – an offshoot of The Abbey Theatre. Well, bully for them! Ruth thought now, her face flinched ugly against the gale. Lady Gregory must be delighted! A petulance she barely recognised.

But as she reached the car-park exit, her body began to falter. Because actually, where on earth was she going to go? She pictured her tiny bedsit, there on Clanbrassil Street, all the papers piled high with the million different tasks she had agreed, wholeheartedly, to do. There was the Social Society annual dinner; the Cheder fund-raiser accounts; the cake recipes for the Shul Visitors' Tea – every day another request, another favour. *Always happy to help!* But she wasn't sure she had the energy for all that now. *And what about some Irish cakes to liven things up? Yes, I know it's not the usual, but I think it's worth a go, don't you? After all, we are—*

'Are you all right?'

In retrospect, it was a miracle she didn't scream right into his mouth.

Through tears she hadn't even noticed, Ruth could just make out the stranger. He was a stocky chap, not much taller than her but nearly twice as wide. He held his hands aloft in apology, or perhaps, in defence.

To their left a man moved through the car park armed with a fistful of flowers. Ruth wondered if they were for the theatre or the hospital. Either way, for his leading lady.

The stranger, though, was busy figuring answers of his own. 'That's where I've seen…' he began. 'You live on Clanbrassil Street, no? A newcomer, up from County Cork?'

Despite everything, Ruth felt a little blush at the recognition.

'Well look,' he went on now, 'I've just finished rehearsals, and I'm heading back to Little Jerusalem. So if you wanted me to escort you I'd be happy—'

'No!' It was her first word. The force of it surprised them both.

The gust hurled bits of Dublin at their ankles, flitters of fag ends and theatre stubs – all of yesterday's highs – until eventually there was a mention of a bar. It was a grubby place, like, upstairs at the theatre; the kind of establishment she never visited. But then, she was also the kind of woman who never cried; who never ran away; never allowed herself to acknowledge the shadows that had slowly crept their way in. So before she could think she turned and led the way around the corner, up towards the main entrance of The Gate Theatre, trying to ignore the curious glance that skidded freely over the wetness of her cheeks.

The bar was grubby as promised. Exhausted paint. A savoury tang on the air you could almost chew. He ordered two halves of Guinness, even though she had still never touched a drop of the stuff; still remembered her mother's rants about the natives' alcoholism. And each evening at the hospital she would watch as the other nurses headed off arm in arm for their sessions in Mooney's, gossip and hangovers giddying the corridors right through the following day. But she never seemed to hear about the outings in time. Or maybe they just thought her a bit old to want to join – the law still remained that women had to give up their jobs as soon as they married, so at thirty-eight she was the only one left on the wage list above the romanceable age.

Ruth Greenberg. Betrothed to her babies.

'So go on then, what has you so upset?' The stranger placed the storm of black and white before her.

She looked down. She had forgotten she was still wearing her smock.

She tried to make her reply sound casual, mortified now for the state he had found her in. She said it was just a bad day at the office, the maternity hospital, like.

'A death?'

'Sorry?'

'A still-born?'

'No!' she laughed, startled by his bluntness. 'In fact if anything, quite the opposite – a good noisy one.'

'Name?'

'Nataniel.'

'Well, Mazel Tov, Nataniel!' He clinked his glass against hers and began to drink. As the locals put it, wetting the baby's head.

She could still see the tiny squeal of a thing, the image calming her now; loosening something in her chest. And then somewhere else too, somewhere lower down. 'Only I called him Oisín.'

'What?'

She shut her lips; busied them with a sip of her Guinness. She had heard they sometimes gave it to expectant mothers, to dose them up on iron.

'Go on...?'

'Sorry, I didn't...' she swallowed. 'I just...well, I like to give the babies nicknames, you see. Register them under their proper title, of course, but then I have my own private list back home, where I name them after whatever story I was—'

And yes! she remembered now – her list – of course! Tucked away in her bedside drawer, still safe from the world. This time she took a hefty glug of the drink, some consolation there at least.

The stranger's name was Harry, though he assured her she was welcome to re-title him as and when she saw fit. He was a History teacher turned actor; the youngest of three brothers who had come to Ireland back when the boys were still wee. The other two were married now, both shacking up with one of the English girls shipped over once a year to give the scutty community a better bit of choice. A boatful of romance.

'And how about you? Why did you leave Cork?'

Ruth stared down at the table between them. A pattern of circles glossed the wood like one of those Russian wedding rings, linked for all eternity.

She kept her answer vague, saying simply that ever since the rest of her family had gone overseas it had been time for a fresh start; a new beginning. 'And of course, after the Civil War,' she added then, steering the sentiment away, 'I had to get out – sure, poor Cork was blown to bits!'

Oh yes, the Civil War had been vicious all right – on that they could both agree. Horrible the way a country could just turn on itself, even after all she'd been through. The fighting had lasted eleven months after the Anglo-Irish Treaty was signed, more bombs and bullets than ever before. Even families were divided right down the middle, the whole country covered in rubble and dust.

But the memory only made Ruth shudder now, the smell of fire and ash too close to home. 'Another round?' So instead she padded across the bar to order a fresh pair of drinks. A bowl of American peanuts. When they came she ate a handful and then another, though still she couldn't taste their taste.

Dear Mame,

Greetings from Dublin all the way to Palestine. Shalom Aleichem!

Ruth looked down at the clumsy Hebrew, the ancient letters so heavy from her pen. Though apparently they weren't so ancient any more, because out in the Holy Land they had started to revive them; to try to bring the language back from the dead.

Ruth thought of Irish, the poor thing – the deadest tongue of all.

Now, I do not wish to alarm you. Or even quite know how to put this ...

She paused again, this time at her clumsy English, like an awkward little sister confessing something that was really her beautiful sibling's fault.

... but I have a piece of good news, and I thought that you might like to ...

She put the pen down completely and leaned back in her chair. To her left on the desk sat a cold cup of tea; to her right her paperweight, a hand-sized chunk of limestone. She picked it up. A flectrum of green ran through the grey like a streak of fat through a steak.

And what about the one where a lonely spinster who doesn't even realise she is lonely finally meets herself a man?

She smiled at the ancient formula as she put down the stone and crushed the page into a ball. She aimed it towards the bin, but looked away as soon as she threw. She knew by now she never made the shot.

And she knew it was a silly idea, writing to Mame like this. Embarrassing, really – a woman of her age. It probably wasn't even true that she had 'met a man', not in the proper sense, like. And even if it was, why this sudden compulsion to spiel it all the way East?

To brag?

To prove?

To please?

The walls of Ruth's bedsit were mostly bare. A small oval mirror. A map of Ireland, the one she never let herself touch for fear she would rub it all away. The garret was on the top floor of a Clanbrassil Street terrace, right in the heart of the community. Trapped on all sides, she sometimes joked. But no, she didn't mean it really – she loved it, of course she did – the frantic babble of market days, pickle-stenched and shrill; cabbage and fish and weekly gossip traded above all else.

'Twelve beetroot for a tanner.'

'Did you hear Lottie Epstein's after getting herself up the duff?'

Ruth looked away towards the window, the glass smeared tearful with rain. It had been torrential all week, or 'Biblical' as the locals liked to say. Though according to the papers it wasn't near as bad as it was down in Cork where the Lee had burst its banks – over half the houses flooded and not an Ark in sight. She pictured their old terrace, the pokey yard now a boggy mess sunken black and deep with memories.

Ruth cracked her knuckles. Writing always made the old ache worse.

The letters came and went about four times a year, usually

coinciding with the festivals. The Chanukah update. The Passover check-in. But of course, according to Mame every day was a festival out East – a Holy day and a happy day and above all, a Chosen Day.

Dear Ruth, May God in Heaven be blessed...

She always began with the same formal opening line, the vague flicker of closeness they had finally kindled towards the end now vanished from sight entirely.

And how is everything in Dublin?

The community doing well?

And the children...?

Ruth stared at the last question that almost sounded like Mame was just a proud grandmother, asking after her next-next of kin.

Of course, she was more than a grandmother's age these days; probably grey and shrunken, sweating into her beloved red dress as she scrubbed the floors and picked the oranges and tilled the fields on the kibbutz, taking much-needed breaks to jot down stiff, unfeeling letters, the ink crusted by the sun before the sentences were even complete.

As for the Homeland, I think we are nearly there. And I heard we have been looking for some advice from your lot? Nu, who would have thought?

But then last time – for once – Mame's letter had actually found a bit of feeling for her younger daughter; a bit of praise, even, for the Emerald Isle.

There had been rumours doing the rounds that the Zionists were planning to send an envoy over to the IRA, to borrow some military strategies. Because if the Irish had beaten the Brits and secured themselves a homeland – everything the Jewish people so desperately wanted – then maybe they could be so kind as to pass on a few words of wisdom; a couple of tips.

Ruth smiled at the connection – the affinity she wished other people could somehow see – so much more than awkward letters linking that desert to this bullet-grey rain. She folded her papers and put them back in the drawer. She drank a mouthful of cold tea.

She had found another box of correspondence when she was clearing out their Cork house, shortly after Mame had caught the East-bound boat. It had departed from the very same port that had swallowed them in, twenty-five years previous – a symmetry of waves if nothing else.

Alone at last, Ruth had read through the letters. There were ones from Uncle Dovid from New York; from Lady Gregory from The Abbey Theatre – a boastful rant about her latest play *The Deliverer* which she wanted Tateh to see, little doubt as to why she had invited him to Dublin. But at the time, of course, his dreams had got the better of him. Maybe even the very best.

Ruth shook her head at the memory and tried to smile. *The Deliverer*, she thought to herself. A bit like her over in the hospital every day, delivering those babies – *sure, that's what they should call me. The Deliverer indeed!*

She looked around. She wished Harry were there so she could share the joke and earn a rare little laugh. But no, she decided – it would need too much explanation; too much history. Probably better as usual to just say nothing at all.

It was six months now since she had stumbled into him. They had made something of a ritual of it, meeting every day in the car park between The Gate and The Rotunda.

'From one theatre to another,' he liked to say. 'A great poetry to that, Ruthie, you know?'

Sometimes they would stroll to The Savoy to catch a film, the audience standing up at the start for a rousing rendition of the country's brand new Anthem. *Ámhráin na bhFiann*. The Soldier's Song – *a nation once again!* Other times they would take a tram back to her place where she would prepare an almighty feast. Chicken soup and pickled herrings – all the ancient mouthfuls. He said he hadn't tasted grub like it since his darling mother, and of course Ruth hadn't had anyone to cook it for since Mame, so there was a common ground in that at least.

While they ate, he would tell her about his rehearsals; about which plays he wanted to audition for next. And she would nod and agree in her way; offer a cameo of her own from time to time: 'Not that it matters, but I mentioned to Dr Solomons about the filing cabinet like you said.' The one item of hers that commanded his attention.

'And what did he say? Has he launched an investigation yet?' Harry took his knife and plunged it into his bread roll, sectioning it open. 'Found the bastards that carried out the attack?'

'Well now, Harry, I would hardly call it—'

'Well, what would you call it, Ruthie?' His voice was suddenly like a fist slamming the table, startling the cutlery awake.

Ruth looked down at her plate, a heap of the uneaten. She saw the pile of ashes again, there where her babies should have been – the contents of the drawer arsonned black. And then she saw the look of horror on her boss's face when she had reported the incident; the sadness between them when they knew it could go no further.

Sometimes after dinner Ruth and Harry would nip down to the Bernard Shaw off the South Circular Road. She had taken quite a shine to the Guinness, the lick of foam along her lip, soap-thick. Or they would curl up on the couch so she could read to him, great tomes of plays he borrowed from the Rathmines Public Library. The rows of due dates on the inside cover looked like a midwife's private list. Harry said it was his duty as an actor to guzzle as much of the canon as he could. Wilde and Chekhov. J.M. Synge. Act after Act 'til the darkness gatecrashed and his eyes sagged shut beneath the weight of stout and tragedy. But she would always be sure to finish, right to the end. To feel the catharsis land.

And sometimes, when he woke and they were well into the night, he would ask if he could stay; would place his hand on her waist and let his breath get a little louder. 'Please?'

Of course, there was a part of her that wanted to say yes. *Yes!* No clue about love, but maybe…And anyway, babies she did know, so how about one of her own? A set of roots down into Irish soil and would that be the end of it then? The belonging at last and not another word?

But every time, she would shake her head. And Harry would nod his to say it was all right, he understood. A conservative woman. A woman of her faith. When actually it was something else that told her to hold back and ignore the swarming feeling in her stomach; to trap the bees beneath an upturned jar and wait, patiently, until they had buzzed themselves to death.

Until finally, it was Closing Night, and the end and the beginning came as one.

The show had had an impossibly good run. *Youth's the Season…?* by Mary Manning, one of the nation's finest female playwrights, debuting here at The Gate Theatre. They had had a full house each night, a gush of reviews; Micheál Mac Liammóir the star, but the rest of the cast had earned notable mentions too, which Ruth read to Harry whenever he felt jealous – an actor's prerogative. And yet, still he had refused to let her actually come and see him perform; had made her promise to wait until the very last night when the thing had fully grown into itself. 'I promise, Ruthie, it'll be the climax of the whole run.'

And, somewhere in there too, the climax of their relationship.

On the day itself she was nothing but nerves; struggled with a pair of twins that insisted on coming out intertwined so that one of them was nearly choked blue by the other's umbilical cord. But eventually she untangled them – felt almost cruel in the separation – then flew into a dress, across the car park, into her seat just in time for the lights to dim and the curtain to *whoosh* to the rafters.

It was only then that she realised it was her first time in a theatre for twenty years. Exactly. She glanced at the man in the seat next to her, just in case someone else had managed to sneak his way in, the reflection of the electric spotlights like magic across his bottle-thick specs.

The play itself was genius. Hysterical. A group of dandies drinking gin and making camp with cravats. And through it all, hovering behind the farce, was Harry. 'Horace Egosmith'. The protagonist's doppelganger and, strangest of all, a mute.

What about a woman who falls for a man who cannot speak? Could she still marry him?

For the whole play an old idea of her father's tugged at her mind.

Or would she stop speaking too – form a code of touches and blinks that only they could understand?

And really, isn't that what we all do with love?

By the end the ovation was like torrential rain, the after-party stuffed fat with well-wishers. *Another round! Another round!* But with his voice back, it seemed Harry had something important to say, so he grabbed Ruth's hand and led her down the stairs out into the vicious freeze of the night, only a few feet from where they had first crossed paths and lives.

She looked across the car park to the hospital. She reminded herself to put the twins on her list when she got home tonight; to try to tangle two stories into one.

'Ruthie, there is...I need to ask you something.'

The white mist of their breaths met in the middle. Above, an Irish flag flaunted its freedom, slapping the wind with a motion both brutal and proud.

Harry told her that she didn't have to answer now, but that he wanted to ask her as soon as possible, to give her some time to consider. Ruth listened in silence, shivering, even if her body was already beginning to warm. Of course, she had allowed herself to imagine this moment, or at least, to think her way through it. She was still no good at conjuring fantasies out of thin air – no, that gift had never come. But Harry was right – there was a lot to consider. Like where they would live? Whether she would invite Mame? Whether he would have to buy a bigger ring to fit over the jut in her knuckle, the deformity covered at last? And then there was also the fact of her losing her job – the thing that had come to define her in recent years. In fact, the first time she had really known how definition felt.

The Midwife.

The Deliverer.

The Rotunda Storyteller.

Though there had always been the niggle that the mothers, for all their gratitude, tended to move on; to forget about her tales and the singsong of her voice whereas Harry would always need her. Sure, who else would listen to him? Reassure him? Read out his reviews and his volumes of masterpieces? Even if they did make her gut pang for another man she once knew, one she certainly had loved. Then of course there was also the chance of a brand new little person – it wasn't too late, she had seen older women come in – so how about her very own fidget of flesh, a legacy that belonged here and only here? Except, she wondered then if botched eyes were genetic; if it could be traced all the way back to the very beginning where things first went mangled and wrong?

'Ruthie, it's the play.'

Above them, the flag flapped another flap, this time a little too high.

'It has just been – God, it's so bloody exciting – it has just been announced that *Youth's the Season...?* is off touring. England. And Manning, well, she wants me to go too. To play Egosmith. Can you believe it?'

Behind the flag the sky wore diamonds, a sparkle on black like a widow's throat.

Ruth stared at Harry, his face pasted with the orange make-up that made his pores look fat like same-shade freckles. 'This is it, Ruthie! Our chance to get out! Everyone in Little Jerusalem is talking about leaving – God knows we're not welcome here any more, especially after your attack. So come on, what do you say?'

Even through the shock, the first thing she noticed was how familiar the words sounded, just the same as her mother's pitch nearly five years ago:

Come on, Ruthie, it is time to go.

But Mame, this is my home.

Home? Do not be stupid, my girl – you do not even know the meaning of the word.

But—

No matter how many stories you learn about it.

'Ruthie, what are you thinking?'

The last lash had smarted the cruellest of all.

'Ruthie, come on, talk to me.'

And yet her answer now, she barely recognised.

'Ruth—'

'You know Oisín didn't actually stay there forever?' Her question went loud across the blackness, over to a taxi where they saw a silhouette with a tiny white bundle in its arms; a beautiful opening scene.

'Oisín,' Ruth repeated. 'In *Tír na nÓg*. He stayed for what he thought was three years but which actually, back in the real world, had been three hundred.' She spoke quietly and calmly, as if over a half of Guinness, instead of out in the midnight shiver poised on the brink of everything. 'Until one day he realised that he was homesick. Can you believe it? Living in Paradise but pining for Ireland still.'

Above them in the bar a savage punch line went off. The laughter echoed down across the tarmac.

'So Niamh gave him her horse,' she pushed on, remembering as she went. 'And told him that he could pay a visit home if he wanted, but that as soon as his foot so much as touched the ground he would be barred from coming back to *Tír na nÓg* forever, and that the weight of all those years would bear down upon him and he would wither like an old man, and die.'

'Ruth, what the hell are you talking about?'

But Ruth couldn't stop now that she had found her groove – the second half of the story – the version that was never usually told. 'But he chose to go anyway; went looking for his family and the Fianna and eventually found his old home, ruined. A pile of bricks, smashed to smithereens. Next he came across some men who were building a road in Elphin, County Roscommon, have you ever heard of it, Harry? And there were a full three hundred of them trying to lift a giant rock out of the way, but Oisín just trotted over and moved the stone aside with one hand, just like that. Only then his girth broke and he fell from the horse and touched the ground...'

'Ruthie, this is ridiculous. Can we please go back inside?'

'...and transformed into an ancient man. Then lay down and closed his eyes. And smiled.' By now she realised she couldn't even hear Harry's words; his furious, frustrated shouts. Something about 'pathetic'; about 'priorities'. Things she had suspected before, but had decided not to see. So instead she saw only the image of that curled-up old man, his flesh loose and saggy with three hundred years of wrinkles. Like he had just been out swimming in the Atlantic Ocean for a very long time, his body pruned and washed up on the shore.

And she smiled.

July

Ever since her visit, Ima's ultimatum hadn't left my skull.

August.

Israel.

Shem?

It followed me around the House, making it impossible to concentrate on anything else, only dither somewhere between terror and disbelief – back and forth like a fiddler's elbow. Because surely there was no way she actually meant it? I mean, it was one thing to bow down to Abba on the matter of checking me in here – letting him play out his experiment for a couple of months – but this, this was something different. This was everything.

Shem, he wants us to go without you.

No, it was pure bollocks, even by his standards – surely she could see that. Only, despite my father's bullying ways, there had always been a strange sense of loyalty off my mother for him; a sort of unquestioning obedience that didn't make sense. Of course, by now I could recognise it was probably just a product of her guilt – trying to make up for what she had done. But every so often I got the oddest feeling like, actually, Abba already knew about her secret, and was just using it against her; like they were in the whole sordid cover-up together.

Either way, the deadline had been set, the countdown smothering closer and closer like the day's breathless heat. Because July had turned out to be a belter, the weather gone beastly hot, a hum off the House you wouldn't believe – the sourness of sweat and fed up. Apparently it was the warmest July since records began; since some poor fecker just sat there and measured the temperature, year in year out; wrote it down in his jotter, a handful of degrees either way – a man after my own gombeen heart.

So the days lost whatever purpose they might have once had, the heat grinding everything to a halt. No use in going outside unless you wanted to fry; no more football to catch on the radio – the Brazilians had lifted the trophy for the very first time thanks to some savage young lad named Pelé; even Scrabble seemed to lack any appeal – sure I had hammered every one of them at least three times by now. So the only decent thing left of the hotchpotch routine was the knowledge that I would be out in the corridor again tonight, scrawling away, the air a little cooler if nothing else.

Because now that I hadn't actually left – hadn't been rescued after all – Alf had wanted to carry on with the telling of his story. I was happy enough to comply, partly out of guilt that I had been so ready to ditch him, but mostly just for distraction – at this stage I would take whatever I could get.

He had come to the morning after the Clanbrassil Street bomb, the whole neighbourhood still frantic on the shock of what had happened. Alf told me he'd been sick three times, his gut flinging itself from the highest height. So then the following day, in a fit of rage (and something probably already approaching grief), he had decided to take matters into his own hands and sign up to the army; to go and get his own back the bloodiest way he knew how.

'Of course, the locals considered me a traitor altogether,' he recalled. 'Joining on with the Brits? Ha! Talk about a kick in the face! But sure, they had always insisted us Jewies were incapable of being loyal to a nation, so I suppose I was only proving them...proving them...' He stopped then, the sentence slipping out of his grip like soap. He glared into the shadows as if someone had come and nicked it straight off him. 'Tip of me bloody...Arra, what was I trying...The War!' he groused. 'I went off to the War!' Lashing the prodigal memory down the corridor, though the echo wasn't quite so convincing: 'Me bloody mind, Shmendrick...' he sighed. 'It's...it's a bloody shambles.'

But despite the hiccups in his head – a couple more of them each night – still his conviction remained strong; still resolute as he recounted how his younger self had packed his bags and stood up for what he believed. 'Oh yes, I was going over to Europe for revenge, Shmendrick, to slit some German throats and bleed them dry.'

And he was vicious with the telling of it now, the bitterness still simmering just below the surface, so that the more I wrote, the harder I leaned against the jotter, trying somehow to do his words justice; a scatter of *!!!*s down the margins to nail the sentences in place.

I looked at the little black marks; tiny bullets for Nazi skulls.

And I didn't know if it was the force of his convictions that was contagious, a plague rising up through the swelter of the air, but after a while I started to wonder if maybe this was exactly what I needed myself – a kick in the face and a boot up the pyjama-clad arse. Because it was all well and good feeling thrown by Ima's ultimatum – pissing my pants in disbelief – but why not actually *do* something about it before it was too late? Why not take matters into my own, clammy hands?

I wiped them on my thighs, *left then right then left then right then left*. I blew up and down each one to dry the bones.

Alf told me how he had gone to England first – two months on a training camp where he stayed awake on watch and did drills in the snow, sicking blood and shitting bile, the two dripping into one. Then he told me how he had boarded a ship to Europe with a pack on his back and a rifle he shot as soon as he landed, firing round after round until he lost his legs in the process, all the time thinking of nothing but that night, that love.

That loss.

So no, I realised I had to cop myself on now. Because if my mother was planning to board a ship of her own, then I was bloody well boarding it too – the long and the fucking short. Yes, I had been happy to give up my voice for her, to give up my friends and my normality. Maybe even, to give up my chance at love. But if it was going to mean giving her up too, then surely it had gone too far – surely something had to be done. I just needed to figure out what the fuck that something was going to be.

That night I stomped back to bed as hard as tiptoes would allow. I hid the jotter away, same as ever. But this time I held onto the pen; took it with me to bed. In my hand it felt snug and tight, the butt of it hard like I imagined a gun.

I barely slept, the noise of the War still loud in my head, so that by morning I was knackered – a buzz next to my ear that wouldn't go away.

And the following night, my body refused sleep again. A bit like a protest, a hunger striker sealing his lips, even though I was desperate for a snooze. But then the next night I was wide awake too, thoughts going like the clappers, and I realised that I would be like this now until I found an antidote; an escape route out of this place. No rest for the wicked or for gobshites without a plan, only insomnia and exhaustion and skin turned grey like gone-off milk until finally the week was dead and buried and I was due for my session with Doctor Lally, my head spinning circles I could barely see as I contorted myself down onto the back-office stool.

'So lad, you'll be glad to hear I've a few new ones for you today...' Across the room Lally paced back and forth, babbling his usual bab, though the space was so tight he could only take a few steps each way before he had to turn around again.

As he moved he spouted all his latest batch of suggestions, a plethora if nothing else. Because even now, months on, he still managed to come up with an infinite dose of ideas; a never-ending list of elaborate schemes for how to make me better again. As if, of course, he had any clue what he was actually dealing with.

'Have you considered a séance, like?'

'A vigil, maybe?'

'Or what about an exorcism? Unless, of course, the Jews don't...' he trailed off, a pause in his pacing; a rare moment of hesitation.

'Or if all else fails, lad,' he barrelled on, 'we could look into getting you a tongue transplant?'

Mostly I tried to ignore what he said, but I felt my lips tighten now into one another, a subconscious twitch as if the suggestion might be real. Truth be told, I wouldn't have put it past him.

I closed my eyes. I felt pure rotten. I needed to lie down.

'Or have...have you heard about Gleann na nGealt?'

As I opened my eyes my head still spun, seeing three Lallies instead of one. But after a while I felt it slowing. He waited as if he could tell. He smiled.

And for the first time all week – or maybe all month – I think I smiled too.

He explained, very slowly, that Gleann na nGealt – the Valley of the Mad – was some kind of lake down in County Kerry, famous like for being in possession of special 'healing powers'.

'Think of it, lad, as a sort of…Irish Lourdes.'

Lally told me that the legend had existed for as long as he could remember, people flocking from far and wide, all certain that redemption lurked in the depths of that murky watering hole. So now the nuns had taken advantage and turned it into an annual Montague House event – charged through the absolute snoz to hire a dinky coach so as to schlep the spastics South, all on the hope of finding a scummy, summer miracle.

'Of course, it's a Christian thing, lad…So I don't know if you…'

But Lally's warning didn't matter to me now, his hesitations or his explanations, because already my mind was reaching for other things instead; things much closer to home.

To be honest, I was only surprised I hadn't thought of them before.

Because hadn't Rabbi Hart told us how Lashon Ha-ra used to cause people to contract leprosy? Rashes and sores from speaking ill; puss that oozed and dripped? But didn't he also say that the only cure was to immerse these people in the River Jordan; wash them off and make them clean again?

As I remembered it now, I felt my smile begin to flare – a rash of its own going hot across my skin. Because fucking hell, I realised – this could actually be it! The thing I had been looking for these past few days! Or really, for these past few years, ever since my botched Bar Mitzvah – another Jewish ritual to start me off again.

Lally must have sensed my excitement, greedy now for the sparkle as he rambled on, flinging as much information as he could. '...and Sister Monica will be sending the permission forms out this week, so you'll be needing to get your parents to sign...'

At this, however, I had to stop; to rearrange myself on the stool. The risk of the whole thing toppling flat on its face.

I closed my eyes and tried to picture my father opening the letter from the nuns, a knife to slit the glob of glue apart. But it was no good; the truth too blunt. Because as soon as he read it I knew he would get angry – wouldn't see any connections, any continuities at all, only a shameless imposition. *How dare they? Trying to bombard us with their Christian 'mumbo jumbo'!* While my mother would just stand there in the background trying to calm him; to suppress the gorgeous ghost of a smile.

But the flicker of that ghost was enough – the gorgeousness I was so close to losing forever.

No, I knew now that this was the only way.

So that night after my session with Alf I sneaked away to Sister Monica's office, right at the front of the House. The place stank of fags. A pack sat open on the desk, poised for the morning guzzle; a kiss like a lover, tongue and all, giving it the Marilyn pout. Next to them on the desk sat the envelopes, arranged in a little mound, all written and ready to be posted – a pile of miracles stacked high and not even a weight to hold them down.

I shuffled through 'til I found the one with my parents' address, the lines that meant home. I opened it.

31st July. The Gleann na nGealt Outing.

I HEREBY GIVE MY CONSENT:

_____

I took the pen from my pocket and forged my father's signature.

Joseph Sweeney

I curled the 'y' at the end for a flourish and blew on the ink to stop it from sweating, or worse, from crying off. I looked at it, marvelling at my handiwork; the sheer accuracy of the lie – still good for something yet!

And the following morning I cornered Sister Frances and slipped her the envelope, the gob of it sealed slick. She looked confused at first, then panicked as she realised – she had helped Alf before, but never me, at least not directly. But it only took one proper look to see just how much I meant it – unholy, really, to even try and turn me down – so she just nodded and folded the letter away, her lipstick-bright lips not uttering a word.

For the rest of July, I was a very different kind of lad.

By night, I slept like a babe. By day, I walked with my head up and my shoulders unscrunched, the full six and a half foot and nothing less. There were bones in me that hadn't been straight in years. And I think I walked a little quicker too, the momentum now of everything that had been set in motion.

Every time I passed Frances in the corridor I had to stifle a kiss.

But even with the plans afoot, still the gangle of me couldn't help but feel a bit pathetic – not quite equipped for the massive leap I was about to take. So one afternoon out in the yard I decided to try something else.

It was hard to believe the nuns were still insisting on our daily hour out of doors. By now the weather was merciless, not a scrap of shade in sight, the sun scalding the bare skulls a jaunty spectrum of scarlet. I looked around. Some even had little blisters that popped.

Usually I would spend my Yard Hour loitering by the weed beds, observing the scene from the side. Or I would hover near Alf's table while he got cocky with checkers, his mind still firmly on the ball there. Today, though, I thought of him somewhere else.

I pictured him over in England at those training camps, preparing for the War; knackering himself out to be sure he was ready for when he finally made it across to Europe. So I found myself a patch of earth away from the others, lowered myself slowly, face first, and pressed. Up. And then down. *Up down up down up.* Working my shoulders and the muscles along the length of my spine, the pathetic scatter of them that barely existed only twinged something vicious at the contortion.

I could manage no more than five minutes at a time, the cramp kicking in after that. Sister Monica watched on wry-eyed, refusing me a drink. Sister Frances didn't dare object. But I didn't let the dehydration matter, or the stiffness that gripped my bones the following morning, only pressed on the next afternoon too. I dug my oversized toes into the dirt to anchor me in place; dusted off two patches of ground for the pads of my hands, savouring the feel of the earth on my skin, my regulation shirt mottling up with the black of it while cakes of yellow hardened underneath my arms.

Every night I left a stain in my sheets that looked like a silhouette, the shape of my body filled in at last.

And I didn't stop. Five minutes became ten. Every day counting down, becoming more and more certain of my plan – so simple and so mad it had to work. I flexed my arm to see. A bulge was beginning to form. At this rate, I would be doing laps of that lake   swim for hours and hours until every trace of my mother's shame had been flushed far away.

Plus, I decided that as well as building me up, it was probably good practice to be baking myself black in this heat – sure, wasn't it going to be even more beastly over in Israel? The Promised Land and the Promised Sunshine, just a boat ride away; me and Ima in our bathing suits, lying side by side, flailing arms and legs to make angels of the sand. I thought of that now as I pressed on, going so low into the dust it almost kissed my lips. I remembered how Alf once told me it was better to be buried face down, just to be sure.

But the mention of his name was the only thing that didn't quite work; the weakest point in my body's plan. Because despite everything – despite the way I had started to grow and grow – I had noticed that actually, it seemed he might be doing the opposite.

In the beginning, it had just been a couple of blips, the same sort of twitches as before.

'Ah, what's the name of...'

'Jaysus, I know the word in Irish...'

But as the month sodded on, the gaps in his mind had started to multiply. Whole phrases vanished and then whole chunks of them too, paragraphs of his memory that refused to come:

'Where was it I grew up?'

'What county was the bog in?'

Like he had given so much to those jotter pages that suddenly, there was less and less of him left.

'And Shmendrick, where...can you tell me where are me legs?' He looked from his lap up to me, his eyes plumped wide with pure blankness. For the first time since I had known him, the shake in his hands had gone weirdly still.

Mostly, I was able to ignore it. To find excuses. I told myself it was just the weather – sure, everyone was struggling to cope – he would be back to his old self as soon as the rain arrived. But then other possibilities started to niggle at me, little pricks on the back of my neck, so I pushed myself even harder in the muck. Ten minutes. Fifteen. *Up down up down up*. Saw stars at the corners of my face that burst in the air and leaked something foul.

One afternoon I went so far I thought I was going to be sick, a tidal wave of nausea that would either explode gobwards or shite out the other end. I weaved my way back to the bedroom for a lie-down, bouncing off the walls. I probably left a trail of stains as I went.

When I reached the bedroom, Alf was already there. At the sound of me he looked up, squinting towards the light. His face was very wet around the edges.

I stood in the doorway, giving his eyes a moment to find me. To click. When it arrived, I saw the recognition, the relief easing his features a bit. And then I saw the exhaustion take over, a frown that wilted right the way through his skin. 'Doctor,' he said eventually, a voice I could barely hear. 'Doctor, I'm...I'm very tired.'

And I remembered then the only story my father ever told me. It was a Jewish story, of course, about an angel of God who visits an unborn babby in the womb. Apparently he tells the child everything – all about the meaning of life and how the world works; about war and love and the sweetness of religion – and then just before he heads off again the angel touches the child, right below the snoz, and instantly it forgets everything it has learned; comes screaming into the world without a clue, only a dent on its face and a blind fucking panic.

That night I didn't wake Alf to take him out to the Virgin. Instead I went alone, all the way to Sister Monica's office, where I rummaged 'til I found an unsent form; a spare one with the spaces left blank. I wrote his name at the top then jittered something illegible for the signature – I decided it only made sense that whoever was responsible for Alf would have a dose of the tremors too; a spastication that fizzed right through their genes.

The following morning, Sister Frances glared bullets when I found her again, an anger that said I was really pushing my luck. But I didn't care, because we had made it this far together now, my friend and me, so God knows we were going to make it out the other side.

The bus jangled South like a cheap toy, a clank and rattle and every screw coming loose. It was five hours to Gleann na nGealt, a veiny trail of banjaxed roads that coursed through the countryside, ruts from other days.

The driver had the radio on. Connie Francis. 'Who's Sorry Now?'

We stopped three times along the way – twice for a communal piss in a ditch, hot steam off the brambles like they had been set alight, and then again for a flock of sheep, the manky fluff of them blocking the road like a cotton-wool stopper in a neck.

Still the weather was killer, the heat even worse now that it was pinned down beneath the bus's windows. And combined with the judder of the drive, it wasn't long before the floor was puddled with sick, more like we were out at sea instead of down the backend of Ireland, headed dead to County Kerry.

My own stomach pondered a chuck, though that was more nerves than anything else. I focused on the view for distraction, the déjà vu of hill and dale and bog.

I thought of Alf and his lover, digging.

He was sat in beside me, gripping the armrests like he might go flying at any moment. He had tried to tell the nuns that there must have been some mistake – that no one would have signed any form – but Sister Frances just smiled at him: 'Don't worry your head about it,' and looked away out the window again, a sadness in her pretty face. Meanwhile, at the front of the bus Father Dwyer was trying to stand, the wobble of him struggling for balance. He barked at the driver to turn off the tunes, much to everyone's dismay, and tried instead to give some kind of sermon, prayers and pontifications to prepare us all for the sacred day ahead.

'We remember how John the Baptist said, "I baptise you with water..."'

Down the back, I only half-heard, my mind already long gone. First it flickered to Rabbi Hart and his infamous spiel:

Thou shalt never spread slander or tales amongst men. Keep your tongue from speaking guile.

Then to Ima's spiel:

Shem, he wants us to go without you.

Both of them as lethal whichever way you looked.

And then there was another voice too, somewhere close by my face:

'Shmendrick...Shmendrick, you've got to tell them I can't go in. Sure, without me legs...I don't remember how to swim.'

And for a moment I felt like a total eejit, maybe even the selfish kind.

Eventually we arrived. The driver opened the door and let the gush hiss out, yellow onto the grass.

The place itself was scabbily unremarkable. To be honest, you

241

might have missed it altogether were it not for the tiny car park and the crooked arrow with 'HOLY WELL' written across it. Only, some genius had swapped out the 'E' for an 'i' and added a 'y' at the end, so now it looked as if the place were some kind of hub for sanctified schlongs.

The air was a twitch of midges that made me dizzy just to look, the view that never quite settled into itself.

Sister Frances had hefted Alf into his wheelchair and now pushed him along the path.

'Franny, I'm thirsty,' he said as he shuddered over the divots. 'Jaysus, why is the yard looking so bloody...*green*?'

We ducked left and right through a straggle of trees, briars and nettles warning us off, before the path spread its legs and a sort of clearing arrived.

My heart was going full pelt with every step. I could feel the pitter patter in my neck.

It wasn't much of a lake – you could have walked the perimeter in twenty minutes; could have even crawled it if you wanted to. Here on the bank, a few clumps of rushes had gathered and a single white cross had been spiked into the dirt, a devout slug smeared halfway up.

I wondered what it would do if it ever made it to the top.

It was one of the lads from the upstairs wards to go first. He was a friendly looking yoke, nothing overtly nuts, like, but apparently he was prone to having fits. And since the nuns took these to being moments of the devil, he had been sectioned away for the rest of his days. I heard he'd spazzed so hard one time he shat his pants and they didn't let him wash for a week.

Father Dwyer took charge of the proceedings, seedy with grins as he led the boyo to the edge. He mumbled a prayer before he sent him under, verbally at first but then with a shove of his wrist, submerging him all the way. Every one of us leaned in, staring down at the patch of bubbles, the scuzz of craziness washing away and marbling in spools up to the surface.

The midges went apoplectic on the unbreathed air.

When the scrawn emerged his clothes were slick against his skin, two salmon-coloured full stops poking out from his chest; a shrivelly lump curled down between his legs.

But apart from the obscenity, and the violence of his shivers, the lad didn't seem any different to before. Still as likely to spaz at any given moment, and no real way to tell, only to chuck him a filthy rag of a towel and send him shamefaced to the back of the line, people moving out of the way as if his failure were somehow contagious.

I tried to catch his eye, but already it was long long gone.

So the turns continued, dunk unto dunk, the awkward cluster of us hoping and praying that at any moment some miraculous creature would rise up out of the lake profaning in tongues and spouting the secrets of the universe. Only, after a while, the novelty began to wear off. The faith. Because the epileptics, the hysterics, the schizophrenics (both of them), all emerged again a little cleaner, yes, but nothing more. Even Tony declared the priest a 'DIRTY CUNT-LOVER!' before his feet had found dry land again.

But despite the persistence of madness all around, I remained totally convinced. Because there was something deep in me now that knew this was going to work – the cure I'd been gagging for all this gagged-up time.

Shem, he wants us to go without you.

Well, Abba could go away and shite, just as long as I could go along too; just as soon as I had sunk under this water here and washed myself clean, purging the truth and opening my mouth and finally speaking some words.

I paused. I realised I hadn't even decided what the first ones might be.

Can...can Alf come too?

I looked around to find him again. He was over at the side staring at the base of a tree, its complex higgle of roots.

But I supposed it didn't matter what I said – sure, that wasn't really the point – only that my speech would mean I could check myself out of Montague House, take my Ima's hand and natter my way to Israel, knowing I hadn't let her down. I would tear up my old flashcards and fling them overboard, a Hansel and Gretel trail through the sea for the fishies to swallow:

I am lonely.

Ima, what's a soulmate?

I'd do anything for you except un-youing you.

'Right, Kikes – are ye having a lash or what?'

When I looked up, it was my turn to swallow. Sister Monica stared straight at me, the butter-yellow canines visible even from here. I checked for Alf. Still he sat away at the side, this time with his finger outstretched, shaking from left to right. I didn't know if it was a 'no' or just his twitch.

'Not that it'll be any use of course,' Sister Monica continued, going smoochy on her fag. 'No amount of lake is going to cure *that* stench.'

As the laughter came from all around I stood impaled into the mud.

The midges were famished now, vultures for the shave of my skull. And the eyes were greedy too, the whole gang of gombeens watching, waiting for me to move. To fail.

A Jewie jumping on our bandwagon? Well, now I've heard it all.

What do you reckon, 10–1 he doesn't make it?

Yes, I knew what they were thinking all right, the doubting pricks – eejits who thought their lot were the first to come up with miracles from dunking. But I knew otherwise; knew I was about to prove each and every one of them wrong.

I rolled my shoulders, preparing them for the dive. Next I clicked my neck, left then right, catching a twinge off a nerve. The swim would be good for it, I thought to myself – loosen the silly thing out.

Only, the longer I stood there, ready to go, the more I started to feel myself distracted. Because the expectation, the all-or-nothingness of the afternoon, the weeks of build-up and the sleepless nights – all of it reminded me now of something else, something from five years ago; something I had tried to forget but which was suddenly weighing me down, a muscle memory that was in me and here to stay.

I looked for Alf. I couldn't find him any more.

And I felt myself grow panicked by this last-minute addition – not part of the plan at all. But when I breathed again I decided that maybe I had no choice – not if I wanted to go through with it, properly like – so instead I would just have to let the memory come one last time, a symmetry to it that, in a way, made perfect, painful sense.

It was a Saturday morning and Shem was walking up the Shul aisle draped in the starch-white embrace of his prayer shawl. The tzitzit fell like eyelashes, too long. His arms ached under the weight of the Torah, the silver handles jutting up beside his skull. As he passed the men they reached out from their pews to touch the scrolls with the tips of their tallit, then press them to their lips. A sacred kiss.

Shem's back was hot, his shins scratchy beneath the rub of his brand new suit. But he knew he had better get used to it, because after today his Abba would never make him wear shorts again. No, after today he would be a man.

From the pulpit, the sea of faces looked infinite. The glint of glasses. The fuzz of beards. The Cheshire grin of his father, numb to the nudges of his friends around him. The older man had been preparing his son all year for this moment; had stayed up every night, practising his Hebrew perfect. It was the most time the pair had ever spent in one another's company, though they had barely exchanged a word Shem understood.

Up in the women's gallery, Shem could see his Ima. Her whole body was stiff – from the nerves, he supposed – and her fingers holding tight to something…a pamphlet? A prayer book? Or no, maybe it was that black leather diary with the glinty indents that sat high on her bedroom shelf, fat with the secrets he had wished, all his life, he could know.

And now?

Slowly, Rabbi Hart unfurled the scrolls across the lectern. Shem looked down. The words were yoked together into one single block – no spaces to break them up, not even any vowels – just a wall of consonants packed in tight. The Rabbi placed the tip of the metal pointer on the page, right at the start of the portion Shem had been practising all year, the one he would recite now like a spell to turn him big before all these people's eyes.

ShmSwnysBrMtzvh…

ThPwrfSpch…

LshnHr…

He must have been up there for a while – he could feel the Rabbi's impatience, a little shove into his side to set him off. Only, how could

Shem tell him that his voice was already echoing through his head? His sermon from Cheder, all those years ago? The one about the power of speech and the shame of slander; about the terrible evil of Lashon Ha-ra?

'Shem?'

Shem tensed his mouth, forming the right shape for the Hebrew.

'Boy, come on now, what's the matter?'

He focused on the scroll, line after line of dense, ancient words. While all the time he felt something else on his lips, poised and ready to shriek.

'Shem, would you stop this nonsense!'

Something that wasn't ancient at all but fresh – a single image from yesterday afternoon, there on the Glenvar Road. It was just a simple thing, really, a woman and a man holding hands, smiling thick with love. And yet they were the only words in the world that he wasn't allowed to say.

'Pet? What's going on?'

Because speaking ill was wrong, and if he did it then she would be ruined. A scandal. The talk of the town and the end of her life, so no, he had to protect her now.

'Shem?'

To shut his lips and keep her safe; to make this vow and seal it tight for as long as they both might live.

'SHEM!'

Or at least, until I found a way to wash the whole thing clean and pure again.

The jump felt like an ecstasy, the clumsy lank of me cartwheeling over the lip of the bank. One by one my limbs followed after, flailing, not *left then right then left then right* but everywhere, colliding with the swarms of midges that splattered onto the paleness of my skin until they were drowned away by the water. It was cold, unintelligibly so, my testicles demolished in one fell swoop – about to speak again but at this rate I would be high-pitched for life! And I smiled at the joke as I shut my eyes and tucked my legs into my body, foetus-tight, thinking now of a Mikveh bath – the one a woman takes when she has her monthly bleeds. Or the one that converts take as well – a ritual to mark them becoming a Jew for the very first time.

I felt the change coursing over me; the River Jordan, come again.

Eventually, the tip of my nose broke up through the water, my lungs craving air. I splashed about, struggling to get my bearings. The group stood waiting on the bank, a curiosity, but most of all a panic smeared across their faces. I must have been down there for a while.

Once I had found myself I clambered out of the water, clumsy with excitement. My shirt was gone see-through, my shorts sopping too. A bit like my first day in Montague House, I thought, when I had stood there, rain-dripping all over the hallway. Only this was different now – the very opposite, in fact – my last ever day in that Godforsaken place and the first ever day of everything else.

'Kike, have you something you'd like to say?!'

At the Matron's command I opened my mouth, tasting the lake on my gums. I saw the scrawny lad from upstairs, shivering despite the heat of the day. I smiled. I decided I would sit beside him on the bus home; ask him what it felt like when he did fits. And then I would ask him a load of other questions too, to try and make him like me – wasn't that how Alf said that making friends was done?

Next I saw Alf in his chair, back again, and God Almighty, all the things I was going to tell him! I pictured the look on his face when he finally heard my voice, the dimple deep and the laughter that would sound so loud.

His hands were shaking on his wheels, the same as usual. I wondered if they alternated left to right – I would have to ask. But I noticed now that his head was moving too, going from side to side, a metronome to slow me down; a beat to catch me up. And then I saw a woman and a man laughing at something I couldn't make out, and a life that would still be ruined if I ever spoke again – a secret that wasn't mine to purge, only to keep – a stupid plan that would never work no matter how hard I lied to myself.

So instead I said nothing, nothing at all; heard the Matron's cackles and made my way back to the bus, my tears masked by the drench of the lake.

For the whole journey home Alf was silent and I shook, unable to stop the shivers. It was almost as if we had caught one another's diseases.

Monday

'Aisling, your eggs are going cold.'

She looks up from the book; misses it instantly.

'Aisling, come on, you have to eat.'

Does she?

'Aisling...' Even from inside her room she hears the sound of her brother's sigh, strong enough to huff the door down. She never heard him go to bed – maybe he has been up all night himself.

'Ash, look, I know this is hard.' His voice sounds exhausted. The jetlag. The concern. But also just a hint of the frustration flicking in. 'You can't stay in there reading all day – you need to give yourself a break.'

It was about half-three last night, ages after Séan left her, that she finally convinced herself to start. Her vodka buzz had drained flat; her head a dead weight on her neck. But her scepticism was still wide awake, ready to slam the cover shut at any minute; trap the night between the pages as if she were pressing flowers. And could you press people too, she had wondered then, to make pictures out of them? Illustrations to go alongside the obits?

But her questions had stopped when she thought she saw something on the book – a word or a name, handwritten on the inside cover. So she had turned the page just to make it go away; her book and her decision to make, alone.

1. *Right from the Commencement of the Journey, One Must Be Open and Honest About the Myriad of Thoughts that Will Undoubtedly Fill One's Mind.*

At the opening lines Aisling had felt her own mind slur. She could half-remember the checklist from that night in the car, the memory of the fight and the anger surging back. But over the page, the proper chapters had begun – new territory, unchartered at least – a slow and steady overview she could just about manage:

JEWISH HISTORY

A LEGACY OF PERSECUTION

NEXT YEAR IN JERUSALEM

And there was a sort of rhythm to the reading, a path through the prose, one that had led her all the way to morning until Séan's voice made her look up for the first time in hours, the other side of the door but a million miles too.

She clicks her neck, rearranging the bones; checks her fingernails for anything that might have grown back during the night.

'Aisling!'

And she almost smiles; almost an irony to her brother standing there repeating that word, given the lines she has just read:

Chapter Eight: NAMES
Upon the commencement of one's journey, one should endeavour

to select a Hebrew name, a fresh title for all the religious and ceremonial moments of one's new, Jewish life. For example, being called up to the Torah; getting married; being buried.

She pauses, half-wondering which name that means you would use for your obituary – how exactly you would like to be remembered. In English or in Hebrew? In sickness or in health? Or maybe you could go for a compromise, a slash down the middle to save every face.

Then/Now.

Derry/Londonderry.

Aisling/?

This name will not, of course, replace or even displace one's birth name, but rather serve to identify one as a member of the Jewish people.

And the more she reads, the more other thoughts are triggered too. Memories. Half-forgotten facts. The glossary we bring to every text. Because actually, she has changed her name once before. It was only a small thing, a tweak to her surname for her Journalism MA, the politician's daughter no longer – too much of an easy target for her classmates – especially with her dad barely out of the news back then. So if her brother could flee to Australia for his fresh start then maybe this could be hers:

Aisling McCreedy. Blank canvas. MA.

Some women, however, will just rely on the fact that their children will call them 'Ima', the Hebrew term for 'mother'.

Or 'Mame', perhaps, which is the Yiddish word, although this polyglot language is beginning to die out.

Then in London, she had even thought about going one better and losing Aisling altogether; leave it behind on the Tube next to the confusion and the loneliness and the constant explanation of how the thing is pronounced. What it means. As if that might somehow reveal her personality to the world.

Ash-ling.

Irish.

'A Vision'.

The Brits always refusing to see how the spelling could be right because, of course, they must be.

But whatever one decides, it is worth noting that the Hebrew word for 'word', 'davar', is also the same as the word for 'thing'. So this act of naming is indeed bound up in the very process of creation, thus in effect you are creating a new Jewish self.

And then inevitably, she considers now, her curiosity stretching a little further, inevitably there is the brand new name some women still take when they get married. *If* they get married. Another name and another identity, layer upon layer like the dining room wallpaper or the new translation of the Mass. But there is still the risk of changing too far, of becoming a different person altogether. And what then? Which self are you left with in the end?

She looks up, the uncertainty getting too much. She sees the strip of light underlining her door. She feels a sink and a relief – her brother must have finally given up.

The morning wades on, the sun from the bay window filling the bedroom. Aisling turns off the lamp on her bedside table, the bulb so hot it would scald your skin. Only, without it her eyes are too tired to manage, so she clunks the switch again and cocks the shade.

No, at this stage she needs all the help that she can get.

Because the text of the book is relentless now, unfurling chapter unto chapter:

SHABBAT AND HOLIDAYS
THE JEWISH LIFE CYCLE
THEOLOGY AND PRAYER

Every inch crammed thick with the archaic text. The illustrations. The diagrams. The swirls of Hebrew script flicking out at the end. She asked Noah once if he could speak the language – the old version or the new – but he said he had only ever learned a bit, just the Torah portion he had had to read for his *Bar Mitzvah*, up on the pulpit ready to be magicked into a man, *tah dah!* So she had got him to teach her some Yiddish instead. *Putz* and *shmuck*, which she already knew. *Shtup* that meant 'fuck' but also a 'tip' in a restaurant. *Stop shtupping the waitress!* Their own little joke, the memory that comes back for her now and almost makes the exclamations in the margin seem to fit.

!!

But these are not part of the design. No, these are something other.

Aisling stares at the little lines; the little dots. She decides she must still be drunk; delirious on indecision. She shuts her eyes and waits in the wooze of the darkness, biding the time she doesn't have.

Only, when she opens them again they are still there:

!!

She turns the page. She must go on.

Over here, though, there are even more of the things, mutating down the side:

??

Curled at the top like petals, or wilting down in the heat.

She stops. She can feel a headache coming.

Outside the window the local birds sit lined up on the wire, listening to other people's conversations. She remembers the bit of Joyce she read in college where he compared umbilical cords to a network of telephone cables – the things that bind us together, stranger to stranger.

But this stranger, it seems, will not give up. Because when Aisling looks again the scribbles have turned to words, breeding and multiplying along the bottom of the page.[1] Pointless irritations, getting in the way.[2]

And look, I know it's second hand…

And it doesn't take long for the memory to find her – the excuse that had almost slipped her mind.

But Mum thought…

The one she knows she could take either way. Because on the

1 NB Ask Joseph? H̶a̶l̶a̶k̶i̶c̶l̶y̶ ̶H̶a̶l̶a̶c̶h̶a̶l̶l̶y̶ ̶H̶a̶l̶l̶l̶l̶
2 Shoping List: Buter, 2lbs Suger, 5lbs Ginger for Mammy's cake

one hand, there is Linda Geller refusing to pay full price for a new edition – easier just to fob the girl off with one that has already been used – maybe then she will get the message? But on the other hand, there is Linda Geller taking the time to find an Irish edition, the only one ever printed. A generosity; a gesture in itself.

And as she considers her options Aisling notices her hands flicking back to the start of the book, searching for where she thought she saw that name.

Only when she finds it, she isn't sure what to do next.

Máire Doyle, 1937

She stares at the date; quickly does the maths. She has always liked the name Máire. She half-smiles – she can only imagine the Brits trying to get their heads around that one. *Moy-rah. Never heard of it – what does it mean?* And usually this would be the point at which her own questions would kick in, the curiosity that comes with the job. The woman's age? Her history? Piecing her life together to try to find the strand. But for some reason, the idea of it now only leaves Aisling exhausted. Again. Because her own story is already enough – maybe even more than she can manage – she isn't sure she can handle another.

She turns back. The gaffer tape has come unstuck, the glue melted from the heat of her hands.

Chapter Twelve: FAMILY MATTERS[3]

---

[3] Doyle family = 4 humans, 17 catle, 14 sheep, 8 chickins, 3 dogs (and tink Piper's about to pup...)

So she reads on, picking up where she left off, forcing herself not to stop. Though she decides she will ignore the margins as best she can, their questions and their doubts just as desperate as her own. No, she needs to focus now – the only way she has a hope.

> *The next ordeal, but one which must be faced as early as possible, is informing one's own family (whom shall henceforth be referred to as one's 'birth family') of your life-altering decision.*[4]

Downstairs she hears the front door slamming shut. She wonders if it is a come or a go.

> *We recommend that the best method to initiate this process is perhaps to write them a letter, in which one explains one's convictions, as well as the complex but confident reasons for which one has made this difficult choice.*[5]

This time, there is a different kind of interruption, her own reactions kicking in. Because she knows the book is out of date – written for a different time – but even for her this sounds impersonal. Just write them a letter? Just leave it at that? She imagines it now, wondering if you would do it by hand or type the thing out at least? Fountain pen or biro; a letterheaded page? And she can just picture Noah suggesting pigeon mail, or even swan if he could, as if one bird would really be able to manage such a precarious load.

4 Birth family. Like adoptid? Magdalin Laundries – same for Jews???
5 Dear Mammy, ~~I've got something~~ ~~I'm sorry~~ I'm after fallin for a fella calld Joseph who's a Jew…

However, no matter the clarity of one's explanation, do be prepared for the inevitable negativity of one's birth family's reaction. For they will display a general sense of confusion and rejection based on the idea that one is choosing this new life over or instead of them.[6]

Aisling thinks now of her parents around the dining table last night, staring gormless when she delivered the news; their clumsy attempts at reassurance, potato-full and strange. She wonders if they discussed it after she left, or even this morning – an excuse, at least, to have a conversation; to look one another in the eye.

Of course, her father will just be terrified about his public image, the failure of his Christian parenthood – as if he hasn't suffered enough blows to last a bloody lifetime.

The sense of alienation and abandonment, that one may 'never be able to go home' (both literally and metaphorically), will plague one for many months.[7]

And her mother will just do anything to make light of it; probably saw an episode of some reality TV show with a Jewish wedding, so wouldn't Aisling be scared getting thrust around on those chairs in the air? And did that really mean no bacon rolls for breakfast?

'Aisling?'

It takes a moment for her to tell the voice apart from the one in her own head. She glances at the margin, as if it could somehow be...

'Aisling, darling? Can I come in?'

6 Máire & Joseph. Joseph & Máire. eriáM & hpesoJ.
7 Tell Gerry too. Get train to Dublin? Wendsday 25th, 6:25, 4s 6d

She looks at the door, the handle nodding. She shoves the book under her pillow and claws her fingers through her hair. Not that it will make a single difference, of course – the cut of her, she can only imagine.

But when she pokes her head through the door, her mother looks anywhere except at her. 'Sorry to disturb, darling. Only, if I ask very nicely, would you come down and give me a hand?' She scans the room, as if searching for something. Evidence? An explanation? Or maybe just for her beloved daughter who has somehow managed to get lost along the way.

'What?' Aisling notices the pearls in her mother's ears, so heavy the lobes sag low.

'The trifle,' she says. 'The one we ate last night. I'm remaking it for Wednesday.'[8] She smiles again, leaning forward on the off-chance it might be catching. 'Seemed like a good idea at the time, but we can hardly go without for Christmas Day, now can we? Plus,' she adds, staring at the suitcase on the floor, the zip undone and its innards splayed from either side, 'probably no harm to get you out of here, honey; let in a bit of air.'

Aisling's feet tingle needles as she stands up, her legs quivering like a lip before tears. As she closes the door behind her she glances back at the pillow, bulging now with the stranger's shape. And with her own possibility, hidden underneath.[9]

Down in the kitchen the ingredients have been laid out, the utensils lined up like a surgical tray or a magician's trick. They do the sponge first, the pores fat and open from the sherry. Her mother has

8 Borscht (Joseph's favorit): 6 beetroot, 5 onins, 2 pints stock, ½ lemon
9 33 hours 52 minuts to go. 2,032 mins. 121,920 seconds. (Mammy taut me maths)

a cooking show on in the background, helping by osmosis, or really just filling in the silence. Apparently her father and Séan have gone up to the driving range – their very own version of together.

Aisling does most of the work while the older woman stands back, watching, trying to read her as she moves – maybe some hint in the way she forces her fingers into the give and bounce of the cake, pushing it tight for the bottom layer.

'Fruit next?'

But Aisling is still back upstairs, really, her mind picking like fingers over the words in the book.

> However, the process of becoming Jewish will not end with one's conversion. One cannot force one's identity to change completely according to a specific timetable. Thus, although the rituals of conversion will formally mark one's acceptance of one's new Jewish commitment, the act of shaping one's Jewish self is a much longer-term task.[10]

'Yes,' her mother says. 'Fruit next.'

They used to bake together when she was younger. She had forgotten about that. Dad and Séan would be in the garden throwing any variety of a ball, while they would be in here amidst a sneeze of sugar and flour. She half-bristles at the cliché of it – the male/female divide – but still she cannot help how familiar the dynamic feels; cannot deny the therapy of it, another layer, the squeak of the gelatin squelching up into her nails, even after she thought she had bitten all ten of them to the quick.

---

10 Always sed 2 babbies. Same as Gerry and me.

'You know Noah used to be a vegetarian?'

She hears her mother now as she shifts her lean on the AGA, trying out a variety of frowns. 'Oh?'

'Yeah,' Aisling says. Another memory. 'For most of his childhood, apparently, or so he likes to claim. He said he locked himself in his bedroom for weeks when he found out where meat really came from and lived on nothing but bread and water.' She stirs the custard next, a nice resistance to the spoon; breaks the skin and picks it out, a flaccid thing. 'Until it drove them demented, Robert and Linda; made them pass notes under his door.'

You are not a murderer.

We love you.

Please, son, do not disappear.

'Pleading with him, like.' She begins to pour. 'Begging him to come out until—'

'Aisling, you know we'll support you whatever you decide.'

She straightens the jug and replaces it on the counter.

'Your father and I…it was just a bit of a surprise, that's all. You know what he's like…'

She looks at her mother, the words dying out. *And do you, Mum,* she wants to ask, more than anything now. *Do you still know what Dad is like?*

'And are—'

But it is too late, the doorbell suddenly ringing, so far away it sounds like it is the neighbours'. The women stare at one another; at themselves.

Aisling smears her hands on a towel and scuttles up the hall.

When she opens the front door the chorus of 'Jingle Bells' has already begun. There are four facefuls of freckles; four rounded mouths twanging out the age-old words, a symmetry of teeth and tongues.

Aisling takes a step back, taking in their Santa hats, their tracksuit zips. The little girl holds a Starbucks cup, her fingernails chipped in red and green, and her top cropped short to reveal a bellybutton pierced with a gold ring and a single white feather, the fluff of it swaying back and forth with the rhythm all the way.

Aisling heard someone mention it in the pub last night   the Travellers' new halting site, down in Dún Laoghaire. The sea air rusting their caravans and the locals going mad.

Aisling watches the feather. She wonders if it tickles.

When they finish she doesn't move, only meets the girl's blue-eyed stare and has an urge to lick her fingers, the last of the trifle's dregs.

'Well now, that was only gorgeous.' Her mother appears, leaning down to put a fiver in the cup. 'A Happy Christmas to you all. God bless!' Loud enough that the whole street might hear. Before she hurries the door shut, a wreath into their faces. 'Always prefer giving to them than to the Romanians,' she whispers, smoothing her crisp blouse down. 'Helping our own, and all that.'

The latch clicks shut. The chain too. Aisling stays standing, lonely for the cool of the outside. The melody. The sound of every December she has ever known. 'I think...I think I'll head back up.'

'OK darling. Just—'

'I know, Mum,' she says as she walks away. 'It's OK, I know.' Even though there is so much these women will never say, more different than it is worth acknowledging.

For most females, the key instance of this will occur with the
arrival of one's first child, solidifying all one's teachings as
one strives to pass them on to a brand new, Jewish being.[11]

Along the landing, Aisling passes the spare room, the gilt of the
handle and the unmade bed. It is three o'clock, the day starting to
give up, yet she suddenly feels further from her answer than ever.[12]

The strain in her wrist shifts sides as the bulk of the thing moves
from one hand to the other. She wonders if the marginalia add any
extra weight, though she is still avoiding them like a plague.

Instead, she devotes herself to the information, another kind of
research to keep her busy. She digs her iPad out of her suitcase to
load up a couple of different websites, more modern versions of
the things in the book. She tries JSTOR. The Dead Sea Scrolls. A
list of Rabbi-run blogs – the sacred keeping up with the times. She
flicks from tab to tab to compare and contrast. Ekosher.com. Total-
lyJewish. The endless resources of a Chosen People. Or as one site
insists on phrasing it, the 'Choosing People', since it is in fact *they*
who decide to respond to God's requests, *they* who take the leap.

And Aisling can feel herself beginning to calm beneath the blanket of facts. Things she already knew from Noah, things she has read
before. But so many new things as well, always more questions to be
asked – a conversation that thrives on never being resolved, enquiry
built into the fabric of the faith.

11 Babby born w big secret? Never meet Mammy & Daddy? Tell the poor
thing there dead???
12 Gerry for goodbye tomorro, 33 Glenvar Rd. Joseph says never see my
brother agen.

Soon enough, though, the chapters before her start to run out, the ritual driving on and on until suddenly, there is only one more step to go.

> *Male converts are required to undergo the Brit Milah, the ritual of circumcision in which the 'orlah' or 'foreskin' is removed.*[13]

She hears her father and brother downstairs, returning home, refilling the place full.

> *Meanwhile, for female converts it is the same procedure as was once used for the freeing of slaves – the Mikveh, or ritual bath. This act will mark the final transition from Gentile into Jew.*[14]

And she would kill for a bath now, she thinks; would fill it up with bubbles, or even a flock of paper swans. Not that 'flock' is the right word for it – it is something else, something she knows. Only, her brain has gone too blurred now to remember. A school of swans, maybe? A hive?

> *Before entering this naturally sourced water (originally a river which flowed from Eden) all attire must be removed including any cosmetics, bandages or jewellery.*[15]

She checks out the window now, anything now to delay the final step. Across the road the neighbours' boat sits in their driveway,

13 Daddy castratin bulls?!
14 Cookd borscht last nite. Joseph sed tasted shite bad.
15 Goodbye pressie from Gerry. Silver necklass. Angel charm.

an expense they can no longer afford. She imagines them sleeping out in it, when all else fails – a life raft for the whole family to gather in.

> *Next, one must proceed to immerse oneself completely with one's feet off the ground, one's fingers and toes stretched wide and one's body crouched into the foetal position.*[16]

And she remembers how Noah once suggested that they should buy a houseboat themselves; moor up on the canal, not far from their Sunday newspaper spot, and fold their lives into a tiny cabin. Shower next to where they read; make love next to where they ate breakfast, a fall of porridge oats along the inside of her thigh.

> *For it is indeed like a return to the womb. A kind of rebirth, akin to the moment of revelation at Mount Sinai when Jews were given a brand new beginning.*[17]

Back in her Dublin house, she turns the final page, and suddenly there is no more room at all.

> *Mazel Tov!*

Only two words she already knew to begin with.

Aisling closes the cover, places her hands down flat and waits. Next she stands, her body stiff with complaint, stretching into the silence. In the distance she swears she can hear 'Jingle Bells', the

16 Swimmin holiday. Lough Erne. April 1933.
17 Story bout midwife who told stories wile deliverin babbies?!

carol singers travelling back. She wonders if they managed to make any more money.

But the only other sounds are the same as before – all the worries and the issues – an echo like a chorus come again. Because just say she wanted to do it; say she had been won over by the ideas and traditions and never-ending debates; say there was something about it all that drew her in. She thinks of that night with his family, of the tension and the scepticism, but then of the opening up and the welcome that wrapped so tight and felt so good.

Only, what would happen to her own family, she thinks now, as she stares around the room? What would happen to all of this? Her MA. Her Mandela. Her childhood memories; her brother she had forgotten how much she adored, and the pride she has always held so close.

'Aisling? Dinner's ready!'

And now her heartbeat going crazy like footsteps up the stairs.

'Aisling, for fuck's sake.'

And a body that fills the entire room.

'Aisling?' Séan's cheeks are slapped red from the wind off the range. 'Ash, what the hell are you doing, it's time—'

'I'm finished.'

He takes a moment, his eyes a little rough with her. But then he sees it, lying on the bed. He stops. 'And?'

The single word manages to prick her eyes, wet for the first time all day. The first time, even, since she came home.

'I...' Though her mouth is totally dry, the taste of salt on her throat like a gulpful of sea. Or like a canal with a houseboat and two lovers cosied together, no space for anything more.

No need.

'Séan...I don't...'

Her brother steps forward and puts his arms around her, gym-hard but sibling-soft. He holds her still. He says nothing. He doesn't have to.

They stand in silence, their breathing slowly matching up. She isn't sure how they have lived their lives so far apart. And the thought suddenly occurs that maybe...maybe she could just ask Séan to do it for her. To choose. A bit arbitrary, yes, but it is an arbitrary deadline, so Jesus, why the hell not? Just to have the whole thing sorted – enough of this, already – to have it ended now once and for all.

He lets go, as if he can feel what is coming.

She looks at him, her eyes wide, a flash of begging in them both. 'Séan, I was...'

But before she can finish he has diverted for the bed. He sits down and picks up the book. He flicks through, quickly, like he is already searching for another way out.

And then he finds one: 'This writing?' he says. 'It's not yours?'

It takes a moment for the answer to come, a bit of a laugh on her lips. 'No,' she says. 'No, that's some other eejit who obviously managed to get herself into the same mess as me, once upon a time.' When she looks at her brother again, though, her smile has migrated, his own dimpled deep and dug into his face.

'And out of interest,' he asks, turning a page, 'what did this eejit decide to do?'

Outside the air is vicious, chasing her up into her mother's 4x4. The stench of cigarette smoke makes it smell like the car is burning from the inside out.

She stabs at her phone to rouse the satnav, an address she half-remembers seeing buried in the margins.

'In fifty metres, turn right.'

Usually she cannot stand the thing – has always resented being told what to do – but for once she lets it take her, down the driveway and out the gates, her eyes struggling to focus on something that isn't just words, inches from her face.

The streetlight comes and washes over her like liquid, like grace, a spool of festive reds and golds along the High Street. She takes the Coast Road, even if she cannot see the sea, the blackness of it shrouded to her right like the dead. To her left the terraces lean into one another. Parks. Taxis, their Lego-yellow glows. Cranes climbing up, putting the city back together again. And in the darkness, the unfinished apartment blocks almost look normal; almost like the inhabitants are just out for the night – a festive piss-up, a Fairytale of New York, *whatever you're having yourself* – whereas by day there can be no pretending, glass walls on either side so you can see right through the emptiness.

But they do say the country has turned a corner; that things are finally looking up, just as she changes gear and indicates left, the contour of the wheel so alien in her grip, her fingers pining for the shape of something or maybe somebody else.

It is Noah who drives them around London, Noah in his fancy car. But no, Noah will have to wait, because her mind can only focus now on that stranger and what she did or did not do; the ending that she did or did not write. A ridiculous whim but what else, quite literally, does Aisling have?

She turns again, half-breaking a red. She passes the canal and takes a hill; feels the sense of speed as it builds and builds and builds.

And she is so fixated she doesn't even notice passing a construction site for a house that has been split in two, a crack down the middle and then a pane of glass, sealing it so.

After another ten minutes the stranger speaks again: 'In one hundred metres turn right onto Glenvar Road.'

Aisling does as she is told.

'Arrive at destination.'

She arrives. She turns off the ignition. Number thirty-three. She unclicks her seatbelt, but her chest does not let out.

The house is redbrick with a black door, the neighbours' extension built so close you would swear they could listen in on every word. A slideshow of television colours illuminates the front room. Greens, purples, blues. The Northern Lights.

Walking the path, Aisling checks for Christmas decorations, as if that will prove a thing. But she doesn't let herself linger, only pokes at the doorbell and waits, back again on the Gellers' front porch, clutching a bottle of kosher wine and hoping for what? For everything?

For this?

She thinks of the carol singers on the doorstep this afternoon, the girl carrying the melody an octave higher than the boys.

'Can I help you?' This girl, though, is a teenager. And unimpressed.

Aisling scans the portrait. The rugby sweatpants. The oversized hoodie. The uniform of a life she used to know. 'Hi.' Next her eyes wander down the hallway. On the floor she sees a pile of shoes, the laces tangled together in a single family knot, or like a mess of hair the morning after love. 'Hi,' she says again. 'I hope you don't…My name is…' And then because she has nothing else – nothing in the world left to give – she begins her little speech. 'So, what I'm wondering...' The thing as ridiculous as it sounds; a struggle to get the strand of it right. 'Was there by any chance a Gerry who used to live here? Gerry Doyle?' But the more she talks, the more she realises that maybe it isn't so ridiculous. Because just the chance to speak to somebody who has been through this before – or at least, somebody who was related to somebody who has – God knows she will take whatever she can get. 'Maybe he was your grandfather, I don't know, but he had a sister named Máire who used to visit him and who...who was...I don't know...' As she reaches the end, her head starts to spin away. She realises she hasn't slept in days. Hasn't eaten either – nothing except for a lick of custard from her fingers; a handful of crisps from a sweltering pub. And more than anything now Aisling wishes the girl would just take her inside; let her slip into someone else's unlaced shoes and worry about no other decision except the usual Christmas dilemmas like which film to put on next and which Quality Street to choose, the wrappers melting in the fire, a neon rainbow against the coals.

'I'm sorry, I haven't a clue what you're on about.'

Aisling looks up. She didn't even realise she was still talking. 'What?'

'This bird. Her brother Gerry. I...I don't know them.'

'Oh.'

'Sorry.'

'No, it's...' Though she doesn't say what it is. She couldn't possibly.

'But if...if you want to leave your number or something,' the stranger offers as an afterthought; a bit of festive charity. 'I suppose I can ask my parents when they...What did you say your name was again?'

Aisling takes a moment, fumbling for the wallet in her jeans. She digs through old receipts, a dark-haired face in a passport photo whose eyes she must not meet, before she spies them. She got them printed when she first moved to London, all pomp and ceremony and arrogance embossed:

Aisling Creedon
BA MA
Current Affairs Expert

Her identity, spelled out before her eyes. The one she is stuck with now whether it is truly her or not.

Once the door is shut, Aisling walks back down the path. The paving slabs are laid at awkward angles – cracked like they have been dropped from on high. And she remembers then the word that she was looking for – the one that has been missing all along. A lamentation. *A lamentation of swans*. And she realises that they must be the saddest birds in the world.

part five | Words...

1941

'What about...'
'What about words...'
'What about words that...'
But the questions wouldn't come any more, let alone the answers. Half-glanced things like an old man's mind gone to mush.

Ruth heaved her weight down onto the footrest of the spade. She paused for a moment, her body suspended on the inhale. The possibility. Until the earth gave way and the *sleán* oozed in – through the white stuff at the top and then the proper, filthy black, layer upon layer like a history. Next she cocked the angle of her wrists, just how Joe, the farmer, had shown them. She leaned back and shoved forward to scoop the sod onto her shovel, jerking left and right to prise it free from the gnarls of roots that tried – so desperately – to cling on.

Ruth felt the weight of her compass swaying in her pocket. She didn't reach for it any more.

She tossed the lump of peat towards the wheelbarrow where some of the other volunteers stood – more of the eager cluster she had managed, somehow, to recruit for the week. Sorting, stacking, drying, smiling. Surprisingly efficient for a crowd of newcomers.

And a decent pile built up by the time Joe finally called 'lunch' and they collapsed into the farmhouse for a round of sandwiches, thickly sliced cheese on white.

'From the farmer down the road,' Joe boasted as he doled out the tea. 'So fresh you can still taste the rennet.'

He had been waiting for them last night when their bus finally arrived from Dublin, welcoming them to Clara Bog with a rousing spiel. He said it was a fine thing they were doing for their country, given she was so desperate for the turf –the coal rations leaving her struggling altogether. And Ruth had tried to feel even a bit of pride as Joe finished up and led them to the barn for a night cap and then bed, only, the draught of the place meant she had barely managed a breath of sleep.

They headed back for the afternoon session now, the January sun rousing a bit of a hum off the place. It was an earthy smell, the very opposite of the sea. Ruth found it strangely nice. The bog rolled out for miles, a browny-green expanse, tatty with heather all the way West towards County Clare where eventually it became the Burren, the ground turned to rock instead; a plateau of limestone; flowers poking prettiness between the cracks. They said some of the species there didn't grow anywhere else in the world. Oddballs. One of a kind.

Ruth paused for a moment; half-noticed a man in the next group, offering a smile in her direction; a funny dent bumped into his chin. She looked away and leaned back into the dig.

When Joe came out next he brought a radio with him, music for them to sweat by. He turned the dial through a limbo of static until a trio of fiddles jigged out, another layer of sound over the clink of shovels.

Ruth had bought a radio of her own a few years back. It was a Crosley, short and squat, with a peaked arch and a gauzed window at the front that reminded her a bit of a cathedral. A reverie of sound. It had been a rare indulgence, but she had decided it was a small price to pay for a bit of company, the place so quiet ever since Harry went away on tour and never came back. She listened to the Post Office Channel. 2RN. Talk of a Jewish station setting up, though nothing had been organised yet and, of course, now was hardly the time.

To her left a couple of the volunteers had started to dance, their jigs high above the bounce of the earth.

And as well as the radio station, the last few years had held so much promise for the community. It was nearly four years since De Valera's rich tones had boomed live on air as he read out the Nation's brand new Constitution. *Bunreacht na hÉireann*. The whole country had tuned in to listen, fifty articles and sixteen headings of independent beauty – Irish sovereignty, the Irish tongue – everything they'd ever wanted! And then right at the end had come the special subclause, just for them – 'The Jewish Congregations' – written onto Ireland's spine at last.

That night the Clanbrassil Street houses had been thrown open to the stars, every stash of Kiddush wine bled dry.

But the hangovers had been quick to kick in. A few months of innocent bliss, of roots starting to take, before Dev began making other radio broadcasts; new alliances, out across the airwaves; a speech from the League of Nations Convention to declare how many visas his government would issue to the thousands of refugees who now wandered across Europe like a pack of blindmen clambering in the dark.

Ruth held the radio to her face, the pulse of the word on her cheek like a kiss:

'Zero.'

Nobody.

Had there been any wine left, that night they would have dregged it dry.

Of course, she had tried her best to defend the *Taoiseach*'s decision – the only one amongst them who would. Because surely he didn't mean it; surely in the months, the years that followed, as the panic grew and the threat of evil went from rumour to likelihood to bloody imminence De Valera would backtrack on his haste; would remember everything the Chief Rabbi had done for him during the fight for Independence and welcome all those poor, those petrified souls – *surely* he didn't mean it.

But no, it turned out that he did.

Surely.

Nobody.

Ruth looked away from the memory now, glancing over her shoulder at the group of strangers, all claps and yahoos and pointed toes. She closed her eyes and wondered yet again what she was doing.

She had tried to keep on top of the news from Europe, despite the Censorship Committee's best efforts. Only a few articles appeared in the Irish press, and those that did wouldn't even refer to it as a 'War', only an 'Emergency'. Somebody else's problem. Even when the fighting started to play itself out up the road in Belfast, still the only bits of shrapnel Ruth noticed were the odd whispers around town; the chat off her co-workers huddled in the hospital canteen, affirming the same-old party lines:

'Ah sure, we're well out of it. A bit of neutrality and like, haven't we done enough fighting lately to last us a lifetime?'

'And what would they have us, join up with the Brits? Talk about a step backwards!'

And in a way, Ruth tried to tell herself, breathing *in-out, in-out* like the almost-nearly mothers, but in a way she supposed she could understand their logic. After everything...And especially...Yes, half of her could almost-nearly understand.

So she had tried to just focus on her work instead; to do what had to be done. But even in The Rotunda it was hard to stay distracted any more. Because things were quiet, so quiet – fewer Jewish women were being fruitful and multiplying – they didn't dare. Their letters to the Continent kept going unanswered, while they were still stashed safely, guiltily here without a Chief Rabbi any more and nothing but dog biscuits for Matzoh bread (the suppliers blamed the rationing), so what kind of a life was this to bring a child into, nu?

The locals meanwhile, for all their 'neutrality', had stopped using Ruth altogether. Would just *prefer* a native midwife, if you wouldn't mind; if it wasn't too much trouble. As if, even after forty years, that half of her just didn't exist.

So then why on earth had she agreed to this? she wondered now as she slumped on with the dig, putting the heft of her sigh to use. Some kind of last ditch effort? To try to convince herself there was a bit of loyalty in her old bones yet? Or was it just Ruth the runt all over again, forever trying to please, even when the other side had turned its back completely?

She took her questions out on the peat, going harder with the *sleán*. She cut a sod and lifted it up, then saw something drop out. When she scooped it with her trowel the fieldmouse's body was still intact, perfectly preserved by the pillow of muck. They were the smallest eyelashes Ruth had ever seen.

As the afternoon stretched on her blouse slicked tight beneath her jumper, the muscles in her shoulders that pulled and pulled. But after a while she felt a new kind of weight land on her body too, the strangest sense that she was being watched.

That face with the dimple; that smile across the way.

She decided she would ignore it; would hunker down to attack the heathery scraw, the rough tufts like a stubble on a chin. Joe had given her a little knife to help – a *scraitheog* – a wrap of twine around the handle and a nick at the tip. She pulsed with the memory of Passover knives stabbed into the soil, ten times in ten different places, to be sure.

Only, when she stood up again the stranger had migrated nearer, taking the distraction too far. Because if this labour was ever going to have the effect she needed it to, then she had to be left alone. To be intimate. To rediscover the layers and layers of her country, the ones she had recently come so close to forgetting.

'So tell me, love, does the turf look a different colour, depending which one you're looking through?'

The directness of the remark left Ruth no choice. She turned to the figure and opened her mouth; noticed her throat was clagged with thirst. Joe had mentioned tea flasks but there was no sign yet, lips as cracked and white as the ground.

Of course, she wasn't actually sure how to be rude to this lad – God knows it wasn't in her nature. But she had no doubt it would come if she just gave it a lash; channelled her frustration towards the blushing jawline. The kippah. The chin-dimple scooped deep like a bellybutton as he smiled and spoke again: 'I've never seen it before, the mismatch, like. But it's…' And then he laughed, a gentle thing, wrinkles cracking round his mouth to match her own. 'Well, if you don't mind me saying, love, but…it's beautiful.'

Ruth felt the weight drop out of her there and then.

For the rest of the day they worked side by side, the afternoon spooling away against the backdrop of the radio. And there was another sound too, the gentle rhythm of his voice, an accent she couldn't quite place.

In the beginning, he just offered little things – passing remarks as they occurred to him, flecked up from the earth:

The weather.

The landscape.

The names of the nearby towns:

Tullamore.

Ferbane.

Banagher.

Ruth thought of the compass in her pocket she could use to navigate.

And she could feel herself relaxing into the stranger, trying not to think how long it had been since her last proper chat. Assuming, of course, the voices on the radio didn't count.

'So how about yourself?'

'Is this your first dig?'

'What do you do for a living, besides recruiting gombeens like us?'

The questions, though, she didn't take to so easily.

She supposed Harry had never really asked much about herself. And then the expectant mothers, of course, always had far bigger things on their minds; tiny little things. So she was unused to the attention – couldn't really understand why a total stranger would have any interest in all of that.

'And what about your family?'

'Have you siblings?'

'Are they in Dublin too?'

All the stories of her life she never dared to share.

She dug on, replying with spadefuls instead. She went lower and lower in the same spot, the earth darker the further she went, walled up around so that the stranger's voice had to go louder now to reach into the hole. And what about a plague of questions, she wondered as she wrestled with a particularly stubborn set of roots, a plague of question marks that hooked into your skin and pulled in every direction...

North.

South.

East.

West.

...'til you were totally ripped apart?

She stood up, cracking her knuckles one by one. The fourth digit on her left hand went *pop*.

She played the notion over again in her head: *A plague of question marks, raining down; a curiosity that rips apart.* It was a nice idea for a story, she decided. To be honest, a bit of a gem. She presumed it was one of Tateh's, from back in the earlier days – the better, brighter ones. Only, for some reason now she couldn't seem to place it; couldn't find its slot in the millions of files she had stashed within her skull, archived away in steel-heavy drawers to be picked out and presented to the delivery rooms, depending on the mother and the mood. But as she stood there in the coolness of that boggy pit, this one seemed to be pointing somewhere else instead, somewhere that even the compass didn't know.

Had she...made it up?

Had she...

Imagined?

She leaned against her spade to steady herself, wishing she could sit down and not sink. Next she breathed in, certain of the error. The fluke – an accident she could never repeat. But then she tried another, just in case, this time daring it out loud:

'What about a woman who drowns in a lake, but then her husband misses her so much he drowns himself too, and they meet again as strangers under the water and fall madly in love?'

She waited a moment, a tingle across her body. She really was thirsty. But then she felt the shadow of the stranger's head peering over the hole, blocking the meagre warmth of the sun.

'Come again?' The eyebrows were high up his face, the becoming-smile.

So she did as she was told: 'What about a woman who drowns in a lake, but then her husband misses her so much he drowns himself too, and they meet again as strangers under the water and fall madly in love?'

The stranger's laughter streamed down from above, a sound she craved as soon as she heard it.

'Or what about a set of twins who speak in alternate words?'

'Or a woman who is bilingual, but then the Irish and the English have a war on her tongue so it shrivels up and falls out?'

Until Joe called 'supper' and hungry mouths dunked fresh-baked bread into stew then collapsed into barnyard beds.

Lying there, Ruth thought she wouldn't be able to sleep, before she lost her head deep deep in the straw.

The next morning, she was convinced it had been a dream, maybe even delirium from the fumes of the muck – forty-seven years of age and she had finally lost the plot! But even on the way to their spot it was just the same, the possibilities already warming her up.

'What about a man who plays the fiddle, but as he grows older a string breaks every year so he adjusts his songs accordingly, until finally he has no strings left at all so just plays a jig of silence?'

'Or a man who sells picture frames and decides to put one around his wife and children and seal them behind glass? Only it makes them suffocate, so they still hang there now, mounted dead upon his wall.'

And they didn't stop, this barrage of ideas. Instead they mingled with her sweat, an endless flow, as her muscles softened and her shoulders peeled back from where they had been hunched for months now, maybe even for years, all the tension of herself and of the Emergency too, unfurling like the wings of the yellow butterfly that flickered on the air between her and her stranger.

She stopped to watch it for a moment, a pale spark against the gross expanse of brown and green and grey.

'Or what about a man who digs up relics from a bog, ancient bits of junk, until one day he finds the body of a swan, buried deep? And when he unearths it, the bird comes back to life and flies away, bright white into the sun?'

At this last one, the stranger stopped his digging altogether. He looked at her until she stopped hers too.

'That…' he said, his tongue faltering on the words. A smudge of black had caught on his lip as if he had been eating the sods. 'That is bloody beautiful.'

By the last day, her exhaustion was complete, her body battered from the work and the utter disbelief. She looked around. The land had been annihilated – giant holes where you could see the layers perfectly, like a pile of mattresses stacked high – lie down and get your best sleep.

But despite the ache in her limbs and the dizz in her head, Ruth insisted on cooking a last supper for them all – a final feast for the weary volunteers. The rusty kitchen only had one sink, one set of utensils, but she told herself she wouldn't make a fuss; said a quick prayer and carried quietly on.

The cabbage was on the boil and the bit of mutton was pinking up, so she just had the spuds left to do when she heard him come in. 'Need a hand?' Her stranger stood in the doorway, his legs far too tall for the rest of his body.

'You're very good,' she said, noticing a blush for the praise. 'But it's all right – only the potatoes and then—'

'But you need some help,' he said, taking a step closer. 'It'll be easier if there's the pair of us.' This time, it wasn't a question.

So they stood in silence as they peeled the thick skins in ribbons, the coolness of the lumps bliss against the blisters on their palms.

Two hours later and the dinner tasted lovelier than any Ruth had ever prepared. She licked her fingers clean, one at a time, no pain in the knuckles at all, only the taste of the bog from underneath her nails, coarse grains she worked away with her tongue.

It was a damp morning to see them off. A soft day, as the saying went. Joe wished them a million thanks before the bus pulled out and pointed them home, a different breed than they had been just days ago.

Despite the thick of her sleep last night, Ruth's body still buzzed, her fingers fidgeting almost as much as her skull. Next to her she could feel the heat of the stranger. Bone then skin then blouse. Jumper then skin then bone.

She realised she didn't even know what he was called.

They hadn't spoken all morning, the loom of reality keeping them firmly shtum. And yet, even still she could hear a mutter off him as they went, reciting the names of each village that they passed:

'Kilbeggan.'

'Tyrrellspass.'

'Rahincuill.'

And what about two lovers who don't share a language so just keep repeating place names to one another, back and forth, back and forth, the only thing they need?

She smiled. She knew she was being ridiculous now, the week obviously driven her crazy; daft enough even to let herself, just for a moment, imagine her Tateh's pride. And she must have been distracted with the thought when the bus pulled into Dublin, because she suddenly found herself asking what she didn't even mean to ask: 'Do you…fancy a cup of tea?'

The surprise in his eyes was only half of what she felt.

She shook as she climbed the stairs and stabbed the ancient key into the Chubb like she meant it harm. 'I've no milk,' she said as they entered. 'So are you all right with honey and lemon?' She filled the kettle and turned on the gas; the bar heater too. She sensed him watching as she glanced around the room.

Home.

The piles of paperwork were cuddled with dust. Folders. Books. Bulk-bought pencils. The museum of a life led only for others. She saw her Crosley radio squat atop the desk. Her fingers tingled for a go of the knobs, a bit of noise to soak the silence up.

But as soon as they sat down her stranger was back on the questions. 'And love, I've been meaning to ask. Those stories you have, where...where did you get them at all?'

She blew on her tea to give her somewhere to look. *Love*. That word he kept dropping in without a second thought.

'And of course, we forgot the one about the Golem,' she said finally, swerving the conversation back. 'The man made out of clay.'

'Ah, but maybe it was peat!'

She smiled, the repertoire between them as if they had been practising all their lives – the one she almost felt she'd been waiting for. And it was so familiar, so natural, that she didn't notice the drift of time; didn't even notice the sudden wet of her lips and the taste of second-hand tea, her mouth wide with a hunger she barely recognised. Next she felt hands as they moved across her blouse and down, gently between her legs, her very first time – a woman of her age! But there was too much death, she told herself now as she began to pant the air between them, too much death going on whereas this here was the opposite, the heat of their skin and the tangle of their limbs knotting tighter and tighter until they reached a better place – a Paradise maybe, or a *Tír na nÓg*, where no one ever grew old; never knew harm or pain, or even a Fifth Province where the stories all came together, faster and faster, higher and higher until she felt. Herself. Say *yes*.

She woke just as the day was becoming itself again. She lay on her side, letting her eyes take it in. His arms. His toes. Her compass on the floor, the face smashed and the needle out. It must have fallen from her pocket last night.

She closed the door behind her as quietly as she could. She

unlocked her bike and cycled *SouthEast*, down past the harbour and the pincer of piers, the clink of boats like glasses in a pub making a toast to better times.

She arrived at the Forty Foot faintly flushed. The bathing areas jutted up between the rocks, while above, the yellow stone of the Martello Tower curved around, the empty windows staring across the grey wobble of the Irish Sea. There was no sign of the Mailboat yet; no, still too early for the letters of the day.

Ruth plunged herself into the water, the bubbles rushing to her ears. Her costume billowed out from her body, a drooping silhouette, but she stayed down, feeling the last of the peat dissolve from her scalp, little trails of brown that marbled up to the surface. It felt like a Mikveh, she thought to herself; a conversion into something that was still too early to name.

She cycled back along the Main Street of Dún Laoghaire, that mouthful of a town. After Independence it had been renamed from 'Kingstown' – *how did the Brits fancy pronouncing that, eh?* Monkstown was next, then Seapoint and Blackrock, all the empty barrels left outside the pubs like offerings to the night Gods that they may be replenished. She hadn't had a Guinness since Harry, not even a half, though it was strange to think of him on this morning of all.

She reached Bretzl's Bakery just as Barty Miller was unlocking the door, the smell of fresh bread hawing out onto the street.

'Early for you this morning, Ruth?' There was a scratch on his lip where he must have cut it shaving.

'A touch.'

'Big day of births ahead, is it?'

'Ah sure…we'll see.'

The bagels' poppyseeds were still piping from the oven, a rough smattering over the rationed flour like a brail that would scald the fingers off you. She paid for two, scrunched the neck of the paper bag and shoved it deep into the corner of her basket; felt a pang of hunger which meant the morning was finally coming to pass which meant, of course, that he might be awake by now and dressed. And gone.

She thrust against the pedals up the rest of the hill. Her thighs were stiff as anything from the dig, but also (a body makes it difficult to pretend) from last night too; almost as if the whole week had been training her for that.

She pedalled harder past the canal, a memory of the energy; kisses that Morse-Coded her neck and a voice that mumbled as he found his way inside. Until she asked what he was saying and he said a *story*, he was telling a *story*. For their baby, he said, their legacy that would be left behind long after they were gone, a root dug deep into Irish soil so that they could never ever be forgotten, never be anything other than—

She heard the blast long before she saw it.

Her bike chucked itself to the ground as the sky erupted, a spray of black and grey like a fall of murdered birds. The dust was everywhere, coating the Little Jerusalem streets, the cries of terror muffled deep beneath.

Ruth closed her eyes and felt a throb in her stomach. It was as if a bomb had gone off in there as well.

She stood up, ignoring the sting in her knees. She left her bike and began to move through the smoke towards the centre of the chaos, a left and a right and then there was Clanbrassil Street, or at least, what remained.

The terrace had a lump missing. A giant chunk, three-houses long and gone. Ruth reached for something to steady her legs. She found a postbox behind her, smooth and green, the letters inside still safe. The Mailboat would be docking soon, she thought, making waves across the bay.

The crater in the street was vast, a jag of brick at either end. One, two, three front doors missing, including her own, and nothing but nothingness instead, the house's innards sprayed everywhere like some grim afterbirth. Only, behind the gauze of smoke Ruth saw that, actually, the cut-off points at the end of the gap weren't quite spot-on. Because if her eyes were right then there it was – half her house, still standing! A line down the middle like a rip or a border with one side perfectly fine and the other…the other…

'Ruth! You're all right!'

'Oh thank God, we had ourselves convinced…'

The neighbours arrived now in their flocks, but she kept moving, looking down and going careful where she trod.

'It is the Nazis, Ruth! They found us! Knew exactly where to aim!'

'I told you we should have left, Daniel. This is just the beginning, you mark my words.'

She stepped over a chair smashed on its side; a pile of crockery shards like an argument around a table.

'I've just spoken to the cantor. The Rabbi's on his way.'

'I had a dream last night about this, you know?'

The crush of glass and wooden slats; splinters up into her soles.

'We need the Golem to come and save us.'

'Do not be silly, what we are needing is a boat. Leave the same way we came!'

Ruth stopped now and bent down, reaching for the ground. She felt the groan in her stomach come again. Hunger, yes, but something else; something very new. She picked up a rock, one from amongst the millions, and rolled it over in her fingers, still warm, the dust settling its way into every groove.

She turned away to find her bicycle. If she hurried she could make it back to the Forty Foot before the morning punters arrived, to see if this thing would float.

In the end, she never found him.

By the time her neighbours picked her up from the water's edge, the terrace had been cordoned off, declared unsafe. She searched all over the city. The hospitals. The morgues. Ran her fingers over records until the ink had smudged off into the rims round her nails.

Without his name, though, there was nothing to be done.

Nobody.

Eventually, the Germans issued an apology for the bomb. They said it had just been an accident, meant for the London Blitz; said that the radar or maybe the bad weather was to blame. But at least, thanks be to God (and to *Der Führer*, of course), nobody had been hurt. No, no bodies had been found.

Ruth hated herself for the hint of pride she felt when the articles appeared in *The Irish Times* – her very own story, written down at last – a petty consolation. But when she read them through she discovered they hadn't even mentioned her name. No, really there was no trace of her at all.

Soon after, the silence of neutrality returned, the Emergency forgotten once again. Instead, there were new stories to read about – Cork United winning the League of Ireland; five cases of Foot and Mouth; the death of a certain Mr Joyce, a festival of mourning where all the restaurants in Dublin served kidneys and gizzards, strange things Ruth had never tasted in her life.

In the absence of anything else, she carried on with her work. She had managed to get a little room in the Rotunda staff quarters, happy at least to soak up the air of birth not death, the screams of new life ringing through the night. And maybe it was the sound alone that started the notions off – she wasn't sure, it was still far too soon to tell. But she couldn't deny that below the sadness there was just the hint of something else; the offchance of a miracle that had planted its seed and the first shoots beginning to creep up.

'Penny for them?'

The voice made her jump, there in the hospital foyer. The place was quiet, the afternoon lull – the babies taking naps inside and out, biding their pre-dinner time. She was on her way to the Common Room for a sup of tea and maybe one of those biscuits that had been touched by too many fingers. Her appetite had been on the up of late.

But now her boss's smile touched her instead. 'Sorry,' it said. 'I didn't mean to startle you.' Despite his many years Bethel Solomons had managed to keep a kindness in his face. A missing tooth. The jaunt of a dicky bow, his chins all wrapped up like a gift.

'No, no, my mistake,' Ruth flustered. 'What can I do you for, Sir?' calling herself to attention. She had to be sure to keep her notions to herself, at least for the time being.

'I only wondered how you were getting on? Any news on the house? Progressing nicely?'

She flinched ever so slightly under the flurry of questions, unused to them all over again.

'Well…there is talk of restoring it,' she tried. 'The terrace, like. They're having some fundraising events at the Shul. But I don't know, I wouldn't like to put people—'

'Ruth, that bomb was a blow on us all.' The Master's tone came sterner with the interruption. 'On the entire country, all right?'

She tried to nod. To stay calm. But even the word itself sent her head spinning off. *Bomb.* Because it had been such a simple day before that – the bus journey back from Clara; the weather and the shudder and the offer to come up – out of character, certainly, but still. Then there had been the tea with honey and lemon, and then the kiss – oh yes, she could still remember the kiss, all right; could practically feel it, imprinted on her mouth. And then there had been other things too, better things, a buzz that ran through her body so loud that eventually she could no longer hear herself think, no longer ask why she was even here any more except that she had nowhere else to go and no one else to talk to; no connection to the place except some ideas that were barely hers to begin with; nothing to leave behind or prove that she had ever even been, unless of course...unless now...this...

He caught her arm as she buckled, saving her from the whack of the tiles. Already they were stippled with dents, years of faints from the other expectant mothers.

'Ruth? Is everything all right?'

Still Dr Solomons held her as she stood, slowly. She placed her hand upon her stomach.

'Can I get you something? Good God, girl, you look as if you've seen a ghost.'

But of course, she knew she *had* seen a ghost; had made love to one too. So now she only smiled and told the Master that he was very kind, but that she was grand – just a bit lightheaded, that was all – she had been feeling under the weather all week. And with a final goodbye she made her way to the ladies' room, trying not to rush; trying, very hard, to keep calm. She locked herself in the stall and sat down. She closed her eyes and waited.

Eventually she opened them again.

She stared at the blood like she had never seen it before in her life. Her spine sluiced ice. She had been six days late.

She leaned forward and held her forehead in her hands, waiting for the moment to pass. The dizziness. But most of all the embarrassment; the double-dose of shame going harsh on every limb. She thought of her shift in twenty minutes and the hundreds of women upstairs – younger women – each one laid out in their wards with their husbands and their monitors, ready for the next big step.

But for her, she knew now – or really, she had always known – there wouldn't be anything else.

No, no baby.

No story.

No legacy.

Just a family who had arrived to Ireland once upon a time and then left again in the very same way.

North.

South.

East.

West.

Never once looking back. A broken finger and a broken heart; a divot from a ship crashing into a port; a mark that had faded away over the years.

Ruth let go of her head as she stood, smoothing her smock nice and flat. She flushed the toilet twice, just to be sure, yanking the chain with each hand. But when she checked again there was nothing left behind – not a single trace. As if, really, she had never even been.

August

By the time August arrived I couldn't feel a thing. They say the cold can get into your bones, so I don't know – maybe the muteness can too. There was no real sadness; no shame; not even a sense of failure for the things I had, or had not, done. Nothing. Like actually, my body had drowned a death in that scuzzy lake after all.

Inside the House, though, the story was very much alive.

Ever since our trip to Gleann na nGealt the tale had been doing the rounds – the drama of my County Kerry failure. It was a joke, because it wasn't as if anyone else had been cured that afternoon – the visit a resounding disaster, right across the board. But for some reason my grand finale had been singled out, an ugly anecdote recounted again and again for cheap, lazy smirks.

'I heard he had a stiffy when he got out.'

'Not that you'd have noticed, his thing is so minute!'

I tried my best to ignore the cruelty; the smut that half-reminded me of all the nasty things Alf used to say, back when I was first admitted. But all of that felt so far away now, a very different time and two very different lads.

August, to its credit, had finally offered the country a bit of respite, a pummel of thunderstorms like tanks rolling over the sky, murdering the heat dead.

The sound of the downpour was everywhere, a stampede upon the roof, until actually, I thought the whole thing might collapse – a flood and maybe an Ark, but of course, no room for the likes of us.

The crazies came in two by two, hurrah! Hurrah!

And all the while, through the numbness, still another boat floated at the back of my mind.

I wasn't sure exactly what date they were off – Ima had said 'August', nothing more. By now their suitcases would at least be packed, all the life they could carry. Her dark, full-length clothes; her lipsticks; her silver necklace with the angel tucked down the side so that Abba wouldn't find it. It had been a present from Gerry, the lad with the tightest grip and the rosiest cheeks – flushed, I had always presumed, from their love.

Despite everything, Alf and I had carried on with our Night Lessons. Neither of our hearts was still in it, though I suppose we were hardly the first to follow rituals we didn't believe. If nothing else I think our bodies just wouldn't have known what to do with a full night's sleep.

His mind was still clinging on, some days bad but some days not bad, almost as if the heat really had been to blame. The only noticeable decline was that his shake had gone bonkers, so violent that he found it hard to even wheel his chair any more without doing a jerky slalom down the corridor *left then right then left then right then left*. If I hadn't been so numb I would have laughed. Bumper cars. Bonus points if you hit a nun.

He was at the part of the story where, with his legs gone in the War, he'd had to crawl his way back to Ireland, a tiny bit of him still holding on to the hope that when he returned he might somehow find a trace of her, lingering.

'Only trouble was, I knew feck all where to look, you know? I had tried to ask her about her family – a million bloody questions – but every time she had gone all cagey on me.' He paused then; raised a finger to pick his nose, though he only ended up juddering it all over his face. 'I think...I think she said her Abba did plays or something. Or no, maybe that he was a...a...what do you call them lads that keep them buzzy yokes? You know, the furry ones that sting?'

So he prattled away to his heart's discontent, not even expecting an answer off me any more; not even caring if I was writing the thing down. I wasn't. Because still I couldn't think of anything else except my own family; my own sting.

With every day that passed, the likelihood was that they had set sail. I supposed I was a bit surprised she hadn't come to say goodbye; hadn't popped in for a final visit. But I decided that that would've only made things harder, and that she had probably written me a letter which Sister Monica had probably confiscated, singeing fag holes in the paper until they came out the other side.

I stared at the jotter. The Martello Tower was long-faded. Another building lost in the fight.

And I wondered if she had gone to the Glenvar Road, to say goodbye to her Gerry. It was a strange thought, but it hovered all the same. I wondered if they had made love one more time, the last of their monthly bliss, her naked except for the wrap of his woolly jumper. And I wondered if she had dressed herself then in silence, tying her beautiful hair back into her headscarf, a regulation garb of her very own.

'Shmendrick, I'm not feeling very well.'

By now Alf had been rambling for almost an hour, questions and answers more for the Virgin than for me. And yet there was something about these words that made me hear.

I kept my head down; pretended to be busy with the jotter.

Because I was wondering now if maybe I should write to her myself. My mother. Even just a postcard, once she had settled over there – just a few words to let her know I was thinking of her; that I would spend my life now doing little else:

Dear Ima, Wish I wasn't here. Ever.

I hoped Alf would still be well enough by then to swipe me a couple of stamps.

'Shmendrick, I really…there's something funny in me…'

I pictured how Ima would take the postcard, fold it up, and put it into the Wailing Wall. It was an ancient thing, right in the heart of Jerusalem, where all the Jews came to pray and cry and slot their precious pieces of paper; to shove them between the stones, deep into the gaps. Because they said that the words would then go straight to God – our very own means of passing notes on High:

Father, Why did I have to see what I saw?
Dear God, I didn't find her.

A direct line, only for the most desperate requests.

'Shem? Shem, please?'

Except, I sometimes worried that the Jerusalem pigeons could just come down at night and peck the notes away; take them out of the cracks and fly them off; use them to build up their nests:

Oh God, I ask you to aid my ailing friend.
To let my hands be still for once.

Though maybe it would only make their nests weaker not stronger, building homes out of other people's doubts; other people's pleas:

What if my silence has been a terrible mistake?
I wanted a legacy, but instead I got nothing. Not even legs.

The early bird, catching the confession.

'Shem!'

The clash of skull on tile sounded like china. Like two mugs, clinked full of tea. His chair rolled backwards into the shadows as if it were running away.

Alf lay collapsed at the foot of the plinth. Still. It almost looked like he was just praying, a supplicant to the Virgin.

I waited, giving him a chance to pick himself up.

But when he didn't I reached across and I poked him, hard, shoving with the butt of my pen. Nothing. Next I reached a little further for his shoulder and gave it a shake, back and forth, as if he just needed waking up.

Still he slept.

I looked around.

Help?

Through the silence now, my heart began to dance a dance. I checked again, craning away towards the nuns' quarters.

Somebody help?

Sister Frances?

Hello?

I supposed I could just run in and wake her up; turn on the lights and clap my hands until the nuns opened their eyes. And did they sleep with their habits on too? I wanted to know. And wouldn't that get in the way of their dreams?

But I couldn't bring myself to move now; couldn't bear to leave him here alone when already he looked like he was in trouble. As if, after all this time, my friend might be...

I opened my mouth, my tongue twitching with the panic.

Dead?

The word mounted in my throat, the ragbags of my lungs suddenly all empty and tight. I wondered if this was how asthma felt, a chest wheezy without air. But there were other words too, getting in the way, as if I just needed some kind of language oxygen – one puff and I would be cured.

ImreallysorrybutIsawmymotherhavinganaffair.

I opened even wider, desperate for a sound. Not for my sake any more, but for his – life and death stuff, like – surely that changed everything?

SomeonehurryIthinkmyfriendhashadaheartattack.

And I thought then that maybe it wouldn't be such a good idea for the Jerusalem pigeons to steal the scraps from the Wailing Wall, because actually, maybe the bricks secretly needed them to stay up, so that when the birds took too many away the whole thing would collapse, a two-thousand-year-old heap of rubble and dust that would make the city wail and wail and wail and never stop.

It took the full thrust of my weight to knock the statue off the plinth. The smash was massive, louder than all the words I couldn't say, until everything, at last, was still.

Hail Mary, full of Grace. The Virgin Mary, shattered to a million smithereens.

'What in the Lord's name?' Sister Frances's voice came shrill from the other end of the corridor. 'Shem? Shem is that you?' Next her body followed, bare feet across the spray of broken shards. 'And who...' Before she stopped. Dead. Seeing the sprawl of it. 'Christ on a bike!' Screaming the things I hadn't been able to scream. 'Somebody call an ambulance!' The things that might have been enough to save my friend, if I had been a better kind of lad. When I looked again, though, I couldn't even see him any more, clouds of porcelain dust coughing up to block the view, almost as if Alf's body had just been vanished into thin air; whisked away somewhere far from me, somewhere he would be safe; somewhere the pigeons could never find him.

For 'Trespassing the Premises' and 'Desecration of Property' the Sisters put me in Solitary Confinement. Two weeks. The cell was so tight I could reach my arms from one wall to the other; could smear them both with the food that was left on a tray outside the door.

When I finally got back to our room Alf's bed had been stripped, the shelf wiped clean. There was a bright patch on the wall where his books used to be, the paint less faded than the rest. Like the opposite of a shadow, a *not*-silhouette.

While locked away I had prepared myself for the worst; had made a little rip in the sleeve of my regulation shirt, just as the custom said. I did it on the left side. Though the rag of a thing was already so riddled with holes you would've been hard pressed to notice the new addition.

The day they let me out I saw Sister Frances around the House a couple of times, but I could tell she was avoiding me, probably feeling guilty for having had me locked up. But I understood – I knew how it must have looked. Like I had attacked Alf somehow; like I had gone crazy and murdered my friend, and to be honest, wasn't that basically the truth? A chance to save him which I hadn't even had the strength to take?

I pictured him now, buried in the ground. I wondered if they had remembered to put him face down, the way he had always wanted.

The rain had finally eased a bit, sick of the sight of itself, so that afternoon we were ordered back out to the yard. They had told us we were to pull up the nettles that had started to clog the flowerbeds – roses amidst thorns or some shite like that. I just held my palms against the yokes instead and let them do their worst; tried to get an even number of stings on either side, even if I didn't actually bother to count.

No more rain, I thought to myself. So it would be good weather for a sailing.

The hours passed us by, the air fresh at least, but then I smelled something sweeter and realised the pretty nun had come up beside me. She spoke very quickly, though her lips barely moved as they whispered a different version of events.

She told me that Alf was still alive, just, clinging on in St Imelda's Hospital a few miles South of here.

'But Shem, you know that notebook you had? The yellowy one with all that…' She stopped to suck her finger. She must have grazed it off a sting. 'Well Shem, Sister Monica took it. I think…Shem, it's gone.'

Through the numbness the sense of failure came throbbing in. I closed my eyes. It was the most I had felt in weeks.

That night I lay staring into the blackness of our room. My room. I could hear a leak somewhere near, the drips slow and fat like a torture.

And do you think they would bury us separately, Shmendrick, if we ever popped our clogs? A special Jewie cemetery, like?

I froze, the silence playing tricks on my skull.

I saw a lad hitchhiking with a coffin once, you know? Down the Killarney Road.

But I would know his voice anywhere, even as it echoed above my head – almost as if the snippets of his mind he had started to lose still hovered, here on the pantry air.

He had a big sign on him, like, begging for someone to pick them up; take them off to the graveyard or maybe just down to Bray for a pint in a local snug!

As it had at the time, Alf's joke now brought me a smile. And then a memory of the lads in school bullying my flashcards the very same way:

'What are they, like, hitchhiking placards?'

'Excuse me, Sir, but could you take me to a place called *"Yes, please"*?'

'Pardon, but I'm headed for a town called *"I'm Sorry"*.'

'A village over beyond called *"I think loneliness feels a bit like hunger, and, Ima, what if someone just ate all their friends? What would they feel then?"*'

I jumped out of bed. The noise was getting too much.

The corridor was ice beneath my feet. After a fortnight in the cell the skin on my toes felt strangely sensitive, newborn baby stuff.

I could have done the route blindfolded, but tonight I kept my eyes open, just to see what they had put up instead. To be honest,

I half-expected it would still be the Virgin, glued back together again – no real damage, just some cracks across her face like she had aged thirty years instead of two weeks.

Mary, the same name as my mother. Though of course, hers was technically the Irish version. Máire. The fada above the 'a' like a crack of its own.

When I got there the figurine was gone. On the pedestal a candle sat instead, the fat, red memorial kind – a tribute to so much more than they could know.

You see, Shmendrick, I have…I have a proposition for you.

As I stood there, another bout of Alf's phrases came looking for me, the sound and the shape of us still imprinted on the air. We had both sat at different heights, yet over time we had been levelled too.

I can nick the stationery for you, on the sly, like.

Sta-tion-A-ry, pet, is when you stand there in the one spot, and I run a-wAAAAAAy…

My mother's voice, though, made my legs begin to slacken. I crossed them over. I needed to sit.

While in solitary, I had been counting down the last days of the month. I used my nail to make scratches in the concrete wall, notches on a bedpost. I sighed. All things considered, the phrase didn't sound quite right.

By now, August was certainly down to the dregs of itself. I wondered if the nuns knew about the deadline; if they had kept me locked up for the guts of the month on purpose. Or worse, if maybe Ima had come to say goodbye, but then Sister Monica had had to tell her that no, she couldn't come in; that I wasn't allowed visitors any more.

I looked away. Behind the plinth I saw a glimmer of white, poking into the blackness – a spare shard of porcelain they must have forgotten to sweep up.

I hoped at least that the crossing would be smooth for her. It was such a long journey – surely weeks at sea. I pictured the boat, an orange-rusted thing, a dot on the horizon going lower and lower until it disappeared out of sight.

I looked up at the candle, burning in memory.

For my mother.

My friend.

The jotter.

For everything I had lost.

And you know what the Irish word for 'survivor' is, Shmendrick? Did you do it in school? Well, I think, if I remember rightly, I think that it's 'fear inste scéal'. The man who tells the story. And sure, isn't that all I am now, eh? The gobshite who's left behind just to make sure the story gets told.

As I crawled back to bed I thought of Alf's words, of his sadness as he had spoken them. But of course, I couldn't even be that man; couldn't tell a single thing. No, it seemed I couldn't even manage to survive.

Apparently, though, my name had lived on – the thing that woke me up the following day.

'Shem? Shem, you need to get up. Sister Monica wants you in her office in ten minutes.'

It took me a moment to hear, my dreams still clinging on, not quite finished with me yet. But when I arrived and registered Sister Frances's words I didn't feel any surprise.

I had known it was only a matter of time now before the Matron called me in and told me she was moving me upstairs. A higher ward. There was no point in me having the double room to myself, and anyway, it made sense to clear a bit of space down here for someone who still held the chance of being 'cured'. The delusion.

I got dressed quickly, buttons and zips. My hair had started to grow back. I spat on my fingers and smoothed the curls slick behind my ears.

When I arrived in the front hallway Sister Frances told me to wait outside while she fetched her superior from the office. I hovered in the hollow light of the morning, the day still shy of itself. Around the House's front door, the glass panels had been stained red, so now the particles of dust on the air glowed a lovely pinky hue.

I went to stand in the shaft of it, to feel the colour on my skin – the same shade as a blush – a bashful kind of radiance. But when I turned around and saw my mother standing there, framed in the office doorway, I noticed she was blushing a bit herself.

'Shem?'

The gush of pleasure that followed was stronger than any numbness could withstand.

'Oh my love.' Ima ran to catch my body before it fell to the ground. She pressed it deep into her own, stroking the length of my back. She was so small she could barely reach the top of my neck. 'My pet. Oh my pet.' Her words were whispered things, somewhere around the jut of my ribs, yet still I kept my hands by my sides, too afraid yet to touch. To believe.

Slowly she led me to sit on the wooden bench which ran along the wall. It looked like a pew from a church, stiff and cold; a plaque on the arm with a stranger's name.

In the wood beneath I noticed another set of letters. 'AH' carved into the grain.

When my mother loosened her arms from around me the panic was quick to rush in, but I saw that it was only to grab her handbag and fumble for other things; tissues to wipe her face and the tear stain on my shirt – proof, at least, that she really was here.

I could sense the nuns hovering in the office doorway. Sister Monica especially, a vulture for the scene.

But Ima didn't seem to care. 'Shem, pet…' Her body was turned at an angle so that it almost faced me but not quite. The light made a little halo around her features. 'Shem, I've spoken to your father…'

My heart knocked now, the same place in my ribs where her whispers had just been.

'Shem, I've…I've been begging with him all month…' Her voice was a little calmer than before, the tears wiped off and sucked away. 'As…as you know, all along he'd said August, but he…he agreed to wait…' A smoothness to them that poured over me like liquid, like grace.

Because very slowly, through the shock, it began to dawn on me what exactly was going on – the last thing in the world I had expected.

I began to smile.

And I began to look around me now, to believe this was really it. I saw the bench below and the console table across the hall, the one with the telephone I had used to ring her, all those months ago. The call my friend had organised – his side of our special bargain.

And then something else hit me, more pieces slotting into place, because 'AH'. Of course! Alfred bloody Huff! So my smile let rip because finally the thing made sense – his initials, etched all over the house – the same-old fear of being forgotten and the need to leave something, any kind of thing, behind.

'...but today's the thirty-first now, pet, so we...'

My triumph lasted a little longer, still only half-listening to what was being said, the particulars irrelevant to the truth. Talk about radiance! But then I faltered, letting the words play again; tripping up on the 'we'. Because something about it didn't sound quite right – not quite big enough for three.

'Shem, we're going tonight.'

And very slowly my smile began to unrip itself, tooth by tooth.

'Oh love, I have no choice!' Ima was facing straight ahead now, so that all I could see was the curve of her ear, the jut of her jaw as it clenched and unclenched. 'He's my husband. And he says...Oh pet, it's just so...It's more complicated than you can possibly know. But it is very *important* that I go to Israel. To be...to be a *good* Jew.' She ducked out of my sight then, leaving the strange words in her wake, though their sense was irrelevant compared to their tone. 'So pet, I've brought you some things...Some photographs, like, just in case...'

Her tiny fingers began to shuffle a little pile like cards for a trick; a last-minute miracle. 'I thought that maybe, if you looked at them you might...' And her voice began to fidget too, going up a pitch as she held out her offerings. 'Look.'

The first was her and me on my sixth birthday, surrounded by balloons. Already I was tall next to her, my mouth wide with two black locks hanging down around my ears and a bright green cone on my head that meant a party. A joy.

The next one I was a bit older, lanky with acne and a large microphone. It was the Cheder Summer Concert, down in the Shul hall where I had squawked a rendition of 'Goodnight Irene' and dedicated it only to her despite how the other boys went nuts with their jeers.

'Do you remember that, pet? You enjoyed that didn't you? Sang so nicely for us all?' She spoke as if to a child, word for simple word, a patronising music I knew was nothing but pure plea.

I nodded.

But the gesture only seemed to make her angry, the music booming louder again. 'So then *tell* it to me, Shem. Why can't you just *tell* me you did?' The wet had returned to her eyes, red-rimmed like bitten nails. But then something distracted them at the corner and I looked as well.

Sister Frances had emerged from the office. She scurried past us, out the front door, before she closed it gently behind her.

The pause held us; a breath inhaled with no release.

But then my mother had to let go. 'Just one sentence,' she continued, breaking it down for me as best she could. 'Just something, love. A line. Come on.' Such a simple request – surely it wasn't too much to ask?

But even now, in the pink of the hallway, I could only feel the same lines on my lips – the very ones I knew that I couldn't give.

Like: *I saw you having an affair.*

Or: *My mother was unfaithful to my father.*

Or: *I am a gossip who spreads hurtful secrets, the worst crime a Jew can commit.*

She carried on. A photo of my first day of school. Us on holiday on a beach in Cork. Always the two of us, hand in hand; always smiling. I tried to picture her over in Israel – surely a much better beach by far – the proper Eastern sunshine instead of the pithy Irish spit.

Not that she had ever been a great one for the tanning, the glare of it harshest on the backs of her knees and the little arcs of freckles that bloomed beneath her eyes. When I was a boy I told her they looked a bit like tears, brown ones that must have got stuck to her face.

A face that was worth saving, that was for sure, even as it fell apart.

'Shem, please.' Her voice was straining thinner, the energy running out. '*Please*.' A sound almost like I was strangling her; like she was begging me to stop. 'Just a word – just one single word. That's all it will take, I promise.' Like the first time I heard her use the phrase *lost for words* and I thought that she meant the number four. *Lost four words*. 'But it's OK, Ima,' I had tried to console her. 'There are still lots of good ones left. Maybe even four hundred and forty-four?' Until she closed her eyes and I knew that she would never understand. And out of everything, that hurt the most.

The car horn beeped from out the front of the House. Sister Frances reappeared at the door. Ima waited, blind. A hope suspended. Before she opened her eyes and stood up; stepped back into the pastel light of the glass. She gathered her things and stuffed them reckless into her bag, not even caring when one of the pictures fell to the floor. And as I watched her it struck me that she looked a bit like an actress, packing away her props.

It was the last time I ever saw her in my life.

Tuesday

T he first thing she hears when she wakes is Shane McGowan's
voice, telling her it is Christmas Eve, babe.

Christmas Eve. So this is it – she is staying?

Outside, she can hear the day already alive; the percussion tock
of the neighbours' heels off into the city centre to join the rest of
the hordes for family lunches and last-minute shopping, the whole
of town heaving like a lung. Then at three o'clock Damien Rice and
the other singer-songwriter types will go back to their roots for the
annual Grafton Street busk, choruses of poetry warbled out onto
the drink-sticky air; a cover version of 'Fairytale of New York' just
to keep the mobs sweet.

Aisling picks at the sleep from her eye. She sees the book on
the floor where she left it last night after their drive; their failed
attempt. Despite the electric-blanket sweat she shivers. Though
when she does finally drag herself downstairs there is a bulge in
the pouch of her hoodie; a reassurance in the weight of the thing
as she goes.

'Morning, darling.' Her mother is ensconced in her armchair
throne. Coffee. Marlboro Light. Three remote controls arranged in
a row, armed for anything. 'How're you feeling?'

The sitting room is a vast, beige thing – an endless vista, broken only by portraits of the four of them down through the years, different versions of Aisling scowling at the camera like she has anywhere in the world better to be than locked up in that gilded frame. The fire is set, a box of turf from some faraway bog. Above the mantelpiece hangs a series of watercolours by a renowned Cork artist, the paint streaked as if they have been left out in the rain. And over it all lies a thin layer of dust, the same as the fuzz that scums Aisling's teeth; scald it off with a mug of tea but she cannot be bothered to face the kitchen.

'And looking to 2014, what the country needs is to embrace a more *philosophical* attitude...' The radio's musings sit her down, some news-show panel clattering from the speakers on the side. '...too afraid for too long of asking the big questions, and sure, look where that's after getting—'

'Christ,' her mother says. 'Bit heavy for Christmas Eve, what?' She aims one remote like a gun to shut it up, then another at the television to bring on the Planner screen. Aisling watches from the side.

The pickings are slim, nothing but reality TV – her mother's newfound fascination – obsessed with other people's lives far more than her own. The pointer dithers between *Sixteen and Pregnant* or last week's *University Challenge* – such an unlikely pair – until here they are, Queen's University Belfast versus some Oxford team, a different college to Noah's but Aisling knows she will be listening all the same.

He used to ask why she never auditioned for the show herself – an encyclopaedic mind and a teenage lust for Jeremy Paxman – the man himself now firing out starter-for-tens until, finally, one sticks.

'Correct,' he tells a group of barely-adults, disdain in every syllable. 'Three questions now on wildlife. First: Which dietary staple is the main source of the flamingo's distinct pink colouring?'

The Oxford lot plummet into a huddle; whispers like hisses until the chosen one emerges. 'Shrimp?'

'Correct,' Paxman says. 'Many species of flamingo predominantly filter feed on brine shrimp, the cartenoid proteins of which are then broken down into pink pigments by the liver enzymes.'

'The shrimp diet?' Aisling's mother says, swilling her coffee. 'Their cholesterol must be through the roof.'

And they mustn't be Jewish, Aisling thinks, for what it isn't worth.

'Question two,' Paxman continues, oblivious to them all. 'True or false: Giraffes are famed for their genetic lack of vocal cords.'

The studio lighting glints off the students' tortoiseshell glasses, making an ugly glare. Aisling wonders if they really have poor eyesight at all, or if they have just dressed up to play the part.

How does a genius look and can I be one today?

The image half the battle.

She never did see Noah's college, despite how he always suggested they pay a visit, even just a road trip for the afternoon – tumble over the cobbles and swoon at the Bodleian; take some snaps by the Porter's Lodge. But she always declined, bitter jibes about how she would probably stick out like a sore thumb, the gormless Paddy imposter – the self-inflicted stereotypes that frustrated him the most.

'True,' the team captain announces.

Paxman relishes in telling him otherwise. 'And lastly, which member of the Anatidae family is distinct in its tendency to retain the same mate for life?'

The contestants are beyond wired now, the final question of the round; the stakes shooting right to the sky. While her own body begins to twitch, wanting to call out the answer or to just rip a page from the book and fold it nine times, exactly how he once taught her.

'Could you repeat the question?'

'Which *member*,' Paxman snarls, 'of the *Anatidae* family is distinct in its tendency to retain the same mate for life?'

Aisling looks at her mother, featureless behind a cough of smoke. She feels the dig of a corner in her rib, as hard and sharp as a stitch.

'Is…is it a swan?'

Paxman gives the points.

Her mother snorts. 'Stupid birds.'

Aisling rolls away into the cushions. She hears a tinkle of coins that have fallen down, a fortune between the cracks, so close now to being lost forever.

Half an hour later there is Séan, the stench of alcohol behind him like an entourage.

'Struggling?' Aisling deadpans.

'Absolute ribbons,' he replies, clutching a poppyseed bagel.

'Town?'

'Lock-in. Deadly craic. Just myself and JP.'

'JP Dawson?'

'Nah, JP Kenny.'

A whole generation of namesakes. Born in the years after His Holiness John Paul II visited Ireland, so all the mammies decided to name their babbies in his honour.

Next Aisling's father joins the scene, bringing his own dose of religion. 'Now, lads,' he says. 'Let's talk about Mass.' He is dressed to the nines, impeccably so, even though they have no plans for the day. 'We could do midnight tonight, or tomorrow morning, but then it depends what you want to do about a Christmas Day swim? Could cycle down to the Forty Foot like we used to – start the big day the bracing way!'

But Aisling cannot listen any more. Hangovers and Popes and Oxford brains; the reality of Christmas taking place after all.

She abandons the couch and makes for bed; maybe for the beginning of the book all over again. Or even another round of Googling to try to track this Máire one down – to see what family, if any, she has left – just in case they might be willing to answer a couple of questions; a couple of starter-for-everythings.

She stands, dancing with the headrush, half-cut on her brother's Jäger breath. She thinks of the Pogues and then the other girl who was in the song as well, Kirsty MacColl. She died young, Aisling recalls; killed by a boat. She isn't sure if she read the obituary somewhere, or if she is just making it up – formulating other lives as her own slips out of touch.

This time, the phone joins in, lamentation shrill. The four of them stare at it like a bomb that is about to go off; to blast the beige apart.

The calls are incessant at the newspaper. Strangers ringing up to 'pitch' their relatives' lives, as if getting the portrait down in print will somehow ease the loss.

'I'd like to propose...'

'I was wondering if you would consider...'

'He had a fascinating life my husband/brother/father/soulmate...'

Aisling and her colleagues will half-listen, jotting down the vague gist on a spare scrap of paper, trying to determine if the tale is worthy of a mention; an irrelevant midweek slot. Playing God, or at least the Gods of forgetting.

Her father answers the call, booming his politician's boom – ever the performer. As if, of course, she is one to talk. 'Aisling. It's for you.'

She looks up, unconvinced. He must have got it wrong. It couldn't be one of the girls – she knows she is etched firmly in the bad books there, having gone completely underground from the moment she returned. But her gut warns against the other option. She doesn't think he has the number. And even if he did, would he really be so bold as to just barge into the middle of her family home?

To make the decision for her?

She takes the receiver, an antique model, mostly for show. A little cavern of cold against her ear and then a voice.

She listens.

She loops the stiff coil of wire around her finger, knotting the circulation blue, before she says goodbye and replaces the handset. 'Mum, can I borrow the car?' Though she is out of the room before the answer can even leave the contestant's lips.

There are no leaves on the trees to block her view so she sees the sign from the end of the street. It is a brightly coloured thing, a pretty drawing of a flower, almost as if the place were for children instead of the opposite. Down the side she spots the EU logo. *Back when funds were flush.* She makes a half-smile then indicates and turns.

The car park is busy, chocked full with Christmas Eve visitors. As she parks she spots an Audi in the row next to her; thinks of the S7, the tack of the leather to the back of her thighs. Apparently Linda and Robert had been furious when he first chose it – *a German make? Noah, what were you thinking?* – history and hurt laced into everything yet, a taste that will not go away.

The voice on the phone had known very little really, only that there might still be a nephew of Gerry's, maybe, locked up in a *Home*. Aisling had faltered on the word, sensing the capital letter even down the line, which made it a different thing entirely.

And it is a feeble lead, she knows – pathetic, really – a wild goose chase she can barely remember beginning. But it is still better than the couch; still a thing she can be doing – explaining herself and asking questions like whether this woman did it? And was she happy? And what would be the price for me to be that thing too?

She takes the book from the passenger seat and slams the door. She sees a SANTA STOP HERE sign in the porch, but doesn't let it put her off. She wonders if it would be any different if people called it a 'wild swan chase' instead, and if, in a way, that's what this really is.

The reception area is a pantomime of tinsel. Banners and wreaths. Comfort and Joy. A backing track of classical music that goes smoothly on her nerves.

She hovers for a moment, savouring.

Her explanation to the receptionist is clumsy, like a foreigner speaking a language she doesn't quite know, but eventually she is led in through the key-coded doors, ignoring the *knock knock* of her chest against the book so loud the nurse can surely hear.

She is surprised by how meticulously the place is kept. A vase of lilies. Some crayon masterpieces: I HEART GRANDMA. A fold-up Christmas tree so that the needles do not shed. Only, the more she walks, the more she starts to register them too, sat in their armchairs, their wheelchairs, their upright beds; their skins as wrinkled as leather, the same texture as the old book clasped to her breast.

And she stops then, suddenly realising. Has she forgotten herself entirely? Too other-self-obsessed to notice? Because here she is, an obituarist in a Home for the Elderly – talk about the Grim bloody Reaper! And she almost laughs; would if she weren't knotted so tight; felt like an imposter already, but now?

When she looks at them again, though, there is something else she feels, something a bit like guilt. Because how could these figures ever match up with the lives she writes each day? Like that lad with the tartan slippers – could he really be the Admiral she did last week? Two wars. Ship's captain. Twenty-five grandkids and a hand-shake from Her Highness and all for what? For this? Or how about that biddy singing softly in the corner – could she be last month's pageant superstar turned feminist? A full pager with a stunning little snap that caught the male journalists' eyes; a gag about necro-philia that left the air slightly spoiled.

So really, Aisling thinks, these are barely even the same selves any more – the people we are in our lifetime, and the people we become. No, maybe we have all changed into something other by the end, whether we decide to or not.

'Well, Mr Sweeney, here we are now and it looks like you're after getting yourself a visitor.'

Aisling looks around. They have come to a conservatory; another batch of bodies and a chair by the window with a pair of shoulders hunched.

'Mr *Sweeney*,' the nurse repeats, a little louder, though her smile stays nothing but warm. 'I said there is a young lady here to see you, you lucky thing.' Aisling notices a flirtation to the tone, which some-how leaves her glad. Because by now she knows that everybody is in need of a soft spot, even if they struggle to admit it.

'Are you going to say hello?'

She isn't sure the old man has actually heard he takes so long to move, too busy staring at the nothing view. But eventually he nods, just the once, and turns his head towards Aisling; a slow swivel of his sinewy neck.

The nurse leaves them be. Aisling watches her go, a sway to her floral hips and the bump of her pregnancy only visible from the side when she disappears around the corner.

Aisling returns to the old man, Mr Sweeney. The son of Máire Doyle. She takes him in, piece by piece. The blanket on his lap. The too-big shirt. The narrow fingers on the armrests tapping an inaudible beat. And when she is almost finished she finds it, mounted on the crown of his skull, and she smiles.

The *kippah* covers his bald patch exactly. It is unadorned – no clip like she sometimes sees to hold the thing in place; no fastener at all. Only gravity. An act of trust. Up close, it is smaller than she expected, the same size as the palm of a hand, and yet, already it says so much.

'Mr Sweeney, my name is Aisling Creedon and I have...This book...It used to belong to your mother.'

She stops herself, though she wants to go on.

Your mother, I see, who must have done it...

Your mother who saw it through...

Your mother who had a Jewish life because you are her Jewish son...

But the son doesn't seem to want to answer. Not yet. His lips are pursed, making a point at the end of his two jagged cheeks.

'Your mother, Máire Doyle?' She tries again, the name this time like a question. And then: 'Your *Ima*?'

Until finally, his eyebrows begin to rise. And then the rest of him.

He pushes up from his chair. He is a giant, even with his stoop. Aisling realises that underneath the blanket he is wearing shorts, two ghost-white shins exposed despite the season.

The legs begin to walk, indicating that she should follow, while the hands drag along the wall like a blind man tracing his way. She half-wonders if he is. She checks behind, as if they are being tracked, but then he turns off and she has no choice but to stop, caught in the doorway.

The walls of Mr Sweeney's bedroom are completely covered. There must be hundreds of them, she thinks, a patchwork of pages all tacked up from floor to ceiling, layer upon layer; white sheets on a washing line out to dry.

She takes a seat and looks around, trying to find her bearings. Of the entire room the window is the only space not covered. She sees how its sunlight has warped the pages on the opposite wall a different colour from the rest, a dull, jotter yellow.

When she looks back, the old man is right in front of her, so close they could almost touch. She flashes him a smile, an instinct and an embarrassment, but he has no interest in her – only in the bundle in her arms.

'Oh yes,' she says, as if suddenly remembering. 'This…I suppose this is for you.' Slowly, she hands over the book, supporting it like a child. 'I'm sure she would have wanted you to have it.' Her own words surprise her; she hadn't expected to give it up, but it seems the right thing to do. Even so, she feels a flicker of jealousy as it goes, then a tug from the curl of tape as it catches her fingertip, almost like it doesn't want to say goodbye either. 'If you look inside you'll see her notes about halfway through, written in the margins.'

But the old man is far past listening now, too busy staring, examining, nestling down into the edge of the bed as he fingers the indents on the cover. His lips move along with the words. Aisling notices pips of white in the corner of his mouth as if it hasn't been opened in days. And from nowhere then she wonders if it must be strange to be fluent in a language that you read from right to left, and also one you read from left to right? And if maybe your mind sometimes goes away and then comes back again, meeting itself in the middle?

She leans into her chair, giving the old man space. She glances over her shoulder where the pages are strung up. She smiles again. The handwriting is exactly like his mother's.

It all started on Clanbrassil Street in 1941, an unlikely place for love.

What about a man and a woman who court via pigeon mail, until the woman falls in love with the pigeon instead?

Aisling pauses. She thinks how much Noah would like that one – she must remember to tell him the next time she sees him.

But the thought only returns her focus, her priorities back in check. Because despite the *kippah*, despite the old man and his room and his hunger for the book, there are still her own questions that need to be asked – other things at stake and not a lot of time. 'Mr Sweeney, out of interest, would you say your mother had a happy life?'

The old man pauses, his lips gone still. Aisling waits. He doesn't look up.

'I mean did she seem...*glad* with her choice, like?' Even she is startled by the bluntness of the enquiry, the hint of interviewer in her tone. 'Sorry, I know it's a personal question…'

Still his head is bowed, so all she can see is that circle. She pictures Noah wearing one. There was an old *Bar Mitzvah* photo of him hanging in the Gellers' hall, the most important day of a Jewish boy's life.

'It's just that my boyfriend…' But this time she has to stop, realising she needs new words. New everything. 'My partner…My partner has asked me to convert for him, like your mother did for your dad. Joseph, wasn't it? So I just wanted to see if…'

Finally, the old man looks up. His forehead is creased, his expression odd, unreadable.

She waits a little longer, giving him space to reply. And she doesn't know why, but in the silence she almost feels that there are people outside the door, listening in; ears shoved against the cracks.

So she decides to just tell them everything, going back to the very beginning. She tells them about the random meeting on the Tube, the leap and then the fall; about the Ikea trip and the houseboat and the book, the expectation. The panic. And as she listens to herself, Aisling realises it already sounds like a very old story, the account fully formed in her mind. 'She ordered it off the Internet, second-hand. I mean, don't get me wrong, it's totally out of date. All very…*Orthodox* you know, whereas Noah's more…so I'm sure we could…' She trails off, some bits less formed than others. 'But it was a good place to start, like, to cover all the basics. And it was the address in the margin that helped me find you – I drove to Glenvar Road last night – Christ, I must have looked a right state.'

She knows she is going too fast now so she bites her nail for time, drops the remnants of it to the floor. She looks at the stranger. He seems to be struggling, far too much to try and keep up. But she knows she has to push on, building up to a climax that, despite the rush, she thinks she can already see.

'And actually, they told me that they were very close, your mum and her brother. Your Uncle Gerry, like. Apparently she used to visit him all the time, even after she had gone through with it – I kind of assumed your dad would have made her cut ties, you know? Leave her old life behind? But it just…just goes to show she could still do her own thing; still be her old self as well.' She takes a pause, allowing herself a moment to see. 'Because, Mr Sweeney, I have a brother too…' And she can picture him now, back in the house, comatose on the couch. Just a bowl of cereal, though, and he will be cured – the magic trick that has always made her smile. 'So I was worried, you know, about what that would do to us. To me. But it doesn't seem to have altered your mother, does it? Doesn't seem to have changed much at all!' And she realises now just how well Séan and Noah would get on. Will get on. The gentleness in them both; the fun that never pushes. They could all head to O'Gormon's for pints, or maybe they will go and visit him next year in Australia. She always promised she would try to make it across, and she and Noah will need some time now anyway to plan. Or just to talk. To be. 'No, it seems you were a very happy family. You…you must feel very lucky.'

By the end she is totally out of breath. It is the most she has said aloud in days. Between her inhales she notices the music has gone silent, a hush that fills the building. Until the next track kicks in, the melody pure and low.

She realises he isn't going to reply.

'Mr Sweeney…' When she finally manages to stand up she is surprised by the lightness of herself, limber without the burden of the book. 'I've got to head.' She glances towards the door. The gap at the bottom goes from dark to light, the listeners scurrying away.

As she crosses the room she wonders if she has time to go home, to say goodbye to Séan; to tell her parents to sit down and talk. But maybe better to just head straight and leave the car there, parked up with all the others that have been abandoned. She read about the Departures Area in recent years, the spaces clogged with unclaimed vehicles ditched for one-way flights. And the poor authorities who don't know whether to clear them away or just wait until the emigrants have finally returned, starting up engines that can afford to breathe again at last.

'But Mr Sweeney.' She stops herself before she forgets, smiling at the old man one last time. 'Thank you. For everything.' For more than he knows.

Only, he is still too preoccupied with the book to reply – totally fixated on this link back to his mother.

Aisling can tell just by watching him that their bond must have been so strong. In a way, it is the only proof she needs.

Back in the corridor the light is already diluting – probably coming up to three o'clock, the Grafton Street mobs getting impatient for the buskers to tune up their guitars and belt out their heart-warming choruses. Old airs and new hits; layers of verses and bridges about the things we do for love and how everything else will, somehow, find a way.

And as she makes it past the receptionist's voice she pictures the carol singers from yesterday afternoon, travelling from home to home. She sees the little girl with the bellybutton and the feather hanging down. Just as the snow begins to come, covering the car park, covering Dublin, the flakes like a plumage too. A whole flock of frozen swans falling from the sky.

Epilogue

T he girl slams the door behind her with an end-of-the-world
bang. The draught makes the pages on the wall flutter so that
their breath blows over the old man's face.

He stares down at his lap. The book looks small, like it is far away.
He tries to measure it. The distance from the bottom of his palm to
the tip of his middle finger gets him about halfway up the spine. He
looks at his nail. He thinks of the girl, demolishing hers.

He measures the book again, just to be sure. Because when he was
a boy it looked so much bigger, up there on his parents' shelf. His
mother's diary – the thing he longed more than anything to read.

But now he has it in his hands and it is a very different story.

Slowly, he opens the front cover. The black tape crunches like a
joint, arthritic and sore, the words of the introduction just as stiff.

1. *Right from the Commencement of the Journey, One Must
Be Open and Honest About the Myriad of Thoughts That
Will Undoubtedly Fill One's Mind.*

His head begins to hurt. He closes his eyes. He gets terrible
migraines these days, sharp, searing things like someone is after

NINE FOLDS MAKE A PAPER SWAN

bashing a thumbtack into his skull. But he forces himself to look again, to carry on with the list. Because he will read the whole thing now if it kills him.

    2. *Be Sure to Contemplate the Glorious Scale of One's Jour-*
       ney's Final Goal.
    3. *One Must Try One's Utmost Not to Flee When it Becomes*
       Too Much. Undeniably It Is an Overwhelming Process,
       but Thorough Rewards Will Ensue Provided One Remains
       Calm and Committed.

He goes very carefully, the sentences as fragile as the pages themselves. He barely notices the light as it drains from the day. But eventually the words are too dead to make out, so he crosses the room and turns on the bedside lamp. He pauses. He thinks he can smell toast.

He reads on in the orange light, hunched at the edge of the bed. After a while it strikes him that maybe he should sit on the floor, all things considered. It isn't an easy descent, an origami fold of hinges and creaks, but he makes it, crosses his legs and rests the book against his knees. He almost smiles then, his body relaxing into the pose; the memory of it.

By the next chapter he spots the comments written along the bottom, just as the girl warned him he would. The sight of his mother's hand lifts his heart, almost too high; almost as if she were speaking to him directly, back from the grave. Back, even, from Israel.

He never did see his Ima after that day in Montague House; never brought himself to send that postcard. He only learned that she had passed away, years later, when he got a letter from the family solicitor. Another heartache. A little sum.

Máire Sweeney née Doyle.

He still remembers his surprise at the words. He hadn't known her maiden name.

He had always wondered if his voice would return once she was gone. But of course, to speak ill of the dead felt even more despicable, so really, nothing changed that afternoon, only that the single light left in him went out.

He made so many rips in his shirt the thing was long past wearing.

He glances up from the page now. Somehow, it is morning. He listens. He thinks he can hear snow. Then he hears the sound of carols from the Common Room, the cries of children ushered in for Granny's last Christmas.

'Time for pressies! Everyone gather round for pressies!'

He remembers the girl that came to see him yesterday afternoon. He wonders if she reached wherever she was going. Although, thinking of her only brings back the echo of her words, louder now than any other sound.

'They were very close, your mum and her brother. Your Uncle Gerry...'

'Apparently she used to visit him all the time...'

'Because, Mr Sweeney, I have a brother too...'

Uncle Gerry, he thinks as he closes his eyes. Uncle Gerry from the Glenvar Road.

A knock on the door makes him flinch. He wipes his face. The nurse is armed with a plateful of Christmas cake and a glass of something red. Even from the floor he can smell the sharpness of the cloves. She doesn't see him at first, then she finds him, shaking his head. He isn't hungry. Instantly she goes awkward; flashes her eyes to the top of his head as she pulls the door behind her. The pages make their sigh all over again.

When he first came to this place he wasn't yet an old man. There had been an enquiry into the country's mental-health facilities which left Montague House condemned – a report that revealed things the government still couldn't quite believe. But by the time he was free it was too late, really, to start again; to try and figure out how an eejit like him could fit into this mess of a world. So instead he had used his mother's money to get a room in here, a nurse who would bring him cake, a pen and a pad of paper whenever he wanted one.

A chance, at least, to repay an old debt.

He looks at the walls now; at their off-white flounce. There are a million different versions of Alf's tale up there, scribbled down through the years. There is the digging on the bog and the loving on the bed; the bomb and the War and the wheels instead of legs. But most of all there is the woman with the different-coloured eyes, the green one and the brown. Because every bit of her now has been immortalised, a legacy of love that will live forever – one of the great Irish tales, never to be forgotten.

To be honest, the old man has written it so many times he knows each moment implicitly, almost as if it were his own story. His own life. But of course it is not. Because his story, he has just discovered, was nothing. Sixty years of silence, for nothing.

He returns to the first chapter of the book and begins again, focusing this time on the margins. When he is finished he tries to stand up, but his limbs have lost their circulation. He does ten thumps each side (*left then right*) to bring back the blood. It resents the request.

When he makes it he fumbles his way over to the wall and begins to untack the pages. It takes him hours, right through the night, his fingers gnarled stiff from the motion of the pinch. Once finished, he bundles the words into an envelope to give to one of the nurses in the morning. He will have no need for them any more.

He is exhausted but sleep holds little interest. He sees the day in, increments and the rest, the place much quieter than yesterday's hullaballoo. He gears himself up then shambles out to foist the envelope at somebody, a fiver for stamps, then shambles back to the book. He missed it in his absence.

By the time his third read is done he has seen enough. He closes the cover and places it down on the floor. Next, he goes to the bedside table where a photograph sits in the drawer, its corners crispy like a leaf. The woman inside wears a swimsuit on a greying beach. She is smiling, one of her lips almost half as big as the other. Beside her in the sand grins a young boy, though he is almost the same height as her. His face is glowing, in the sunshine yes, but also just in her presence – it is clear how much he loves her – so much that he would do anything for her; would run into the freezing Atlantic right there and then; would give up his entire life and not say a single word if he thought that it would save her from disgrace.

If he thought wrong.

The old man places the photograph back into the drawer. He reaches up to the top of his head and takes off his kippah; drops it to the ground and gives it a little kick. Exposed, his bald patch feels very cold. One last time he looks around the unwritten room, the walls he barely recognises, before he crawls beneath the covers, face down into the feathery pillows. Because he had a friend once, in another life, who told him that it was better to be buried this way, just to be sure.